Antonella Sbuelz Carignani

GRETA VIDAL

A Season in Utopia

Translated by
John Gatt

STORIA

Originally published in Italy as *Greta Vidal*
by Sperling & Kupfer Editori/Frassinelli SpA, 2009

Published by
Troubador Publishing Ltd
9 Priory Business Park, Kibworth
Leicester LE8 0RX, UK
Tel: (+44) 116 279 2299
Email: books@troubador.co.uk
Web: www.troubador.co.uk

ISBN: 978 1 780881 89 8

Typesetting: Troubador Publishing Ltd, Leicester, UK
Printed and bound in Great Britain by
Clays Ltd, St Ives plc

To Silvia and Giuseppe. Again.
But also to Mark
– who counts for so much though he hasn't been here long –
and to Alice who's no longer here.

The two epigraphs are quoted respectively from Claudio Magris, *L'infinito viaggiare*, published by Mondadori (quotation translated into English by John Gatt) and from Wisława Szymborska's poem 'Could have' in *View with a grain of sand* (selected poems translated by Stanisłav Barańczak and Clare Cavanagh), published by Harcourt Brace and Company.

"the hopes of a generation in a particular historical season
are part of that season's history and have thus also
contributed to making us what we are, even if they have
been unfulfilled or belied by the course of events…"
CLAUDIO MAGRIS

"Listen,
How your heart pounds inside me."
WISŁAWA SZYMBORSKA

FOREWORD

Why this story

Some years ago I revisited the places where, as a child, I had spent a long and happy summer: Abbazia (Opatija) and its surroundings, on the Carnaro (Kvarner) Gulf of what is now Croatia's Dalmatian coast on the Adriatic. The garden in which I had then played, giving on to a bay with white cliffs, is naturally much smaller than I remembered, but the house still retains traces of a beauty which time, far from smothering, has only made more touching and precious.

That first visit to Abbazia – and to Fiume (Rijeka) – was followed by many more, and getting to know the story of those places became an imperative for me.

I thus set out on a journey of enthralling research and reading: everything I read generated new stimuli, led to fresh curiosity, raised questions to which simple answers seemed impossible. Even as a child, I've always been suspicious of simple answers.

So I made landfall at a moment of the Story – of History – which looked to me like the eve of a Big Bang.

I think that's just it: there are moments in History that immediately precede the points of no return, being positioned at a nodal shift in the ramification of human affairs.

The years after the First World War – immediately following the Russian Revolution and immediately preceding the rise of Fascism – are one of those crucial turning-points: which way would things go? Pacifism or rearmament? Conservatism or reform? The development and consolidation of liberal democracy or the overthrow of the parliamentary principle? Each bifurcation could spark off an infinity of variables and set in train an infinity of possibilities, as in that marvel of combinational calculus, the Rubik cube, which so entertained us as children.

So, in that tormented post-war period, many doors still remain open, many cards are still in play, the possibilities remain unexplored. A significant portion of the world is almost a clean slate, the new international order has yet to be decided. A new future can be forged. A few years later, this will no longer be the case.

In that decisive phase of European History, Fiume and its surroundings – including adjacent Abbazia – is one of the most strategic points: a multicultural and multiethnic territory soon to be contested, disputed, dismembered.

This book recalls those moments and those places, centering on the Fiume enterprise.

An embarrassing episode which is usually tucked away in a few lines in school history textbooks. But the complexity and the contradictions experienced in the Fiume crisis seemed to me an exemplary reflection – a stripping down, rather than a metaphor – of the complexity and contradictions of the Italian, and perhaps of the European, situation in the wake of the First World War: opposing and exacerbated political agendas, new social and cultural ferments within a climate of widespread violence, hopes of a transformation and upheaval of the old world, an aspiration for order and peace coupled with the inability of many people, after years of warfare, to fit anew into that peaceful order.

At that dramatic moment – while in Paris the victorious Powers were discussing and signing treaties which were to foment new tensions and ignite new conflicts – Fiume not only constituted an expression of fiery nationalism – potentially dangerous, as nationalism always is – but also an outburst of rebellion and utopianism, of social and sexual transgressiveness, of artistic ferment and heterodox thought. In the course of five seasons – between September 1919 and December 1920 – the town in fact attracted a welter of dissident and rebellious spirits, uncompromising and restless, of various kinds and origins: libertarians and hotheads, students and ex-combatants, intellectuals and artists, monarchists and republicans, reformers and dreamers seeking alternative ways in a world that had just been torn apart by the carnage of the Great War; and they came from the most diverse countries – Italy and France, the United States and Ireland, India and Egypt, Belgium, Albania, Montenegro...

Of course, it mustn't be forgotten that these included above all nationalists, adventurers, ex-commandos intoxicated by years of warfare and accustomed to violence.

But what impelled me was to explore the less familiar aspect of the Fiume experience, telling the story of the idealistic, utopian soul of the anti-conformist, visionary wing in Fiume, probably a minority. What matters is that that soul was there, it did attempt to impact on the course of events, and was humiliated and beaten. Quite possibly, its humiliation and defeat influenced the way History subsequently unfolded, including the rise of Fascism.

In this respect it is emblematic that some of the actors in Fiume were to embrace Fascism, while others were to combat it strenuously or opt for exile.

We are all aware of the dark sequel: in 1924 Fiume was annexed by Italy, which had by then been transformed into a dictatorship. The brutal fascistization of the town began, including bloody repression of the Croat and Slovene minorities and of the political parties opposing the regime. But this was to take place in a profoundly changed context.

However, I wish to emphasize that I am not an historian. I am a writer who loves to explore History most of all in its cones of shadow, its hidden creases, the impact of the iceberg of "grand" History on the diminutive keels of the "little" Stories, of the submerged lives, of the everyday microhistory of all the countless and nameless Everywomen and Everymen.

That is why strong tales of individuals also run through this book: stories woven of enchantment and disenchantment, of expectations and struggles, of anxieties and errors, of suffering and love.

Although I've attempted a faithful recreation of the climate and events of the period, my novel does not aspire to historical authority, nor does it intend to offer a personal interpretation of the narrated events. Rather, I was concerned to reconstruct the atmosphere of a crucial and extremely complex moment of our past.

For those who may be interested in finding out more, I refer to my notes at the end of the book and the related suggestions for further reading. As regards myself, I can only add that in digging into that complex post-war period – into the colonial partition of the planet, the mandate system, the configuration of geopolitical theatres in which many of the subsequent developments of our History sink their roots – I have at times had the impression that I've understood more of the present: of my world, and of my way of being in the world.

Frankly, with some uneasiness.

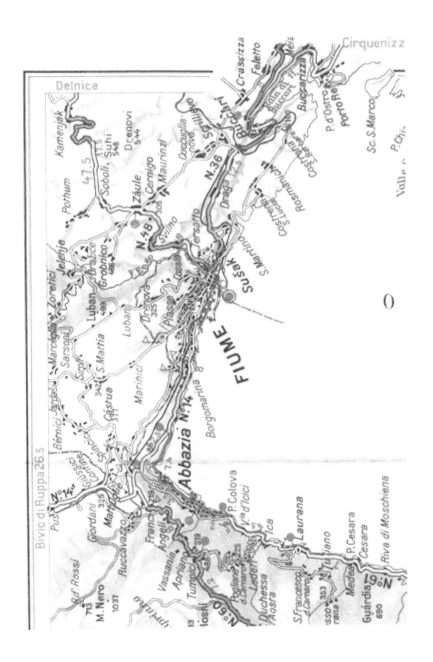

Prologue

Abbazia (Opatija, Croatia)
May 2000

Maybe my coming here was a mistake. But I had no other choice. I felt that nothing was more urgent than all this, which is now my life.

A short while ago I got to the house, which is now a tumbledown ruin, and I slipped into the park through the ramshackle gateway. Never before have I been here, but the old stone fountain at the foot of the broad stairway didn't seem foreign to me, or unfamiliar: as if it had appeared to me in dream, or somewhere in my imagination. I sat on its edge and from there surveyed the trees among the brambles, the steps half overgrown with nettles, the villa with its collapsed roof, the cracks and the patches of moss on the body of the amputated putto placed there to spout a jet of water which must have dried up long ago.

And suddenly I recalled the small boy I'd seen in a

refugee camp, years ago: he'd lost his arms in a minefield and his eyes glanced vivaciously, as if substituting wrists, palms and fingers.

I came back out, and walked on. Strange: I didn't feel tired from my interminable journey. What I felt was the unexpected sensation of finding this place familiar.

Now the lane has just become a long sunken footpath which winds through vegetable plots and gardens, trunks of Mediterranean pines and clumps of sage and rosemary. It descends in steep curves, going to the bay. *Her* bay.

A stronger gust of wind shakes the boughs of an apple-tree that protrudes over a dry-stone wall, marking a boundary.

And straight after, I sight the sea.

Then the picture is vivid and brutal, like the shadows cast by this raking light that slides along the sides of things. It's a sharp, real picture, even if only I can see it.

… The girl sits alone. Her back leaning against a rock, her legs crossed upon the shingle and her feet bare, stretched out to the lapping waves: the tide is just coming in.

She gazes towards the far end of the bay, towards Fiume. Or maybe not. Rather, she's reading, or studying.

Maybe she has an open book upon her knees, and the book is a Latin book. That's it, that's how I imagine it: a heavy Latin book. And she's struggling with the translation.

She picks out subjects, hunts for verbs, vies with her glossary in memory, checking through declensions. Her hair is gathered in a bunch, her gaze is alert and her hands long and slender. Seventeen, possibly eighteen. Her name I know. It's Greta.

Then she suddenly notices something that seems to sneak upon

2

the silence, but so imperceptible and faint that at first it's barely an impression.

She searches the sky, far away, and sees them. Two tiny specks amid the clouds, scarabs that catch the light and seem to pierce the horizon, travelling close together in a line, in between the last rays of the sun and the seascape.

She closes her book, places it on a rock. The daytime warmth still lingers in the whiteness of the rocks and the shingle which she now strokes with the wet soles of her feet. She lifts her hands up to her forehead, shading her eyes, and follows the two specks.

They are approaching rapidly, coming from Fiume.

The girl watches one of the biplanes which is moving away from the other one, banking and heading towards her bay. She follows its trajectory, its new flight path: the plane descends, comes nearer. Perhaps she props herself up with her hands to maintain her body balance as she throws her head back to look, and she even manages to glimpse the aviator's face looking down and his hand waving her a greeting.

The tossed object takes her by surprise: a waxed paper package. Why, I wonder, do I imagine that the package is tied up in the pilot's scarf. A green scarf, of military hue.

Or, no, a brighter colour: blue or red. Her name is on the parcel: simply Greta.

As she treads barefoot towards the object which she has already spotted somewhere between a rock and a clump of broomplant, the biplane suddenly wobbles like a marsh-bird shaking water off its plumage, and Greta reads that controlled roll as a greeting gesture.

So she too raises an arm, gives just a wave of a hand.

The aircraft resumes its trim, rejoins its fellow, falls back into line, flies on. Greta examines the parcel she has picked up, undoes the knots, unwraps it. When she discovers its contents, her eyes open wide, *and the air of astonishment on her face makes her look as if she's still a child.*

Finally, standing erect amid the rocks, she gazes up at the sky. Maybe she laughs.

★ ★ ★

Is that how it really happened – she with her book, the dropped package, the biplanes flying across the bay – or is it a momentary mirage, a trick of my imagination?

I remember the first untruth told me as a little girl by an adult.

"Your mamma's just gone to sleep."

"I believe you I believe you I believe you. I believe you, I swear I do. I believe you."

And at the same time I was wondering whether I'd ever again be able to believe what anybody said.

I slip my hand in my pocket and feel that folded paper whose text I now know by heart. I feel it confirms this choice, my motives for being here today. It's an article nearly ninety years old, but I've only just recently read it, and have only just recently grasped its full meaning.

The Fiume League, constituted in that town in 1920, takes upon itself the right and the duty to represent, in every form and manner…

A bird flies up out of a garden. I follow it as it glides over the sea.

… the rights of defeated and of highly marginal peoples…

Defeated and marginal peoples. I suddenly recall the little boy sitting at the edge of a street in Mostar. Behind him, the walls of a large building: three blasts had ripped it apart. He was holding a football and looking at the river close by. Hit by bombs during the autumn, the old bridge over the Neretva had ceased to exist months ago.

… to be admitted, in Paris, to a Conference and to Treaties which claim to make peace…

I can still see it, that face that knows no peace: a young woman, slumping. Her head could not stop shaking. In the genocide she had lost everybody. It was Rwanda, 1996. That was where my NGO was operating.

…peoples who lack sufficient raw materials or oil to arouse the interest of the victorious Nations…

Defeated nations, victorious nations… Mozambique, 2003. I was there that summer, along with others, for the Maputo Protocol which had to be supported in every way, ratified, made a living thing: at last African women could see acknowledged by statute their right to life, to education and to contraception, to their integrity as human beings. At last genital mutilation, which at a single stroke rent soul and sex, body and dignity, was being outlawed.

I know, there's still a very long way to go. But to have started is already something.

I've left my sandals on the shingle. The chilly water makes me shiver. I find a rock to sit on and rest on my knees the book I've been carrying for days: a gust of wind turns the pages, opens it at the black-and-white photo which I've tucked in between the pages of verse.

I look at the girl in the photo who's smiling between her two male companions, her long tress of hair standing out against her light-coloured bodice, one arm resting on her hip, her eyes gazing at something behind the camera. I touch her face with the tip of my finger.

It's her that's the real reason for my journey.

It's because of Greta that I'm here now.

Autumn

*The skies are streaked with grey like the fur of tabby cats, the
winds blowing off the sea and the shadows lengthening along the
shores like the beams of the lighthouse.*
The red of the shrivelled leaves crumbles into fiery streamers.
*The waves get bigger and bite into the bollards at the end of the
pier.*
*Beyond tufts of reeds, occasionally a stork rests, its stilts long and
slender as stalks beneath its snowy white feathers.*

Flavours are strong on the palate.
*The juice a touch tart of apples, the sweetness of grape clusters, the
pasty pulp of persimmons which drop with light thuds and smear
orange patches on the endmost meadow grass.*

So Elisa wrote down those colours. Or leastways tried to.
Then tore out the sheet; words aren't up to it.
She then thought beauty cruel if it can't be spoken.

Fiume
12 September 1919

Greta flurries, feeling out of breath, as her heart pounds against her chest.

She can feel sweat on her temples, wipes it away with her finger-tips. Her feet seem to fly over the broad limestone slabs that pave the road, where the lime-tree fronds project sudden shadows in their regular intermittency.

She stops: the running has finished her. She draws deep breaths. She has a stitch.

She glances ahead to gauge the distance that still separates her from her goal, at the end of the tramlines that go from the Sussak bridge at her back on towards Cantrida.

A twinge of anxiety, a knot of tension. She can't delay further: it's too risky. What if her father were back? She starts running again towards Piazza Adamich, her feet pounding the cobbles, measuring out spaces she knows well: the row of stores along the pier, the town centre full of cafes and restaurants, the stone and brick buildings frowning down at the piazzas and streets, the old bell-towers soaring upwards, sticking out like long fingers beyond the red-tiled roofscape.

She slows down again, panting. How much further to the boundary?

Old Furio – more household factotum than chauffeur – is waiting for her there, at the checkpoint, at the wheel of the family's Lancia: only Greta had papers and documents permitting her to enter the town, only she could get past the pickets of the *carabinieri* in their khaki uniform with their stiff aeroplane of a hat the size of a cocotte's screen. Further on, helping them patrol the checkpoint north of Fiume, was a knot of English sailors with light rye hair just peeping out from under their caps, and in impeccably spotless uniforms: one of them came up holding a mug of tea and murmured to her smilingly: *"You can go, mademoiselle, you can go…"*

And he enveloped her in a blue gaze that seemed to roam among her apparel.

"Are you visiting…" he held her up further, *"are you visiting someone, here in Fiume? Maybe… maybe your fiancé?"*

Greta smiled back, and, taking back her permit, replied mouthing some of the little English she's learnt during these last few months: *"Who knows, sir, who knows…?"*

Then she was off in a rush, her eye on the clock tower of San Vito to calculate how much time she still had.

She could feel the Englishman's blue eyes somewhere on her back and could imagine where.

Finally she got to her destination – the old hospital pavilion – and delivered to *zia* Ingrid all the stuff that had been carefully packed into a bag whose bulk and weight – and importance also, or so at least it seemed to Greta –

matched a bridal trousseau. The asylum medical officer only grudgingly gave his permission, and only after humiliating pleas and hints at the certain gratitude that the family would demonstrate. That the family in fact knew nothing – was totally in the dark about the whole thing and god save us if it wasn't – Greta kept strictly to herself.

But now that she's brought it off, she feels the urgency to get back.

She turns off briskly at the Roman arch, comes out on to the central avenue, skirts the tramline.

Outside a little café, two women seated at a table – wearing broad-brimmed hats and light-coloured dresses – are eating fruit preserves coated in thick red sauce. A rose stands on the white table-cloth between their crystal bowls. She watches them, slows down for an instant, suddenly realizes she's hungry. She crosses the tramlines and starts running in earnest once more, while she feels sweat trickling down her temples.

That's just when it happens. Or at least when she becomes aware of it.

At first it's the vague impression of something new, over there: the windows of one house are thrown open, a woman appearing in a balcony leans out pointing into the distance, a boy, hopping on to a bike, pedals off like crazy. Then, a feverish bustle, loud cries, voices calling out to each other, it all seems to come to a head down that way, at the end of the main avenue. Finally there's a burst of euphoria, exclamations and excited yells, shoving and rushing and children leaping: and at doors and windows and terraces people have started waving the Italian tricolour.

A shove makes her stumble. Greta leans against a wall,

and at last she sees them. For an instant alarm and astonishment almost take her breath away: the line of trucks stretches so far that she can't make out where it ends.

At its head comes a red car: but it's almost grey with dust, and its wheels are coated with mud. A man is standing in the open car and stretches out one arm, waving his hand. The white snout of a hound also appears, it's panting, perhaps from thirst.

Then the column comes to a halt, and as if in response to a signal – which, however, no one appears to have given – dozens and dozens of soldiers leap out of the trucks waving their hats and flags amid the cheering crowd: and all around them, on the street, looking out of windows or crowded on to balconies, men and women throng from all around, while clusters of small boys who have clambered on to ledges look on curiously, their skinny legs dangling like the pincers of sea-crabs.

The trucks get moving again amid the flanking crowd that makes way for them.

A new song gradually fills the air. People have strewn the road with sprays of laurel plucked straight off the trees as a sign of homage as in ancient times: they squeak gently underfoot and are ground into slivers beneath the wheels.

One soldier leaps to the ground beside Greta, casts her an ardent glance. A woman has come up close and proffers him some wine.

Greta finds herself there in a daze, dry-mouthed and with aching feet. A wave of shoving people presses up behind her and seems to thrust her aside: brusquely attempting to get out of their way, she climbs the steps in front of a large building and stands with her back to the door. What is going on round here? What do those guys want, here in Fiume? Where have they come from? And, first and foremost, who are they?

But amid that dizziness that has overwhelmed her like a blast of hot air she hears the chime of bells reminding her that it's already midday.

She skips down in alarm. She's already expected at home, and she certainly can't tell them why she's so late this morning, when everyone thinks she's somewhere else.

Trying to keep clear of the throng, she starts running again to get to the checkpoint, which she suddenly thinks must have folded like the houses of cards which she built up bit by bit as a child, more and more lop-sided under the added weight. And she recites prayers and charms at every stretch: that her father isn't home yet, that Furio hasn't driven off with the Lancia in a panic, that that strange motorcade of trucks hasn't blocked her path, that her way back home is clear.

And above all that no one in the family has discovered what she's come to Fiume for.

13 settembre 1919

To General Pietro Badoglio
For His Eyes Only

Fiume is in extreme danger Stop risk of most serious
international incident and unimaginable consequences
Stop possible flashpoint new war Stop Your Excellency
appointed Military Commissioner Extraordinary for Julian
Venetia with absolute command over north-eastern
frontier forces Stop You are ordered to assume command
immediately Stop At this grave moment I rely your
complete devotion loyal servant of our fatherland Stop
    Francesco Saverio Nitti
    Prime Minister of Italy

Badoglio folds up the telegram, and smooths it down with
his hand.

The train he is travelling on has been scheduled
specifically for him: a high priority special express, arranged

in little over an hour since his meeting at the Braschi Palace, which houses the office of the head of government.

A strictly personal meeting, to which he was summoned in great haste by the prime minister's office that same evening with a phone-call to his Rome office as second-in-command of His Majesty's Royal Army.

As soon as it reached the capital, the news of the *coup de main* had been immediately jumped on by news editors: news-vendors were swarming like flies along the street and yelling the news at the top of their voices, even finding their way into the Palace itself, with the newspapers selling hand over fist.

The rooms inside Palazzo Braschi were cool: a relief to come in out of the sun. But the meeting had rapidly dispelled the sensation of relief of a few moments earlier. This meeting comprised four men, stiff and tense, with grim faces: sitting beside Nitti, the Prime Minister, was the War Minister, Albricci. Opposite them, General Diaz.

They had been waiting for him, Pietro Badoglio. He had arrived on time. Then he had carefully perused the telegram which Nitti handed to him:

Column grenadiers commandos with armoured machine-guns led by d'Annunzio at 11.45 hours swept aside all resistance and reached Fiume Stop

Events taking serious turn compromising our international standing Stop Please inform whether they have secret Government backing otherwise request means to act with maximum effect Stop

Signed

General Pittaluga

Badoglio hadn't batted an eyelid as he handed back the folded sheet. He had asked no questions nor made any comment of any kind: the very expression on his face had remained almost unchanged. He had merely listened to the curt, lapidary exposé.

Then – tight-lipped Piedmontese that he was, even more than soldier – he had nodded his acceptance of that sudden and unexpected appointment which he could sense oozed trouble: Military Commissioner Extraordinary, in command with immediate and absolute authority over the whole of Julian Venetia. The territory only just redeemed for Italy. That was the official appointment. As for the implied corollaries, there was no need to spell them out: put everything back in its place, restore order and discipline as quickly as possible and with as little damage as possible.

Badoglio hurriedly took his leave and prepared for departure on a specially scheduled train.

Only once he was on the train did he study the map of Fiume, the railway line from Trieste, that stretch between the blue Adriatic and the ochre of unfamiliar lands, criss-crossed by frontier signs that look like rough stitches on torn fabric. Then, here in Bologna, the unforeseen occurred.

First, it took him by surprise, then it caused him no little alarm on account of the swiftness of the reaction and the violence which it sparked off. An utterly new kind of violence, which he's come to know just these last few months: agitations, strikes, lock-outs. New wounds opened by the war and others, much older, which have never been healed. He sits up to listen, stiffening, looking out through the window into the fog that swirls over the station, past the cordon of *carabinieri* surrounding the stationary train and trying to hold back the surging throng of youths.

Even from there in the train he can hear a chorus of slogans that grow more furious with waiting.

It's students, he's been told. And they've heard about the train, who it's carrying, where it's bound. The word spread rapidly since news of the march on Fiume was trumpeted by the press.

Badoglio doesn't really want to, but he's forced to hear those voices chanting a name insistently as if hammering a nail: *D'Annunzio d'Annunzio d'Annunzio.*

In between there are only the epithets dealt out to the Allies. It seems to him that the least offensive is the cry of *cheats and bastards.* Badoglio draws his head back, reclines against the back of the seat.

Yet, up to a few days earlier, the great majority of Italians didn't even know of the existence of a town called Fiume, so far out to the north-east, beyond Trieste which had just been won in the war which was just over: and suddenly, lo and behold, it's the epicentre of a new visionary revolt.

And from there the blaze could spread. So now it's up to him to put the fire out.

Then it all happens in a flash, unexpectedly: a body breaks away from the mass and shoots forward, past the line of *carabinieri*, with an animal impetus and a sudden burst of rebellion that overcomes every barrier: he climbs and clings to the train, flattens his face against the window, now rivets his eyes to Badoglio's. For a few instants they stay like that, general and student, staring at each other through the diaphragm of that window-pane as if it were a sheet of litmus paper.

Simply intent on looking at each other, on

understanding. On studying each other across astronomical distances.

No gesture of violence, or fury. Just that one word, chanted in a whisper. The solo performance of the chorus of slogans still being chanted out there. Then a sudden blow descends on the youth's back: Badoglio hears the thud, the fall, the crumpling of the body – like an old bread-bag – on the edge of the track below. In the distance, there's the crack of a gunshot.

The general just has time to crane his neck, to quietly drink in that sight under the lamp's pool of light: the young man on the ground, in a body bag, the two policemen bending over the body, intent now on dragging it away, his glasses splintered, crushed beneath a boot. Then the train recommences its journey and the weal of darkness reabsorbs and sutures all things.

For an instant, Badoglio shuts his eyes.

There's a thorn in his mind: *d'Annunzio.*

He knows d'Annunzio well. He's known him from wartime, when they were both fighting.

He esteems him as a soldier, as a literary man he couldn't really say. Literature isn't his trade.

But it's the man – d'Annunzio the *man* – that most troubles him: the visionary, the rebel, the radical. Always walking on the razor's edge, always living at the extreme, at his ease amid the most absurd risks and dares of sheer madness.

A genius and a lunatic, an angel and a scoundrel: in a word, a poet.

He folds up the map of Fiume. It's uncomfortable, this role that he's accepted, this task that he's been set.

And undoubtedly it's thankless, embarrassing: one Italian officer against another Italian officer, just a few months after the end of a war that has left behind millions of dead and wounded, a flood of enraged returnees, social problems and tensions that march on without stopping, in step with inflation.

No, this is not the moment for Italians to be fighting Italians.

Abbazia
13 September 1919, evening

The man abruptly raises his arm and violently agitates his hand as if to drive away something visible only to himself.

His face creases into a grimace, and the throb of who knows what image quivers for a few moments beneath his closed eyelids.

The train is going at full speed. The man's sleep is profound. Around him, in the coach, other bodies are huddled up in an effort to sleep – or at least to get some rest – side by side in that darkness.

The vibration is like a wall of air against the Nieuport's wings.

His hands clutching the joystick and his eyes searching through the clouds in a now familiar spasm, Tullio leans out of his cockpit and searches.

Beyond bursts of violent white flashes that look like pure phosphorus he can now discern the spreading columns of smoke, the enormous spouts of rock, the craters violating the landscape, the snaking line of fire – a grass-snake drawing itself to its full length and then contracting – from the hilltops of San Gabriele down to the shores of the sea. And the hilltop bunkers, the grenade pot-holes, the barrage balloons with their ungainly wallowing over the horizon, gut-full of hydrogen, their skin glinting.

Beneath him, the earth shudders. Gouged, torn, smoking. Scooped down to its marrow.

Then a thump seems to make the whole front quake and yellowish fumes well up like swarms of insects or like pus erupting who knows where: and they roll downhill, creeping into the caves and gullies, filling the ravines and the trenches. Asphyxiating gases. Phosgene.

For a moment, precariously, he manages to see his brother Elia as if he were there in front of him: his musket in his hand, his pack on his back, his face plunged inside its mask, his dagger stuck in his bandolier: a quarry pursued down the long entrail of mud, waiting to emerge into emptiness.

Then there creeps into the corner of his eye the ghost of a shadow.

The other plane has popped up all of a sudden, above him and just a bit behind, out of a tall mass of almost black thunderclouds: Tullio sees its silhouette grow larger in the little mirror of his instrument panel.

He grips the joystick hard, jams his feet down on the pedal. His eyes are glued to the crosses on the wings of the Austrian Aviatik which seems to have come out of nowhere.

21

It all takes place at feverish, lightning speed. From above, the biplane banks and descends – a brutal lunge, nose-diving – and pops up again in front of him, so close to Tullio's Nieuport that he catches sight of the machine-gunner a few metres away: the pallor of the long gaunt face, the eyes behind the goggles, his coat collar turned up. Tullio gives a start: he resembles his brother. The man resembles his brother, Elia.

For an instant, as though encased in plaster, Tullio senses his reflexes have slowed down. The machine-gun burst hits him just above the right wing. He feels the heat surge suddenly rise to his head, the blood throbbing in his temples, the tingling in his hands. Pain bursts his eardrums with the instantaneous change in pressure as he loses altitude in a nose-dive, and now the vibration of the biplane is suddenly so violent that he fears it will break up.

But the aircraft recovers well from the air pocket, its oscillation diminishes, it regains stability.

Tullio re-sets the trim and banks sharply, dipping suddenly beneath the other's tail. Then he climbs. He climbs and takes aim. His clenched knuckles hurt. The gun-burst roars inside his head and its stutter violently assails his eardrums.

The Aviatik bucks for a moment or two a few metres away, then thick dark smoke issues from its engine: and in an instant the biplane is a black pyre spinning as it shatters and rends the sky.

Relief draws a sharp yell out of Tullio. The pilot is a twisted shape. The other body drops into space.

He follows its trajectory and sees it fall – a disjointed puppet – beyond the Italian lines, its arms flung out as on a cross: then the soldiers' swift leap out of the trenches to rush upon what's left of that young man on the ground: bayonets thrusting senselessly, the rage of months of warfare in the work of ferocious hands.

Elia. He resembled his brother Elia.

And suddenly the plane loses altitude and starts to vibrate madly, and terror tastes like blood filling the palate and the mouth. As nausea seems to flood him, he realizes he's falling.

Tullio opens his eyes wide all at once and awakes to the rolling of the train that is braking amid jolts and long-drawn-out clanking.

For an instant, just one instant – still befuddled by the dream, caught between sleeping and waking – he feels at war again: his senses alert, his nerves shaken and tense, his body ready to attack. He is fully roused by a voice enjoining him to get off the train. He alights swiftly, without a word, his kit-bag on his back, jacket and book in his hand.

A sudden shaft of light that continuously slices through the night picks out on a signboard the name of the little station.

MATTUGLIE. MATTUGLIE ABBAZIA.

Several Italian soldiers are moving feverishly about: they board the train, open bags, search through the seats, crawl beneath the wagons, groping everywhere with their hands. You can feel the tension in the air, commands come like whiplashes.

From somewhere in the darkness behind him comes a pistol shot.

Tullio catches sight of the officer violently shoving along a passenger, sticking the pistol into his back: they disappear beyond the station, past a closed door that seems to lead into a warehouse.

He eyes the young fellow next to him. He'd already noticed him on the train: a long mop of hair over his blue eyes, quick, nervous hand movements, white shirt, well-cut jacket.

He must be about his own age. No younger than twenty-five.

And all at once it dawns on him: his companion's apparent slowness in making out words, his copying what the others do through fear of having misunderstood, his enquiring looks all around so as to make sense of what's going on... it's not merely a momentary anxiety: he's feeling lost in the language no less than in that new environment.

So Tullio goes ahead. He has no precise reason, he's just following his instinct which, he knows, has been sharpened by war. The shaft of light has now moved away, illuminating the edge of a wall at the far end of the station.

Out of his pocket he grabs his brother Elia's medal – he's always kept it with him, ever since that day – then turns to the lad and swiftly pinning it on to his jacket whispers simply: "Just leave this to me."

There isn't time to add anything: the two soldiers are getting closer.

Tullio instantly spots the collar badges they're wearing on their uniforms, indicating their battalion. That tells him where they've fought. On the Carso plateau, along the Isonzo, on the slopes of San Michele – the battle-front facing Trieste.

"He's with me," he says, showing his papers and nodding towards his companion, "but my mate's dumb. A souvenir from the Isonzo battle-front."

He's well aware that such-like traumas are not at all

uncommon. The war that hadn't long been ended had not only mangled bodies. With his eyes on the soldier who's holding their papers, he adds: "He was at Plava, in May of '17, altitude 383."

No one who's fought there can forget the lives lost, the massacre. For an instant, Tullio can see it once more, the two whole days and nights of non-stop bombardment, beginning at daybreak of the 12th of May: the same that returns in his dreams, the same that he is unable to forget.

The soldier scrutinizes their faces, lowers his gaze on to the medal on the chest of the lad standing in front of him.

"Where are you heading?"

"Abbazia."

"The purpose of your journey?"

"Business."

"How long are you staying?"

"No more than three or four days."

The man hesitates an instant, and Tullio seizes the opportunity to stretch out his hand: his gesture seems warlike, expressing aggression, but also authority. The soldier recognizes it instantly: it's the gesture of an officer.

His reaction is immediate and natural, drilled by years of warfare and subordination to his superior officers: he quickly hands back their papers and gives a parting salute.

His fists thrust back into his pockets, with a feeling of relief that relaxes his tension at last, Tullio moves slowly away. He skirts the track, then turns off, leaving the station behind.

Only then, beneath the lime-trees of the avenue, does the young man walking beside him address him and hold out his hand.

"Paul Forst. American. From New York."

"Is that the name on your passport?"

"No, as you've already guessed. That reads Paolo Lamborghini."

"Not bad," says Tullio with a wink. "An excellent Italian name."

Then he grasps and shakes that hand warmly, thinking that it still feels strange, months after the end of the war, to exchange civil greetings.

There's a white full moon over the sea, radiating a fiery halo, like a disc of red-hot metal with an icy heart. He remembers: he used to gaze at it as a boy, when out fishing with his father. They would get up quietly in the darkness, stumbling into chairs and steps – through gritted teeth, his father would swear at yet another bump, at the noise – and eventually they stepped out into the night as a dog started barking. Like sentinels guarding the watercourse, along its edge stood paunchy mulberry trees with dry spikes like long thorns, and atop those thorns, at their very tip, a moon like this one dandled to the rhythm of his sleepy footsteps. He hasn't been out fishing since that time. Since his father died he never again took up rod and line.

Paul's voice, with its broad drawling syllables, brings him back to the present: "Could you explain to me now the meaning of that word *dumb* that you applied to me?"

Tullio keeps on walking. "This area, for Italians, or at least for *certain* Italians, is a real… hot zone. Censored. And they certainly don't welcome the idea of too many foreigners turning up and snooping around where they shouldn't."

"Well, thanks, then," murmurs the other. " *Beatus vir qui scit amicitiam.*"

He stares at him in silence, in amazement. He wasn't

expecting Latin. But the foreigner is right: lucky the man who knows friendship.

He looks around for the first time, for an instant he scans shapes and things.

A log recently cut, smooth as an altar. A wisp of smoke from a chimney which the wind blows into untidy curls and then rapidly disperses into the sky. The outline of great dark houses, gardens in the stillness of night, the occasional lane going down towards the sea. Further down, an archway. To the right, some steps. As they approach, a cat cringes, eyes them, slips round a corner.

As if steeping in the briny air, he scents the fragrance of bread. It suddenly comes to Tullio's mind that he hasn't had a bite to eat for hours.

Then he hears Paul's voice, just a bit quieter, hesitant, with its foreign twang: "Actually, I ain't heading for Abbazia. I'm really going... well, I'm going to Fiume."

There's a moment's silence between them. The sudden call of an owl. The sound of footsteps not far off.

Tullio turns towards Paul. He passes him a cigarette, lights up. "I never took you for a tourist." He inhales a long puff. "And I'm heading for Fiume, too."

They stop and observe each other for an instant, studying one another, in silence. Then they slap one another on the back and burst out laughing together.

Tullio suddenly realizes that's something else the war's done: it's wiped out the frontiers between languages – between all those different nationalities – in the name of one single language: that of violence or that of solidarity.

An army truck passes them on the road. They start walking again, keeping closer to the walls.

The scent of the lime-trees now prevails, the scent of bread is gone.

13 September 1919

To General Pietro Badoglio

Military Commissioner Extraordinary for Julian Venetia
For His Eyes Only

Top Secret

Fiume is in the hands of the rebels STOP Your Excellency should consider whether it would be wise to go to Fiume where you might be held the city being subject to actions rebel soldiers STOP Perhaps it is wiser to take over command of all troops Julian Venetia and promptly organize them establishing cordon sanitaire completely isolating Fiume STOP That done send no food to Fiume and let no trains reach there STOP

Francesco Saverio Nitti
Prime Minister of Italy

Abbazia, 13 September 1919, evening

"*Fiume is like a bright beacon shining amidst a sea of abjection...*" Her father is quoting from memory. He combines the inspired air of a prophet with the agitation of someone afflicted with *delirium tremens*. He appears to be drunk, but is not. He has hardly touched his bean and cabbage soup, and his stewed beef is going cold on his plate, swimming in its thick brown juice, but he really doesn't seem to notice.

Greta swallows her last morsel of chocolate mousse – of all desserts, her favourite – and observes her father's whiskers: until yesterday they sagged, grey streaked with white, as if they'd given up. Today they're slicked up and grey-black: what concoction can he have used to make them look younger and hoist them up like two figureheads? He concentrates, continuing with his story.

On the 12th of September the poet Gabriele d'Annunzio arrived in Fiume at the head of a military convoy – they say, suffering from a fever – on a Fiat 501. A convertible. A red one.

Greta lowers her head, smiling. She takes good care not to tell him *"I know. I know because I saw it, and because I was there."*

The trucks were crammed with miscreants of all kinds, whom d'Annunzio had dubbed legionaries: former commandos, monarchists and socialists, officers and privates from the war, all united in that expedition which had suddenly descended on Fiume. All of them determined not to back off. That's what people are saying. And here he takes a sip of wine.

He doesn't seem at all troubled by that motley crew, by that medley of uniforms – and jumbled origins – united under a single command. He seems struck rather by what holds them together: Fiume.

Then Greta concentrates on listening while she tries to picture to herself the diverse sequences of the enterprise.

Everything was so sudden and crazy that no one managed to intervene, he continues, downing a mouthful. Some did try, in fact, on the journey from Ronchi to Fiume, while the crocodile of trucks was inexorably going through the streets of startled old settlements and dusty little townships, where the children flocked the streets wide-eyed to follow that unexpected procession, the jolting vehicles lurching into puddles and quagmire and the soldiers waving their hands or their muskets, chanting their warcry: *A la la.*

Monfalcone, Prosecco, Opicina. Then opening out on to wider and straighter roads, with blue vistas of sea. Trieste, but lately redeemed for Italy. Stern and indecipherable, somewhat haughty, the names of its streets and squares rechristened in Italian when the war ended, some months back.

The attempt to halt in one way or another that band of irregular troops, unauthorized by any government, took place at Castelnuovo, her father explains. There the road was blocked by a detachment of *bersaglieri* light infantry.

D'Annunzio then alighted from the Fiat, snapped into a military salute, stood amid dust and potholes in front of the bemused *bersaglieri*. Then he just talked.

But that man is such a smooth talker that he can lubricate an engine, her father adds with satisfaction. And certainly he was convincing, since the very *bersaglieri* that had been sent to arrest him heard him out in religious silence, half astounded and half mesmerized. Then they too enlisted as legionaries of the bard.

He preens his whiskers, does her father, while not yet ceasing to talk.

Other units of every kind – commandos, mountain troops, grenadiers – were leaving the regular army and going over progressively to swell the poet's rebel force.

So on the 13th of September, at noon, d'Annunzio officially took over as military commander of the town of "liberated Fiume". Her father tells the story excitedly, with his Adam's apple quivering between his starched collar and his double chin, while he relays to his family the speech which d'Annunzio delivered from the balcony of the Government Palace amid a boisterous crowd. He even recalls entire passages.

Greta looks at him, reflects.

Everything seems to have gone awry, ever since the war ended, really.

And there, on Italy's eastern frontier, things seemed far from that return to normality which they had hoped for after what her father called the crash-bang-wallop of the collapse of Austria-Hungary.

Whenever he travelled to Trieste on business – grain exporting and financial investment were his daily bread – he came back each time with fresh alarming news, but it wasn't always easy to gather whether the reports were really to be believed. And he'd also bring other things from Trieste, when he came back home: boxes of Virginia cigars and bottles of vintage wine and packets of fine Moka coffee which he would get roasted in the kitchen: then he would drink it, strong and bitter, reclining in his armchair like a pope, before the fireplace in winter and out on the veranda in summer.

It was then that he would rattle on: tittle-tattle about some acquaintance – in which case she wouldn't even listen – or serious stuff, real news.

And then Greta really did pay attention, eager to know and to understand: for instance, the mess after the war ended when Yugoslavia rejected the London agreement which Italy had signed three years earlier, and laid claim, besides the Istrian peninsula, to the towns of Gorizia and Trieste.

But if she hazarded any questions, her father shot back in annoyance: "You keep your mouth shut, this isn't your female twaddle."

And with that the reportage came to an end.

But now this nameless march on Fiume, led by a *condottiero* poet, has thrown everything up in the air, and once again everything looks uncertain, strange: her father, who can't stop talking; her mother, silent as ever; little Elisa in dismay, staring at them intently with an expression that Greta knows all too well.

She'd like to pull a face at her so as at least to make her smile – her sister smiles too little for one who is only nine – but senses that this isn't the night for it. So all she does is wink at her, with a sidelong glance at her father. Then Greta's glance comes to rest over there, on that chair between her father and her mother, on that space which, ever since it has fallen vacant, seems to have grown beyond measure.

No one has yet got used to that – Arturo's empty chair: and no one has ever sat on it since his sudden death, which was so absurd and so hard to accept.

It's been eleven months, she calculates silently, that her brother's been gone.

But this evening her father has a sparkle of former times in his eyes, and he goes on refilling his glass and pours out wine for them also: even a drop or two for Elisa, who's never yet tasted it and gives a start with astonishment. Then he stands and proposes a toast, which to her ears sounds like a proclamation: "To Fiume. To Fiume free and Italian."

She raises her glass: "Well, then, to Fiume."

The tinkling of crystal is a fragile chord between their fingers. The drop-chandelier hanging from the ceiling seems to take it up and release an echo. The glass panes of the French windows looking out on to the garden reflect shapes and outlines in the fixedness of that moment: her father's massive frame, her mother's rigid self-control, Elisa's red locks swaying slightly on her shoulders as in turn she raises that glass and finally drinks her drop of Terrano wine.

Then Greta seeks out her own reflection among the others on the window-panes.

Her hair gathered up in a bunch, the oval of her face slightly tilted forward, her damning gaze on her school blouse – so demure and severe – and on her boarding-school skirt enfolding her eighteen-year-old body which is now really a woman's body, though at home everyone vies in treating her still and always as a child. She pictures – rather than sees – even the tiniest details of her face: the sprinkling of freckles on her nose, the tiny, fairer locks of hair that slip over her temples, her right incisor, white and healthy, but with a tiny tip missing, heritage of a day long past. She likes herself not quite enough, but nothing can be done about it.

She gets to her feet, wraps herself in a shawl.

"Where are you off to?" asks her father.

She'd like to tell him, I'm going to Fiume. I'm going to see for myself what's really happening, I'm going to work out for myself with my own eyes whether it's worth a toast or not. I'm going to make up my mind, I'm going to get to the bottom of it.

But she's got to suppress it all in an acceptable reply, like a well-brought-up daughter who knows how to behave: "I'm going to get a breath of air in the garden."

Within the sudden silence of the sitting-room, Greta has the impression she can hear waves crashing upon the rocks, yet outside there seems to be no wind to carry the sounds of the bay. Maybe she's just imagined it.

But with her very first steps beyond the patio she feels the profound peace which, ever since she was a child, that greenery and that fragrance, that sparring of shadows and moods, instil in her.

Looking out over the bay of Abbazia, the garden which

her grandfather had laid out around their spacious house is now irremediably losing its original balancing symmetries and is bursting into anarchy, with thick brambles, fronds and undergrowth: cedars of Lebanon, clumps of bananas, camellias growing right up to the steps and magnolias whose violent scent almost makes one swoon, smelling more languid in dry weather and sharper when it blows from the north. But for her grandfather, as she knows, the garden had been a real park, the luxury to be indulged in by a man accustomed to hard work but also ready to allow himself to be tempted by new delights and passions, whereas Greta's father has always seen that mock-up of an equatorial world – an amalgam of essences, mosses and exhalations – as just gloss, a whim to be abandoned without hesitation or regret.

So the park, in proud decay, now seems no more than a forest, and the gardener's cottage has been deserted for many years: just two stone-built rooms at the bottom of the park, at the end overlooking the sea, amid a tangle of canes planted as a discreet windbreak and now overgrown in a riotous thicket buffeted by winds from south and north. She can still remember the gardener, wearing his leather apron, his hands the size of dockside cranes and his face like that of a Balkan brigand: but he would teach her the name of every flower and would pick her sprays of that sweet-tasting mint whose savour she prolonged by sucking it gently between her teeth, taking care not to chew it.

The great house stands high up, on the opposite side, at the top end of the park. It's comfortable and spacious, but severe. No orgy of stuccoes or neo-baroque ornamentation or *Secession* frills: the family lodestars have always been sobriety and dignity.

But what she loves is not the house. It's where the house ends, where enclosure opens out, allowing the gaze to extend as far as the sea and to glimpse other limits, other horizons.

That's where she wants to go now. She just wants to sit upon a rock, to gaze at the lights of Fiume.

An irregular little gravel avenue traverses the entire garden – fragrant with sage and rosemary, with resin and lavender – but then narrows into a pathway leading to the white hollow that looks like the house's solid womb: there you go along amid a few rocks, then you come to the stone steps that go straight down to the sea. A rocky beach, with deep clear water and seagulls diving in from time to time.

Greta takes off her shoes and socks, lifts up her skirt a little, and sits carefully on one of the steps, with her feet in the water which still feels warm from the day's sunshine.

A small crab shrinks back to hide under a rock.

Little wave-crests and foam lap at her ankles.

The semi-darkness that has descended upon her is nibbling away at the edges of things: the tops of the trees in the parks that slope gently down from the neighbouring villas towards the sea, the brow of the coastline amid boulders, the outline of Monte Maggiore rising behind Abbazia. And in the distance, barely divined, the islands of Cherso and Veglia, which give perspective to the horizon of the great gulf of Carnaro.

Breathing the sea air, Greta now looks into the distance: there lies Fiume, across the bay, right opposite Abbazia, set like a conch between the slopes of a mountain and the rugged flanks of the Carso plateau, as if to figure the very heart of a natural amphitheatre.

And now its lights are twinkling, this city claimed by Italy and by the newborn kingdom of Yugoslavia, the most bitterly contested city since the end of the war, the most hotly discussed in the newspapers.

Strange indeed is its destiny, Greta reflects, dipping her fingers in the water and slapping it gently: the Paris Peace Conference has subjected it to the military control of an inter-Allied command – with forces from France and Italy, Britain and the United States – but now it's been occupied by a poet *condottiero* who speaks like a prophet and acts like a centurion. What will her fellow convent boarding-school girls be doing now in the town? And the nuns – will they be scared? And Lucia, who sits alongside her in class and has been her friend since the beginning of primary school? And what will her best teacher, perhaps the only one she truly respects, the one who teaches her history and philosophy, think of it all?

And all at once nothing is in its place any more, in the midst of this extreme confrontation: here's the house with its park – a shell that's always protected her amid Istrian stone and tropical plants – and there is the newly undecipherable world that has suddenly opened out just outside Abbazia, on the other side of the bay at her feet.

Whatever has become of Fiume? An unexpected scene of miracles? Or a version of the utopian City of the Sun? And who are these legionaries? Idealists in pursuit of a dream or soldiers habituated to the use of force and drugged by years of warfare? How can one get to understand if everything reaches you via a father's inflexible filter or that of an elderly teacher or some unchallenged authority? Greta gets up, wends her way back up to the house, gazes at that great white moon that seems ready to plunge into the sea.

She's decided what to do.

Tomorrow her father is leaving on his usual business trip. He'll stay a few days in Trieste. He often comes back from there a different man – younger looking, sideburns better trimmed, even the unusual tang of a stronger, sharper perfume – but Greta hasn't noticed in her mother's expression any new tell-tale signs after these long absences, which have grown more frequent of late: only the resigned detachment from the humdrum everyday which has now become too burdensome, impossible to bear.

But what does she really know about her parents? No more, it suddenly occurs to her, than they ever get to know about her...

The garden swarms with shadows now. Greta goes up the steps among the rocks, takes the little pathway. The sudden call of an owl makes her tremble for a moment.

Tomorrow her father will be off, and this means one thing: that her mother will be even more withdrawn into a world of her own, perhaps staying in bed from after lunch until evening. That Elisa will be with her nanny, busy with the final preparations for the imminent reopening of school. That the house will be as it were plunged in a time mindless of anxiety and clocks, disconnected from duties and rituals.

So no one will pay any attention to her.

It's the perfect opportunity, she tells herself again. She'll find a way of getting back to Fiume.

13 September 1919

To Admiral Cusani
For His Eyes Only

Top Secret

I order Your Excellency to use the vessels at your disposal to blockade Fiume by sea so that no supplies can reach the city. If any of the vessels present fails to give an absolute guarantee, Your Excellency is to effect its immediate departure.

Signed
General Pietro Badoglio
Military Commissioner Extraordinary for Julian Venetia

Fiume
13 September 1919, night

F ar off, through the foliage that from time to time allows a distant view of the sea, Tullio has glimpsed the ships at anchor in Fiume harbour.

Or maybe he's only imagined them in his anxious haste to get there, mistaking for outlines of hulls vague shapes of concentrated darkness. Beneath his boots dry grass and roots parched by the summer now crackle sharply.

To his right, in the still pale night, the gulf's expanse of sea appears in sudden vivid glimpses.

He mops the sweat from his brow and adjusts his back-pack.

He left in a rush this morning, and didn't bring much with him. Among those few tightly packed clothes are his most precious possessions: his camera, some books, his fountain pen in its leather case.

But he needs nothing else, he's sure of that. Years of warfare have trained him to travel light in life: he's learnt to do without anything inessential, not to believe in extras. By his side, Paul trudges in silence, his mop of hair aslant his forehead, his grey eyes fixed on the ground, with swift strides in boots that seem to make no sound.

Tullio edges towards him, speaks quietly: You know, I've been asking myself what is someone like me from the Friuli region doing heading together with an American for a town that's occupied by Allied forces, reoccupied by irregulars, and encircled by the Italian army?"

"Looking for trouble?"

"Exactly right. But what about you?"

"It's okay for me. In trouble, I mean… okay."

"Your Latin marches better, polyglot."

"Why don't you learn English?"

Paul slows down a bit, looks at him, repeats more quietly: "Why not?"

Tullio smiles into the darkness.

"Because in that case, the moment we get to Fiume, d'Annunzio will have us thrown into the sea. Don't you know what he thinks of the English?"

By this time their guide has outpaced them, so they speed up behind him.

Getting past the boundary imposed by the blockade right round Fiume certainly hasn't been a problem.

Tullio casts his mind back to the station, to his journey as far as Abbazia: beyond the brambles leaning towards the train, great wooded depressions gouged like wounds into the broad undulating plateau.

Not far from the station they quickly found a guide: a little lad of about fifteen, his face already bronzed by the sun, who is now leading them through that ample curve so as to slip past the frontier patrols. So far he hasn't turned round, but has simply marched at a steady pace through familiar stretches.

There isn't a breath of wind. Occasionally a bough quivers, a bird suddenly takes flight.

The grass is sparse and the ground dry and hard, here and there cracked by the heat, with clumps of sage and rosemary intruding among the crooked, gnarled trunks of the olive trees. In places, a thicket of holm-oaks, a clump of junipers or broom-plant, the boundary of a little overgrown orchard enclosed by four dry-stone walls policed by the boughs of a fig-tree.

Tullio's nose scents new odours, and his mind goes back to the first time he saw the sea: a low expanse of reeds and lagoon, barely separated from the marshland amid spits of sand and bushes, at the mouth of the Tagliamento.

Then Paul sweeps him down by the shoulder and pins him to the ground beside him, and Tullio finds himself huddled on the dry bed of a watercourse. Only then does he too hear the sound: suddenly, circumspectly, it approaches. Twigs snapping, footsteps on the ground? Hunched close to the other two, muscles fully tensed, he's ready to attack, or escape.

He concentrates on a torch beam scything forwards in the darkness, igniting boughs and bushes all around them in flashes of light. Then he picks up the sound of footsteps that grows louder and nearer and then suddenly seems to slow down.

Finally he catches sight of them among the greenery: a military patrol. And he remarks on the strangeness of feeling himself stalked like that: not in flight, as he always has been, but crouching in a muddy ditch, his face pressed into the ground, feeling the terror of a cornered quarry, a hare with the hounds on its scent.

His mind goes back to his brother Elia and the lot that befell him: dead meat. A beast to the slaughter. He with other privates, beasts like himself. Compelled to dash out of their potholes and rush forward towards other potholes beyond those fortified trenches, beyond the crumbling, pock-marked slopes, beyond the hollows and the gullies, with sparse bushes so low and so damnably stunted and few and far between as to offer not a ghost of cover: the enormous empty expanse ahead of them, spreading out like a savannah.

Which they had to cross alone, alone in masses, through the hell of shell-bursts and gunfire.

He's aware of Paul's grip, of the young lad's sweat. Now the sound of footsteps reaches them from their right. Tullio feels his jaws set hard, his finger-nails sticking into the palms of his clenched fists. Even to go on breathing suddenly seems to him too noisy.

Then the tread of feet moves off and the last shafts of light disappear into the scrub.

They still remain flat to the ground, listening with bated breath to the noises of the night around them: a sudden rustle in the grass, a call that sounds unfamiliar, the creaking of a twig or plant litter under the feet of some animal.

He couldn't say how much time goes by, but to Tullio it seems endless: in silence, they continue their march. The night feels as though it's spread into wider spaces, in shadows suddenly suspect, in sounds which you have to strain to hear.

At last their guide comes to a standstill, turns to look at them, waits for them. As soon as they're up to him, he points out the railway line which has suddenly reappeared ahead of them. Past the checkpoints, past the frontier. Their destination, the agreed spot.

So Tullio pulls out the banknotes – the right amount, rolled tight like cigarette paper.

The boy doesn't pause to check: he slips them straight into his pocket, then waves them farewell before disappearing into the bush towards Abbazia.

Tullio and Paul sit on the ground against a tree-trunk, waiting. The American takes a paper bag containing two bread-rolls out of his back-pack and hands one to his friend. As they eat, they keep their eyes on the railway line, each immersed in his own thoughts.

It's a matter of minutes, then the noise grows louder and nearer.

The locomotive's red eye gets slowly bigger and dilates as the train slows down, clanking. Swallowing his last morsel, Tullio smiles at the thought of the complicity of the train crew, who, by braking at that point, make it easy for anyone to get on board: it's true, then, they're on the side of the enterprise.

He gets up, rushes forward, slings his backpack over his head, with a final upward thrust he manages to spring and climb on board and instantly realizes that other bodies, as if issuing from thin air, are doing exactly the same as he is. Tullio slides along the hard flooring, rolls on to his back, gets to his feet.

Beside him a lad the size of a wardrobe – a wardrobe in khaki uniform – deals him a slap on the back that almost catapults him off the train. Then, half smirking in complicity and half smiling, his broad face opens out into a warcry for a bayonet charge: "For our commandant, *Eya Eya Eya Alala*."

From the train's open window, head dangling down from the roof in an ape-like apparition, another face appears, black-bearded, which enthusiastically takes up the call: "*Eya Eya Eya Alalaaa!*"

15 September 1919

To Prime Minister Saverio Nitti
For His Eyes Only

Top Secret

Both in Trieste and in Fiume d'Annunzio's action is deemed to be the only solution remaining to us to avoid being smothered by the Allies... d'Annunzio is seen by all as their idol, the new Garibaldi.

His ascendancy is such that one word from him suffices to determine a solution.

The situation is therefore supremely delicate. An impulsive action or bloodshed would undoubtedly lead to an uprising in Trieste. But what is most serious is that I cannot yet guarantee that my troops will march or raise their weapons against their comrades. Overnight we will issue the proclamation allowing a period of five days before they are declared deserters.

But I must state frankly that I do not have much faith in it...

This, Your Excellency, is the situation, without veils.

Signed
General Pietro Badoglio

Fiume
20 September 1919

Greta walks without knowing where to look.

She seems to be swimming in a dream, amid shapes that are familiar, yet new.

She's always thought of this town as her own: on account of so many childhood memories, on account of the convent school at which she is a boarder here, on account of her Fiume grandparents' house, which stands facing the sea, old and stern like a retired Feldmarschal. It was her grandfather who'd had it built, fifty or so years ago, after having left his native Vienna and roamed the empire and sailed to distant parts: Africa, the Americas, China. He had ended up right here in Fiume and perhaps had found here a synthesis of all he had seen in his restless wanderings round the world: sea in front, mountains behind, islands studding the horizon, numerous languages and numerous peoples mingling in the one city. And he had found it perfect to reside in for what remained of his life.

But today Fiume is different: a foreigner.

She feels suddenly ill at ease, as she paces slowly along the Corso, between the grand buildings that she's known all her life, their balconies and windows draped with flags, everywhere packed with people: everyone looking as though they'd come out together on to the streets, more for the sake of feeling part of a single moving body than to get anywhere in particular.

What, Greta wonders, has become of the familiar, hard-working Fiume?

She recalls the broad, clean streets, the feeling of order and peacefulness, the girls leaning over their looms in the alleyways of Città Vecchia, the kids sitting in the sun amid a tangle of fishing nets and cordage, the fishermen busy hauling their catch: garfish, tunas the size of logs, squid and scampi, mullets and sardines; and the steamers weighing anchor for Bombay or Thessalonica, and schooners heading for Chioggia, their holds crammed with kaolin, timber from the island of Veglia, coal from Arsia. She recalls, too, those tiny details that are the soul of a place, its way of being different from other places that appear so identical: the mobile stall of a pipe-vendor, the iced coffee with swirls of whipped cream in large crystal goblets, all the newspapers in several languages spliced into long bamboo canes, waltz music played in the cafes by musicians from Vienna or by a Magyar violinist.

There have always been so many languages spoken round and about. Italian – or rather, the Venetian of the Istrian peninsula – but also Croatian, and German, and Hungarian.

And people have always lived in peace. As far as she is aware, ever since ancient times. Good-neighbourly relations among people who are naturally used to the idea that a Free

Port such as Fiume is also a port open to so many peoples, to interchanges of accents and customs – even of tastes and dishes – no less than of merchandise of every kind. But today everything's changed. New faces in the street, new smells.

Even the sounds seem different, a single language predominating.

A girl brushes past her, goes up to a group of soldiers, picks out some cockades with the Italian tricolor out of the basket slung from her arm, and pins them on to their uniforms. From the courtyard of an inn come jarring notes of a patriotic song in place of the usual noise of cards being slammed down hard and dice being vigorously shaken.

Soldiers wearing their fez at a rakish angle and a short musket hanging behind their shoulders guard banks and important buildings, as she noticed in going through the town centre, and even certain piazza corners and some intersections leading into main thoroughfares whose walls were lined with posters with black lettering.

The Allied forces stationed in Fiume are now leaving the town in the hands of the new arrivals.

She finds herself studying their faces, scanning their expressions. What she thinks she reads in them and in their very manner of dress is impatience with impositions and rules, a taste for defiance and adventure, the challenge of open rebellion, now thrown down to the whole world.

She senses that she's being watched. She picks out the gaze of a young lad amid comrades of maturer years: he lights himself a cigarette whose only purpose seems to be that of making him feel more of a man, and he eyes her as he puffs out the smoke with an assurance he doesn't feel. The matches slip from his grasp, scattering at his feet.

Greta hastily averts her gaze from his embarrassment.

But the image remains strong and vivid.

A legionary who's little more than a boy, wearing a uniform that's too flimsy: and such a young face he had, without a trace of beard or moustache on that adolescent's smooth pallor, and with all the air of a schoolboy wagging school so as to miss a test... How old might he be, she wonders. We might be the same age, she surmises.

And suddenly she finds herself thinking that that is the face of someone who believes in being there on that day in Fiume. And me? What do I think? What do I believe in, in the thick of all this? But she doesn't know what to answer, just yet.

There's a young woman standing apart beneath the archway leading to a courtyard: she's carrying a basket of apples and holding a child by the hand.

Greta catches the questioning tone in the few words of Croatian which the child addresses to his mother as he tugs at her skirt to win her attention. Before his mother can answer him, a soldier in khaki bends down to the little fellow and, with a gesture halfway between play and slap, ties around his neck a tricolour neckerchief and then pats it down sharply as if to make the cloth cling to the frail chest of that child who doesn't dare to duck or react, but remains dazed and breathless.

Then the man winks to a comrade, stares at the woman, moves off with an overbearing swagger, with long strides and a tough-guy look. A lilting song drowns out every other sound in their vicinity.

"*If-you-don't-know-who-we-are   just-look-us-in-the-face,*" Greta watching the soldier from behind, "*Sussak-is-a-hell-hole but-this-is-a-heavenly-place.*"

She remains rooted to the spot.

For an instant, there they are: the child rigid and bewildered, the mother cramped against the wall, apples tipping out of the basket and rolling at her feet.

Then Greta gathers them up quietly. She goes up to the young woman, puts the apples back into her basket.

There they are, looking into each other's eyes, without words to utter.

She feels only a bitter taste in her mouth, a dryness rasping her throat. Then she bends down to the fair-haired little boy, undoes the knot, removes the neckerchief. The woman attempts a smile. In fact, they both do: but Greta realizes that both of them find it hard to smile.

So she starts walking again, allowing herself to be carried along by the crowd: it's difficult to escape that tide that invades the piazzas and streets.

Then she hears a voice calling behind her and turns to find herself almost smothered in an embrace that feels warm and familiar.

"Lovely to meet you here instead of at school, my nerdish classmate…"

"Nerdish, Lucia?!" laughs Greta. "But then you don't much mind my slipping you the Latin translations…"

"Forget Latin, for today. Here we're talking a completely new language. All it took was courage, and now there are those who've had the guts."

Greta looks at her: is she being serious? But Lucia's already taken her by the arm and is now launched on a breathlessly feverish account of the town's last few days, her eyes lit up with excitement and her hands drawing pictures in the air with her characteristic gesticulation, while Greta thinks to herself *oh god, not again,* and resigns herself to hearing the news over again, blow by blow, which her father had spun out only yesterday. She doesn't aver to Lucia *mind I was there. Mind I saw those trucks, too, the people cheering, the legionaries.* She prefers to listen in silence, grasp her point of view, and put aside, for the time being, her need for nuance, the doubts she registers. But something in her friend's tone of voice makes her uneasy: perhaps an elation she cannot comprehend, a loud-mouthed enthusiasm that almost scares her: the same that the whole city is breathing.

"But who are they, exactly?" she asks her. "Who are they really, these legionaries? What sort of people, I mean?"

"All sorts. And their opposite. Some of them, you'll see, all polish, in impeccable uniforms, nice. You can tell from miles away that they're ex-officers, sons of good families. And some of them are so young that they must have run away from school to get here. Others are the sort you'd pray not to come across on a dark night… some ugly mugs, some ugly looks… But there are some not at all bad-looking," she ends, with a sly, matey wink.

Then Lucia takes up her story again and guides her along, cleaving a way through the stream of people that has formed around them. But Greta has stopped listening. Taken up with her own thoughts, she's busy making sense of what she's seen so far, trying to make up her mind about what's been happening around her.

So, they're all sorts. Hotheads and ex-officers, proletarians and middle-class rebels, possibly gentry, even, and students. But they're bound together by something, a common goal that unites them.

An ideal, then? What ideal? Annexing Fiume to Italy? Or

is there more to it that she hasn't yet grasped?

She pulls herself together, listens to the final details: the crews of the naval ships anchored in Fiume harbour have joined the cause and supported the enterprise. And Lucia hands her the leaflet bearing d'Annunzio's words: *The Carnaro is ours. It's a Dantesque seaway…*

Greta looks at her friend, doubtfully. She wonders whether or not to say to her that this cheap rhetoric certainly won't get us far. Then she asks herself what good will it do, and adopts a lighter, neutral tone.

"And to think that you've always loathed Dante…"

"On the other hand I rather like this new warrior poet. Have you heard that today the Fiume Town Council has handed over to him civic authority?"

"And what does that mean, exactly?"

"That folk here believe in him, and that the top political institution has placed its future, the city's fate, in his hands. Including relations with the Italian authorities and with the Allied forces, my father says."

"What else does your father say?"

"He's pleased. He says this is the right man to shake the government out of its inertia, out of its neglect of us and into the annexation we're asking for. Also, he says the man's a poet – and he can't quite swallow that – but he added that after all he's lost an eye in combat when over fifty. And he also says that he's got more than enough guts and that he's the perfect spokesman for the people of Fiume and their feelings. Hasn't the American President Wilson said so or hasn't he, that every people in the end must have the sacred right to decide for itself, to decide its own history?"

Greta stares at her in astonishment.

"Since when have you been interested in politics, Lucia?"

"Since it's been interested in us."

"It's not such a simple question…"

"On the contrary, it's dead simple. Fiume wants to be part of Italy, it's been demanding that loudly for months. Don't pretend you've forgotten that that was what our Town Council requested. Hearing someone shouting it out to the whole world can give us nothing but pleasure."

"But Fiume isn't only Italian. It's also Croatian, and a bit Hungarian. We're not the only ones here…"

"And don't even pretend you don't know that we Italians are in the majority in the town."

"In the town, maybe, but what about the surrounding area? And things could have been sorted in some other way…"

"Like how?"

"By diplomacy."

"Tell me something: do you also still believe in Santa Claus?"

"And who do you believe in? In Santa d'Annunzio?"

"I've seen him, Greta, and I've heard him."

"Well, then, come on, tell me… What's he like?"

"Intellectually, a giant. One dribble from him would drown the both of us."

"And physically?"

"Well… just a dribble."

And they double up with laughter, light-heartedly, regaining their mateyness in that contact of their bodies once again so young and so close.

Tullio is looking at the gigantic poster which has been pasted on to the side of a building above the portraits of the King and Queen: an outsize close-up of d'Annunzio surveying Fiume like a pagan god.

"That man has flashes of genius…" he murmurs.

"What did you say?" asks Paul, close by him.

The turmoil and the excitement are mounting all around, and the hubbub of the crowd filling the street drowns out their words. Tullio again looks at the poster, and points it out to Paul.

"I was just thinking out loud… d'Annunzio has sensed new realities. Take politics: he's transformed the way it's done so that suddenly it belongs to everyone, a sort of strange work of art to dish out to the masses, to those who were fighting up to yesterday, to the man in the street. And people need this too, not just more bread and more justice: politics served up for them…"

He doesn't manage to say more: the intersection is a bottle-neck. The movement of the crowd separates them and eventually swallows them up and carries them into an unexpectedly violent swirl.

An ever louder tramp of feet, occasional shouts amid a clapping of hands, a wall of people coming forward and overwhelming Greta and Lucia: it's a tide from which there's no escape, that crushes the space between people and drives all in a single direction, until – now struggling to walk, now running with the crowd and risking a fall at every step – the two girls find themselves down at the pier.

An impressive portrait of d'Annunzio, above those of the King and Queen, seems to dominate with his dark eyes and to hold your gaze: but suddenly something has disturbed the force-field and that face almost two storeys high is no more important than the bodies that now collide with hers, or than the voices which she hears round about, or than the child in his mother's arms sucking his thumb as he looks at her. Then she makes out in the distance the khaki blur of the soldiers and a long line of armoured vehicles arrayed on parade along the pier.

Suddenly elation sways the crowd, bursts out in volleys of shouting. The red car moves slowly forward: round it, the flood of people heaves and masses like one single bundle of nerve-tissue until the wave of excitement that runs through the multitude – women and youths, clusters of soldiers – travels, vibrating, to reach her.

"It's him!" yells a woman's voice. "It's him, the Commander! D'Annunzio!"

The crowd presses forward and becomes almost a tumult: Greta finds herself being shoved forward and then stuck amid all the others, in one single tangle of arms and legs and hands.

All at once a violent blow to the chest knocks the breath out of her and clouds her vision: as she flurries and creases up, winded, she instinctively reaches out one hand.

But she realizes it's wasted effort: she can't stretch out her arms to protect herself from other bodies and make room for herself and breathe.

Then panic takes hold of her, her legs go soft as warm butter.

But someone holds her by the waist, helps her staggering gait with his powerful, secure grasp. Little by little, Greta recovers, gets images and colours back in focus.

Then she turns round, and he sees her: she's a young woman, and she's smiling. He must have divined her indisposition, and is now holding her hand in a warm, natural clasp.

Greta feels a calm closeness and an unfamiliar elation in that new contact, in that knot of bodies around her: it's almost an epidemic of elation which instantly annuls boundaries, barriers between men and women, differences of class and the more banal differences of age.

She catches snatches of songs which suddenly grow louder.

She smiles at the woman beside her, finds herself singing: quietly at first, with a slightly unsteady voice, then more and more confidently.

She doesn't know the tune, or the words.

But all she has to do is follow that rhythm, join in with the rest in a verse already under way: all that's needed is the desire to be there, in that song, there, amid that rally.

Caught up in the flow of the multitude and forced to move with it, Tullio and Paul find themselves on the pier. The air is thick with voices and strong odours, with excitement and expectation.

A song seems to be spreading like a flood, winning over the most reticent: some beginning to sway their bodies in the strange mime of a dance which combines echoes of a march with hints of a primordial rite.

Then the crowd parts and the red car moves towards them. As if in glory, skirted by two streams of devotees.

Tullio finds himself in the foreground, among the folk shoving and pressing forward behind him, so that he has to brace his legs to avoid losing his balance altogether, while he hears bursts of shouting and sees outstretched arms around him. Then he manages to see the medals pinned on the man's chest, the hand held out in salute, the jubilant expression on a countenance that really looks just as he expected it to be, were it not for that guarded expression, hard to define.

The car keeps moving on, draws away. Tullio, in its rear, is still watching it.

Afar, the golden sunset looks like an ocean of honey.

Greta sees the car come forward, its red paintwork glinting, people parting before it. Then, it's just one instant, a fleeting glimpse through the crowd of that little man standing up in it on whom everyone's attention is focused: the long, sharp face, the monocle concealing one eye, the goatee beard beneath a jaw that's a bit drawn even when it broadens into a smile, the white gloved hand raised in salute to the visor.

Then the car carries him on towards the podium that has been set up for him and that looks like the pavilion for a mass religious gathering, but all draped with flags.

"What's he doing?" someone asks loudly of the person standing in front of him, who has a better view.

Greta picks up broken phrases amid a chorus of shouting.

Finally, that voice, over the loudspeakers. D'Annunzio's voice, clear and ringing. Then something happens in the silence that immediately descends: Greta senses it in the air. She looks around, watches all those upturned faces, their eyes on the podium, her gaze dwells on their fixed expression under the evening light: all of them intent on listening, enraptured. And all at once she feels she understands.

Nothing at all about d'Annunzio's appearance seems to reveal the charisma that everyone attributes to him, but, from the very moment he's started speaking, something has come into being between him and the throng that surrounds him: a bond as between bosom friends, or lovers. Fellowship and passion fused together.

Greta, too, finds herself listening. And it's as if she can see that voice, almost touch it: it's steel, lava, down. It vibrates like violin strings, modulates in waves of sound, soars upwards and then sinks so low that the silence becomes absolute so as to hear it still: and once more it comes from the chest – deep, assured, intimate – and gives way to a confidential tone, as if revealing a secret.

Suddenly she realizes that it's there, right in the womb of the voice, that the essence of a character is laid bare: not in the facial features or in the eyes. Nor in the way the hands move, or the postures of the body, its claiming light or shade with assurance or modesty. It's in the way all of its own that that breath, following its own inner rhythm, embodies thought as sound.

Tullio didn't catch the words – which he guesses were in Croat – directed towards them, but he saw the lad in uniform dash forward and then strike the man who had just spoken: and that man, smitten, double up, a trickle of blood running down from his nose and streaking his chin and his hand which he had instinctively raised to his face.

Instantly, a brawl's broken out: the two legionaries are the younger, the other two more adult and heavier.

Tullio feels their rage, their fatigue. The exchanged insults, the provocations. He's ashamed for them.

He senses a sort of wave of violence in their rough movements, in their voices, in their egging each other on that spells death to him, in all the people that have gathered round, eager to throw themselves into the fray, ready to come to blows. He finds himself in the thick of it even before he's decided to.

This isn't the way, this isn't the way. It's not them. If we have enemies, it's not them. We've nothing at all against these people, in Fiume. Haven't you had enough killing during the war, haven't we had enough of being forced to kill each other for interests that aren't ours, in the name of these flags?

And he doesn't know whether he's really shouting out loud or whether it's just going through his mind, as he tries to prise apart that melée and to pull out one body and then another: but he tells himself, no, this is not how he imagined things would go, this is not the meaning of his being in Fiume: not contending nationalisms quick to declare further wars on one another, quick to knife one another.

And as he notices the blood on his lip, he sees Paul – or simply senses him – like himself straining to keep people apart, to fling them back, to raise a fist, maybe to yell.

Again Greta is swept along, still dazed by the sensation of being unable to control her legs or gauge distances in that constant stumbling amid all the shifting and shoving forced on her in the scrimmage of bodies around her. The young woman beside her keeps clasping her hand.

The water swarms with transparencies, the setting sun now sits low down on the sea.

The light oozes from the roofs, thickens on the outlines of the ships at anchor in the harbour, at a distance.

At last they manage to stop and slip away from the tail of the march. Greta now notices that she's sweating and out of breath, that her feet are aching in her leather ankle-boots which are unsuitable for long trudges. Then she glances at the girl next to her, the way she undoes the hairpins from her tousled hair which she now rearranges in a chignon.

And now she holds out her hand. But quickly regrets that curt gesture which strikes her as a jarring note, as if their acquaintance was more genuine amid the crowd – walking side by side, singing, sharing the shoving and the emotion – than in that conventional and rather belated formal handshake.

So they stand there for a second, not knowing what to say, as if the elation they had just experienced was gradually dying out as they withdrew into their everyday roles and kept their usual distance.

"I have to go now," says Greta. "Really, I was with a friend, but I've lost her amid all these people. I'm sure she's looking for me."

But the other girl shakes her head, clasps her once more by the hand and goes backwards, dragging her along, as in a children's game.

"Hang on… It's still so early… This is such an important, special day."

Well, really, why not? thinks Greta.

It's all so simple and in its own way so natural, though she feels she's inside a dream and doesn't know how it will end. She goes along – no questions, no resistance – until the two of them are beneath the balcony of the Società Filarmonica building, where a group of young people are making music and others have started dancing. Some street lights have been lit and illuminate the space between the buildings, projecting sharp shadows on to that improvised dance-floor. Greta looks around and stops: people are chatting, laughing, looking on.

Some couples are dancing arm in arm. Some young men are smoking, up against a wall. Here and there a figure is silhouetted against a window, perceived only if it moves.

Her companion, quite at her ease, joins the throng. But something holds Greta back. Shyness, aloofness? She can't tell. Perhaps it's a sense of guilt, she muses, and the awkwardness of still being there, without her parents' knowledge, though her father's away at present.

Then she spots Lucia a little to one side, sitting on some steps, busy talking to a young man in uniform on whose right sleeve are stitched a sword and a garland, an emblem that Greta has previously noticed. She feels uncertain: should she join them or leave, pretending she hasn't seen them?

But Lucia notices her and comes up to her smiling, with an air of bravado: "I really can't believe it… you here, too, ready for some fun like ordinary mortals?"

Greta looks her up and down without answering. Really, she's starting to feel irritated by her friend's new persona, her playing the woman of the world, whereas, up to the start of summer, she was just a gauche schoolgirl like all her classmates, wrapped in that black apron that makes them all look as graceful as a sack of coal with a chignon attached.

And as she watches her walk away, Greta stands there on her own pondering to little effect on the meaning of how things had gone that day, on Fiume's mad metamorphosis, on how an unfamiliar world had burst in on her world. She's not ready to enter the turmoil, to pretend everything's fine. And she doesn't feel that confidence which seems to enable Lucia to take these experiences full on without inhibitions or misgivings, without having to give an account of herself amid that novel elation.

Her one great need is to understand, to rearrange every tessera of the mosaic so as to see the picture entire. But as she turns back she feels someone touch her shoulder. She spins round in amazement, somewhat indignant at being touched.

"You were forgetting this, signorina."

She looks at the young man who smiles as he proffers her a book. He has an open countenance, dark keen eyes, a lip that looks swollen. Next to him, slightly more in the shade, another young fellow is looking at her. Neither of them is in uniform.

She glances at the book, amazed: she reads the title, *Romances sans paroles*.

"No, I think you're mistaken. It isn't mine."

"It is now," says he. "I'm giving it to you."

Now she stares suspiciously at him. "I always choose my own books."

"I'm sure you do. But this is special."

Greta backs away, raises a hand. "Really: I can't accept it."

"Sure you can. In fact, you must. How can anyone not accept a book in Fiume, the only town I know that's governed by a poet?"

Greta's gaze hardens. "A poet that's entered Fiume at the head of armoured vehicles and soldiers: men who carry muskets, not inkwells and idylls."

For an instant he appears to falter, but doesn't take his eyes off her face.

"But Fiume has welcomed him with open arms and has entrusted him with full powers."

"Maybe there's only one Fiume, but there are all sorts of Fiume people."

"I don't yet know what sort you are. I'm the sort that loves books."

In the gaze with which he holds her, Greta suddenly perceives so many things: surprise, disappointment, hesitation. But not anger, nor ill-will.

Now his friend speaks. Greta is for a moment nonplussed by his accent, a foreign one.

"My God, Tullio ain't got no musket. Just a few books, a few ideas. Would you like…" he pauses, perhaps trying to find the right word, "… would you like to search us, si-gno-ri-na?"

Greta knows she's flushing. She takes the book, leafs through it. Anyway, it's a good excuse for her to face down and avoid their gaze while putting on her dignified look.

"Let's start at the beginning, what do you say?" the voice beside her is saying. "I'm Tullio, and this is Paul. Shall we now put on the agenda just a touch of cordiality between us?"

Now she smiles. "Just a touch."

She doesn't sit down, she doesn't even think of dancing, but she finds herself talking. A bit uncertainly at first, a bit hesitantly, then finding it increasingly natural to be in a crowd, by the light of the street-lamps, with waltzes and polkas providing the background for the conversation and the sudden sensation of a new door opening upon other lives, other horizons, other ideas. Upon other ways of reading the world, which for her has up to now always been one and the same – loved and unquestionable – and viewed from only one angle, contained between Fiume and Abbazia.

The face of a mature man – with beard and whiskers, top-hat and tail-coat – reminds her suddenly of her father. She comes out of her reverie.

It's getting late, it's almost dark: the lights are on in the windows and the features of the young men in front of her are visible only intermittently: a profile illuminated by a lamp, the flash of white teeth in a smile.

So she's now hurrying along the street, having firmly refused all offers to escort her, in an atmosphere of warm damp scirocco which makes her hair stick to her face.

Possibly on account of the anxiety that grates on her breathing, distances seem warped and the streets seem suddenly longer. But they're crowded and noisy and still brimming with life: knots of legionaries wearing fezes, odd patrols of commandos or bersaglieri, girls quietly laughing beside lads in uniform, children in swarms – filthy with dust, free, dropping with tiredness – yelling and wielding pea-shooters.

All at once she has the queer feeling that she's being watched, but turning round suddenly she can't spot anyone among the crowd who seems to be interested in her.

Finally, the last stretch, getting darker. The large buildings give way to private houses, the street-lamps are fewer and further between, the street narrows in a bend, while she is getting farther from the centre, feeling just a touch anxious: but she's almost there, she knows. The agreed rendezvous is a few steps away. As ever, Furio is waiting there, perhaps smoking a cigarette, already sitting in the driving seat.

Then it's an instant, the lunge of that arm that clamps her shoulder, emerging from the wall of a house.

The words muttered through clenched teeth smell strongly of wine.

She feels trapped, without any escape. She attempts in

vain to shake the grip off her flesh between her shoulder-blade and her neck, but the blade-like fingers clutch her tight and she already feels the man's weight upon her, his face grazing hers, the pressure that squeezes her against the wall. Her legs kick the empty air and her instinct is to bite and claw, but the anger that invades her body doesn't translate into a real struggle under the impact of that violent brutality. She feels her knees sagging, the rough wall that grazes her shoulders and a cheek and scuffs the skin off her hand.

Then all is unexpected, confusion. She senses only that all of a sudden she can move and breathe freely while at her feet two bodies are entwined in a furious struggle.

She hears the grunts, the panting, a hoarse cry. A shape finally gets up, takes a few steps, goes away. Only then, labouring to recover her breath, does Greta realize that standing in front of her, somewhat bent but intact, is the young man who gave her the book.

So it was he who had followed her, it was his gaze that she had sensed, though unseen, upon her at times in the gloom of the street.

She is too scared to speak: all she wants to do is run away.

It was all so sudden that she can still hardly take it in, believe that it's happened to her and that it could have turned out quite differently, which she can hardly imagine. She sees her hands are trembling. She rubs her clammy palms on the rumpled fabric of her dress.

Meanwhile she listens to Tullio whispering, still breathless, with his frank face, and his long, lean, hermit-like body leaning momentarily against the wall: "Shall we put it on the agenda... just a touch of appreciation, now, between the two of us?"

She is grateful for his light-hearted tone which helps her out of her embarrassment and takes the melodrama out of the situation. She manages half a smile as she holds out her hand and smooths back her hair.

At last her voice is almost steady: "Just a touch."

25 September 1919

To Gabriele d'Annunzio, Commandant of Italian Fiume
For His Eyes Only

Top Secret

Dear d'Annunzio,

… pending my coming to Fiume – just for as long as necessary, be it understood – my ideas are as follows:

1   To march on Trieste.
2   To declare the Monarchy defunct.
3   To nominate a Governing Directorate, with yourself as president.
4   To prepare elections for a Constituent Assembly.
5   To declare – of course – the annexation of Fiume.
6   To land troops in Romagna (Ravenna), in the Marche (Ancona) e in Abruzzi, in support of the republican uprising.

These are my ideas. I submit them to your consideration.

… I salute you.
Signed
Benito Mussolini

Fiume
25 September 1919

He sees it emerge from the debris like the tuft of a yellow cob of corn at the edge of the rubble: Tullio gets down on his knees, feels it hesitantly with his hands, grasps it and slowly unearths it. Gently, carefully.

Then he stays a long while on his knees, his body motionless and his head bent forward, with his sister Anna's rag doll just a shell between his fingers.

Around him the debris is an expanse of shattered stone as far as the eye can see.

Only to the right, further up, at a distance, a wall has been left standing: the mock-up of a theatre wing. Beyond the one window, nothing but sky. Here and there twisted ironwork sticks out, the chipped snout of a brick, the wooden skeleton of a fixture. And a few tattered ends that could have been anything: a linen bedsheet, a blanket, a bit of old grey felt from a beret, a lady's skirt or an infant's wrapping. Up that way a dog sniffs through the rubble. Tullio stares at him without finding the strength to yell at him and drive him away.

Then up comes a dry wind that seems to swarm over the rubble and gather strength in the gap, offering no resistance: not to boughs, not to roofs or steps, not to the occasional dry-stone wall marking a boundary. It's a wind that does not set things creaking, doesn't sneak whistling under window-panes, doesn't whine through the hearths, doesn't squeak through joins, doesn't lash boughs or awnings or laundry on the line: no, it wallows freely in the empty space, over that expanse of rubble which had previously been the school, his father's printing press, the cooperative, the church, his home. Which had previously been his district – Sant'Osvaldo – on the outskirts of Udine, Italy's forward base during the war.

He knows how it happened: he knows it all.

Three explosions, with two brief intervals in between. After the third, emptiness.

The ammunition depot was hit first. Shells and debris were hurled sky-high, as an enormous mushroom of soot billowed up from the ravaged earth and apocalyptic whirlwinds and maelstroms rose upwards sucking up masonry and glazing, sweeping aside lofts and balconies, tearing up church porches like hairpins. But some people actually tried – tried to escape.

But the second bang was more powerful, and immediately after, implacably, came the third explosion: the gelatine depot. The explosive used for packing into tubes to be pushed through the barbed wire entanglements so as to tear open gaps in the trenches. Then it really became hell, and swallowed up his entire district.

How many died, no one knows. The figures have been

censored. And where would you look for bodies? How far from home? And how reassemble the corpses, how give them a name, how give definite shape to scraps scattered everywhere?

All he knows is that amidst all the others, they're there too, together or apart: his father, his mother, his sister. And he discovers himself murmuring their names, and with theirs also his brother's: Elia.

He gets to his feet, casts his gaze over the rubble and as far as the neighbouring fields: trying to map out distances, restore contours, go back just a few instants so as to see everything again as it was before and where it was before, when he hardly even looked at it because it was always in view like an old, over-used garment, which you slip on without even noticing... Over there, the school yard, the baker's, the butcher's, his father's printing press, which had previously been his grandfather's: you went down three steps to enter it and you had to lower your head slightly beneath a sharply protruding wall. To the left was the house and garden, the old apple tree guarding the courtyard, the porch looking out on the square.

Then he realizes that it's no good, he can't do it. How can you reconstruct everything in the middle of nothing, without any landmarks, without a centre and a circumference, without even a single wall to mark the boundary with the void or the heart of a piazza or to keep out that wind that won't stop blowing?

The doll feels heavy in his fingers. He bends down, picks up a stone and flings it away: he follows its trajectory, watching it cover the distance. The dog raises his head, following its course. A bird flies off in alarm.

On the horizon, the Alps stand out distinctly against the sky like a crown.

To howl, to rail, to curse. To tunnel out a path for rage. To find something, anything, round about, on to which to off-load his grief.

But he stays there motionless, slumping, his fingernails dug into his palms, his body huddled in emptiness.

Then the earth begins to quake.

Tullio instantly opens his eyes wide.

His throat is parched, he's in a sweat. He's already more than once experienced flashbacks to the memory of that day in a phantasmagoria of inconsolable grief: a grief which never relaxes its grip on him.

And the details become ever more cruel with the passing of time, as if the growing distance from the event made everything more distinct. His father's perpetually ink-stained fingertips, the apron worn by his mother to do the house-cleaning on a Saturday morning, his sister Anna's crystalline, flawless laughter.

He gets up, gives his face a splash, puts on his only shirt that's still almost clean, or at least not too grubby.

Luckily, it's already time for him to meet up with Giulio.

Here he comes, with his unmistakable fast stride, his hair more unruly than ever, his beard and whiskers almost one great tangle, his baggy linen shirt dangling out of his breeches in his perennial rejection of all uniforms and dress-codes: a sort of Franciscan friar who's had his sandals replaced by a pair of old leggings.

They've arranged to meet at the pier. Tullio hasn't yet

met him since he's been here in Fiume.

He stands there waiting for him, watching him from a distance, assailed by misgivings and queries and even by an unexpected anxiety. And suddenly he's wondering about many things. Whether Giulio will have changed much, whether they'll still feel as close now as they had felt then, whether this strange new mission will have affected the way he is and his life-style which Tullio knows so well.

It's the war, he reflects, simply that: it's knowing a person in war-time conditions at their most extreme that enables you to see him naked, stripped of every mask, every pretence. That's when you know what stuff he's made of, you know whether you can rely on him or not. And perhaps the war is always to blame if his instinct has become so keen in judgement of deeds and persons: a high precision instrument which Tullio would gladly do without, considering what it's already cost him.

He and Giulio only met during the final months of the war, but he feels he's been his friend for a life-time. They've shared a lot, always at speed, with the constant sensation of having to race through life, with no time to waste: fears, enthusiasms, relief, memories of high ideals before going to war, the reality of its everyday horrors while they were in it together.

Their war was different. An airmen's war, fought out in the sky.

Tullio at times felt uneasy about it, as if he was really enjoying a privilege, up there in the clouds rather than amid lice and rats and mud, in the bowels of the trench system. Yet he knew every time he took off – with the sharp gush of air, with the bucking and blasting, with the sudden slides amid the scream of gunfire and air pockets – that the risk of not making it back became more real with every sortie and the fear more piercing.

And then both of them, the war over, experienced the unexpected difficulty of fitting into peacetime life, that peace they had so longed for. And terror was no longer that dark shape that darts out from behind the clouds, the impending racket that perforates your pressured eardrums, the uncontrollable spasm of your nerves as you continually look over your shoulders, with the nightmare that your engine could at any moment burst into flames.

But there was another dread, far more subtle, and really more demeaning: the suspicion that it had been a mistake to believe in an ideal which had in the end shown itself in all its appalling nakedness. Not a just and a justified war – the culminating point of the Risorgimento, Italy's national rebirth, its final annexation to include its *natural* frontiers – but a shambles without absolution. Millions of men in uniform driven to slaughter each other without hatred and without any genuine reason.

The suicide of an entire continent. This sums up its balance-sheet today.

But what Giulio thinks, he doesn't know.

Then there they are, face to face, momentarily incapable of speech.

Their handshake is brisk, as they look each other in the eye without daring to express their pleasure at seeing each other again. But at once the sudden thump on the shoulder is the familiar sledgehammer blow that Tullio recognizes as he hears his friend exclaim, already exercising a powerful grip on his arm: "There's something I must show you, old chap. You couldn't even imagine it. I bet you ten to one that you'll crack up with envy. Are you on? Deal!"

Now Tullio grins, but more to himself than to his friend: no, Giulio hasn't changed one bit.

He's still the same old Giulio, half bohemian, half quixotic, one half soldier and one half intellectual, always anti, always out of line. Probably he gives a course in painting, studies Croatian or Hungarian, talks the waiters in the taverns where he eats in the evening into joining the Proletarian League. And he does everything with the selfsame passion, because passion is his god.

Meanwhile Giulio has led him to a motor-cycle parked not far off and is now inviting him to climb on while he is already starting up the engine under the gaze of some little lads.

Then Tullio gives himself over to the whole experience: the air blowing on him, the mild, grey sky, the power of a landscape that is still new to him, the shadows being sliced in the dust, the motor-cycle leaning into the bends, a shudder as it skids, then the road mastered anew. Finally, they dismount. They're here.

Giulio leads the way through the greenery with feverish impatience, then comes to a halt with an air of triumph and turns to enjoy his astonishment, while Tullio, wide-eyed, whistles his disbelief.

And all at once he once again sees here, in the clear sky over the Carnaro, the suicidally, absurdly mad duel sought out and willed by Giulio as a challenge to himself and to destiny: the memory is so vivid and precise that Tullio effortlessly relives every moment of that adventure, which now lies nearly three years in the past.

"You're crazy!" Tullio had yelled out to him, shaking him vigorously by the arm and making him stop as Giulio was checking the fuel tank and the magazine for the Lewis machine-gun set on the upper wing, as he was getting ready to take off in his Nieuport.

"In war, the future belongs to the crazy," the other had replied, shaking himself free from Tullio's grip. Tullio had barely been able to stop himself punching him, in the instinct to strike out and inflict pain, the urge to shout you idiot, d'you want to act like a kid, or play the hero? Then he had silently told himself that after all everyone has the right to look for his own way out, his own short cut out of the anguish and the fear of death: and in war-time, during *that* war, more than ever.

So his arm dropped back, and as his only farewell gesture he had given Giulio his own helmet, as if it were some kind of amulet which could save him from mayhem.

"Here, take this," was all he'd said, "keep my leather helmet for your moronic skull…"

"My heroic skull. For a hero of the skies. Thank you," Giulio had grinned in reply. And then he had winked at him through his goggles as he boarded the biplane.

Tullio had watched him take off, his eyes narrowing to two slits against the strong, harsh light from the sky over Trieste: and the yellow Nieuport had climbed up, banked over the sea in a broad sweep, righted itself after lurching in some turbulence. A prehistoric bird, yet alive, its fuselage a strong, naked body, the ailerons of the upper wing flashing as they caught the sunlight, Giulio's far-off face leaning out, sensed rather than seen, behind the outline of the machine-gun which might or might not serve its purpose. His gamble was on.

Giulio had thrown down the challenge knowing that it would be taken up. Of that, he'd had no doubt: he knew the flyers too well. He'd thrown down the challenge on a sheet of paper in a leather case which he'd parachuted under cover of darkness over the little Austrian airfield which was not far distant.

And the paper carried that challenge to a duel, complete with signature, as if in a medieval tournament: to take off close together, a strange pair – an Austrian and an Italian biplane – vying with one another in a contest of courage in that new dare – flight.

To display – during a lull in the war – their courage and valour.

No longer just sheer strength, it was also the game itself that counted: if only to find other reasons – light-heartedness, dare-devilry, high spirits – beyond the reason which had been blown sky-high amid the carnage which now pitted them each against the other, on either side of that absurd frontier which, if it was so flimsy amid the mud, the barbed wire, and the trenches, up in the air was a mere abstraction. Tullio had kept telling himself: that's Giulio, and if that's what he wants, it's fine by me. But then he'd stayed there in anguish, at the mercy of a blank helplessness that seemed to block all action, his eyes glued to the sky where Giulio had not yet returned: calling himself an idiot for having let him take off. How long had he remained motionless at the edge of the airstrip tucked away in the countryside of Friuli, amid plane-trees and rows of poplars, in the cool, dry evening breeze? A brook flowed along the far edge of the paddock. At a distance could be seen a stack – dry branches, uprooted undergrowth, withered brambles – which looked set up for a pyre. In a ditch, a frog was croaking.

Finally, he had made up his mind, and had run to his biplane, identical to Giulio's, so light and tiny that they all nicknamed it *baba*: going back to infant syllables was a charm like touching wood, maybe one of many ways – like amulets in a breast pocket or a woman's photo on the instrument panel – to keep fear under lock and key.

Giulio might have been hit. He might somehow have attempted an emergency landing. He might still be alive, across the border: he could rescue him.

Having checked that he had the area map in his pocket, Tullio had climbed on board his plane.

But when the propeller was already at full throttle and he had already started his take-off run, the biplane's wheels bumping along the dusty turf of the runway, more by instinct than by eyesight he had somehow spotted him in that quarter of the sky that was already giving way to dusk.

He appeared from behind a cloud, silhouetted against the livid violet of the sunset and was starting to bank gently on the way to gliding down in a slow descent. Then everything came into focus: the long fuselage, the winged snout.

It was indeed Giulio's biplane.

And following behind him, as a token of farewell – paying homage to his courage, to his craziness – came a German Fokker as his escort, keeping high up in the sky, getting into his curve, preparing to return to base. Tullio had turned off his engine. Then had looked on, the tension concentrated in his temples, his jaws set so hard that he could feel the rage in his teeth, his fists clenched on the joystick. Giulio had climbed out unhurriedly, removing his helmet and then his goggles, as all the others crowded round him in a frenzy of embraces and hurrahs.

Tullio was among them. And when they were face to face he had caught in Giulio's eyes a look of unclouded triumph and a complicit wink.

His fist had shot out instantly, allowing no time to restrain the blow. He'd struck him under the jaw: just one blow, but a liberating one. A friendly blow, really.

Under the hangar, with Giulio at his side, Tullio now admires the biplane. Two others stand further back, in the shadow. Motionless in that space, it gives a sense of restrained power, a promise of might, at the ready. An Ansaldo SVA2.

Tullio walks around it slowly, looks at the stabilizers, reaches out to the rudder, touches the propeller and strokes the fuselage. He feels their shapes with his fingertips, the hardness of the different materials: he strokes them in a kind of caress as if on an actual body. Finally, he comes to the winged snout painted in black on the starboard side: the emblem that the Nieuports of their squadron carried during the war. And, beneath the emblem, the brief legend in red still smells of fresh paint: *Ardisc.*

"Ardisc?"

"I'm still working on it," goes Giulio. "The word's incomplete."

Tullio resumes his inspection. He glances at the machine-gun and then at the streamlining used to mask the mountings – that's a good slipstream arrangement – and then at the semicircular openings that he's spotted in the upper wing and also at the wing base. "That gives better visibility," he murmurs, entranced.

"Right. Both above and below," Giulio's voice confirms.

"And this engine…" he runs his fingers slowly over it, "… at least a hundred and fifty horse-power."

"Two-twenty, to be precise."

"Speed?"

"Two-twenty."

"Faster than the Albatros, the Brandenburg, the Aviatik…"

"…yes, faster than the Austrian fighters. But…"

"…but less manoeuvrable?"

"Exactly right. This is a reconnaissance chick. But it can also drop nice presents."

"Range?"

"Three or four hours. The reserve tank is in the upper wing."

Tullio thinks back to his Nieuport: eighty horse-power engine, one-fifty kilometres per hour, maximum range a couple of hours. His only comment is a long-drawn-out whistle: all envy and admiration..

He's never flown an SVA, but his war-time flying experience has left in him a passion of which he suddenly feels ashamed, as of a boyish weakness, as he reminds himself that what stands before him here is not a giant toy but a weapon of war, for real. He turns to Giulio and gives him a long stare: "What do you want to do?"

"A whole heap of things. One of which is already clear in my mind. Don't stare at me like that: I know you, and I know what you're thinking now. I'm not going to drop any more bombs, old chap, but I'll make even more noise. And this time, trust me, the target will be the right one. Will you bet on it? Give us your hand!"

Tullio looks at him in silence. No, Giulio hasn't changed a bit. Whatever plan he has in mind, he won't be able to stop him this time either.

26 September 1919

To the Prime Minister of Italy
Francesco Saverio Nitti

For His Eyes Only

I hear that Marinetti and Vecchi have turned up in Fiume with a Republican programme rejected by d'Annunzio Stop But it is certain that if decision not taken immediately there could be nasty surprises especially if Yugoslavs attack in strength Stop As result my position here daily loses prestige and power Stop I therefore request Your Excellency if solution is procrastinated to order my replacement Stop
  Signed
  General Pietro Badoglio

Fiume
October 1919

Greta walks hurriedly, silently: she turns past the nearly dark entrance, goes all the way along the corridor, starts up the stairs trying to ignore the metal grilles.

Each time, this is what happens to her: her heart beating in her chest and the irrational desire to become almost transparent, not to emit a sound with her footsteps, to walk hugging the wall in an attempt to avoid those eyes which always seem to her to strip her naked.

Only intermittently does she pay attention to that voice that stubbornly goes on talking. This is the most trying moment during her visits to this place: covering the distance that seems to stretch to infinity, to cross the entire wing so as to get to *her* as quickly as possible. And to do so unaccompanied, this last considerable while: her mother is certainly no longer able to bear this new anguish, to shoulder the added burden of another's sorrows.

But today, just as last time, the doctor has insisted on accompanying her. It's not to ensure her safety, Greta sensed that a good while ago. Rather, he seems to latch on to her because he sees that she comes on her own, without adult supervision. And today he keeps on talking.

He speaks in a bass voice, slightly nasal. At times he squeezes words out at length, as if to extract from them non-existent pulp. Cerebral alterations, clinical analysis both empirical and abstract, the Brever theory, the Kraepelin hypothesis. And then, malaria therapy, cardiozol shock effects, the merits of frontal lobotomy: she has the distinct impression that the guy is going all out to impress her, with a display of high-sounding words that excite him with their pyrotechnics.

Greta says nothing, makes no comment, doesn't react. He seems to read that silence as interest, as admiration: so he goes on, enthused. Electrotherapy. What an achievement! Has she perhaps already heard of it? She has no idea how many patients recently have received electric treatment. It's extraordinary for treating neuroses affecting ex-combatants. And on he goes with his detailed descriptions – little miniatures – while Greta gets the shudders at the thought of those vivid word-pictures, like those of Flemish art, passionately drawn: electricity applied with wires, sudden convulsions, the final catalepsis.

A very promising therapy. Indeed, be it said: quite revolutionary.

So she turns to look at him: his geometrical goatee beard, the thin curve of his lips beneath a moustache as stiff as two carob pods, his severe and self-important nose with its pince-nez perched upon it. He doesn't look as if he's talking about people, sick men and women, beings still capable of experiencing sentiments and emotions.

To avoid listening to that voice, Greta clutches at a memory, she retrieves an old nursery rhyme that she used to sing during her childhood games. She lets the rhythm and the words surface gently like snippets of peace and harmony and lull her mind in a medley of sounds.

Ding dong, the church-bell rings…

An open room adjoining the corridor, with a woman sitting inside.

…three little lassies they sit by the door…

The woman's eyes follow her. Her gaze looks to her like a death-throe.

One of them spins, one of them sings, one of them kneads babes of dough…

It upsets her to return her gaze, makes her feel guilty to avoid it.

One of them prays the good Lord to send her a fine man to wed…

No gesture here can find peace, no gesture has a place, an agreed meaning.

★ ★ ★

Then she sees the man at the end of the corridor. He's walking slowly towards them. His right arm is stretched forward and his fingers curved as though he were grasping something: and he traces large signs in the air, at times calm, at times excited, as if engraving the space around him.

He's elderly, slightly doddery. Under thick grey eyebrows his eyes stare into the distance. He must be a harmless patient, otherwise he wouldn't be there but strapped to his bed or locked up in another ward.

Greta senses the doctor by her side stiffen and slow his pace. "He's agitated today," murmurs the doctor, "today he needs the strait-jacket…"

Greta notices him making a slight nod with his head to an orderly who's just come out of a room. She's already once before seen him use a strait-jacket on a woman: she's seen the ties pulled tight to prevent all movement, to pin down the arms and hands, to bind the trunk as in a vice. She feels pained and powerless, and can't take her eyes off the old man who has come up to where they are.

He keeps up his untiring gestures, his sweeping slashes through the air. Distraught, angry arabesques: thrusts of the wrist, of the fingers. When he gets to the end of the figure, he begins all over again, breathlessly: from left to right, without a break, mumbling a few mangled syllables.

And all at once, it all seems clear to Greta, and somehow obvious, natural.

From left to right, without a break.

It doesn't take much, she tells herself: it doesn't take anything at all to realize. The orderly is approaching, the doctor stands and watches. Greta turns to look at him, touches his arm, whispers: "Please, doctor: just a moment. Just give me a moment. I think… I think I understand…"

His expression is at first one of profound surprise, immediately followed by hard-faced anger and bad temper.

She's already groping in her bag: her cheeks are burning, but she has no intention of giving up her modest intention, her wretched intuition. "Please give me just one moment. And then, I swear, I'll go away."

At last she finds her pen. But she has no paper. She pulls her book out of her bag – she always carries at least one – and quickly tears out a page. She feels the doctor's eyes on her, his barely contained rage, the orderly waiting.

Then Greta goes up to the old man. She asks herself what she should say, how she could act. She wonders if there are any bridges, if there are ways of communicating between distant shores so foreign and unfamiliar. And all at once she feels ridiculous, helpless and yet presumptuous: even if there were a way, she's not the person who would know it.

Then she just follows instinct: she grasps the old fellow's hand, holds it for a few instants between her own. She feels it trembling, sweating, and she squeezes it with a calmness which she certainly doesn't feel. She gently opens his fingers and slips the pen between them, then patiently guides them into gripping it securely. The old man's memory hesitates, then slowly returns: he regains confidence with the gesture, he seems to her not to be trembling so much.

This is the moment to take hold of the paper. Greta rests it on the book that she holds up before him. The pen pressing down, the word.

ONLY.

And then, *I*.

And finally, somewhat crooked, it spells *YOU*.

Greta writes holding in her own hand the old man's hand, inert.

For an instant they remain there, both heads bowed, without speaking, the skinny old fellow trembling in his baggy hospital outfit, Greta propping him up with her body. Then the man backs off, paper and pen in hand: just two or three steps, slightly sidelong, until he slides with his back against the corridor wall.

She stands there looking at him. He sits down, stretches out his legs, leans slightly forward: and laboriously, his forehead creased with the effort of concentration, writes something on the page which he is resting upon his thigh. His face wears a twisted smile, and saliva is dribbling slowly out of his half-closed lips. With her heart in her mouth, Greta approaches him, squats, peers at the paper he's holding in his hands. Then she reads a higgledy-piggledy name scrawled in large block capitals: UGO.

She looks round at the doctor, who's standing silently behind her.

"Is his name Ugo, this patient of yours?"

The other hesitates. The orderly replies: "Yes, his name is Ugo. Ugo Poli."

"May I ask what he used to do, in the past?"

The man shifts his gaze towards the old fellow, who now seems to be at peace. "Teacher. School-teacher."

At long last, Greta is on her own again, walking down the corridor. And she feels the silence does her good: it helps her collect her powers and sort out her ideas before she enters that room and again faces that situation.

She's thinking of her, of Ingrid: her aunt.

The death of her only son – a few years after that of her husband – snuffed out her spirit though not yet that already feeble body, which she feels she can hear rustling like leaves on the back garden path or like dry chestnut husks, as she bends down to hug her tight and whisper *Zia, I'm here. I'm Greta, and I'll stay with you for a while.*

And every time she leaves she has a sobbing in her throat that won't come out and such intense heartache as to curdle memory. Heartache over a future denied, over what could still be – her aunt serene, her cousin living – if that absurd and accursed war had not mashed up an entire world.

She's got to the end of the corridor. She stops and draws a deep breath, with her hand still on the door-knob. Eventually she tiptoes in.

The light inside the room is strong and harsh, outlining things sharply. There's her aunt, seated as ever. Behind her the bed, the wall, the slightly flaking iron bars in that single window full of light.

Motionless, with slightly bent back, head leaning to one side, hands resting on her lap: like a well-behaved girl who looks and listens demurely without being a nuisance. A model patient. Isn't that what the doctor said?

And wasn't it this after all – her listlessness that makes her inoffensive and the family she comes from, which, on account of its social standing, can't be ignored – that afforded her the privilege of that rather secluded room of which she was the sole occupant?

"Here I am, Zia. I've arrived, and I'll spend some time with you." She speaks bending down in front of her, just brushing her cheek with a light caress and finding it diaphanous, chill.

Ingrid's body remains motionless, her eyes staring into space. Perhaps there's just a faint quiver in one hand, but so imperceptible and brief that Greta is quickly convinced that she'd only imagined it.

She sits down on the bed, and sighs. She casts her eyes over the canvases, paint-brushes and paints resting against the wall in the corner beneath the window, which she'd fetched for her upon a sudden instinct some time back, on the day when d'Annunzio arrived: an attempt to reconcile Ingrid with her great life-time passion. A wholly irrational hope that the memory of her painting might produce a burst of light and might somehow bring back her memory of her own identity. But if she'd mentioned that at home, they'd have thought she was mad.

And her father would actually have stopped her from making that hopeless attempt: a sense of decorum and of the ridiculous is his top priority. Maybe that's the very reason, she suspects, why he was so quick to consign her to this institution, to cover up that grief and that nameless malady: away from them, far from home, screened off from indiscreet eyes. Her mother didn't have the strength of will to oppose him.

As for herself, Greta: does she count? She's still regarded as a child.

And there'd be trouble if her father suspected that she's been coming on her own to this mental institution, without asking either for permission or an escort, almost every week for several months now.

And yet, deep down, Greta is convinced that while she's talking to her aunt during these regular meetings a spark of contact lights up between them just for an instant: and though she cannot be sure of it, every time she talks to her with fresh vigour and despairing tenacity, with endearments, squeezing her hands. This time, too, she leans towards her, bends down over her.

What does that gaze harbour? A terror of remembering, of the past, of her loss of control over what is left of her future and her personal dignity? She would so like to understand.

She has always seen herself in her aunt, her mother's only sister, who lived with them ever since she was widowed.

It's not so much their physical resemblance that makes them look so akin – same eyes, nearer grey than blue, same freckles, thick dark hair. It's more their underlying character, their serious approach to the world, the same secret persistence in seeking private avenues of escape from their bourgeois family's mercantile horizons – businesslike, solid, concrete. And it's to Greta, right from early childhood, that Ingrid has always devoted all the love and tenderness perhaps reserved for the daughter she never had, whereas, Greta now reflects, her own mother always concentrated all her attention upon her only son, Arturo, as if foreseeing that he would be taken from her early, far earlier than he should have been.

So it was in Zia Ingrid that she confided, as a bosom friend, she was the person who gave her her first books of poems, the great French novels, and that strange book – *The Interpretation of Dreams* – by a Viennese doctor: Greta read it eagerly, drawn by something profound that helped her absorb even the obscurest passages.

These are her thoughts, as she gets close to her aunt. How much more they would have shared if only things had gone quite differently. She smiles at her, takes her by the hand. She cradles her aunt's hands, like a nest, within her own.

They seem cold, helpless, lifeless, but when she starts stroking them – very gently, on the palms, with her forefinger – Greta feels them quiver.

And she starts talking to her as one talks to a child: about everything and about little nothings, about the present and about their past, about her sister Elisa, who's often sad, and about her father, who spends more and more time away from home, and about her mother and about the cat's newborn kittens and then about those soldiers – the legionaries who've come as far as Fiume and want to annex it to Italy and are taking on all comers and I can't work out whether it's right, whether it's an ideal worth supporting, Zia, but I've seen that there are people who are ready to fight after coming here from distant lands for the sake of something which hardly concerns them and then I thought that what unites them is a dream, a dream of utopia. But I can't judge, not yet.

Do you remember, Zia Ingrid? Utopia… it was you that taught me that word.

And now something happens. For an instant her aunt's gaze shifts from that void in which she seems to have been immersed for months, and fixes on her, really, on her niece.

And deep in Ingrid's eyes, Greta reads everything, not only her individual suffering but also other burdens, other sorrows: the anguish of all humanity. Her mother's long-standing grief, the raw grief of her sister Elisa. Even the cat's distress, which dragged on for days, after her kittens were removed and, with tortured mewing, she scoured every corner of the park and spent an endless time exploring, fruitlessly, every nook and cranny among the rocks and along the walls.

Greta then senses that her voice issues almost on its own, freely.

You sensed it, didn't you? You know.

You sensed that I and your son could no longer see each

other simply as playmates or think of each other simply as cousins. You sensed what I myself felt. So you know what I've never told you, what I haven't confided to anyone, what I always kept to myself while he was fighting on the Carpathians. We never even exchanged a kiss. And how could we have? I was just fifteen, and he wasn't even three years my senior.

Come on, then, help me to understand: how can one suffer so much on account of a love that has never existed, that has only been imagined, that maybe the two of us imagined?

Then Greta is on her feet, at the door, out of there. She's back at the end of the corridor, runs down the stairs, dashes outside into the open air, to feel that she is part of the present again, of the world remote from all that.

Only then does she pause a moment to get her breath back, to calm herself.

She hears the sound of a hoe coming from the far end of the spacious garden, a regular, rhythmic beat, which reminds her of the tramp of soldiers during the final days of the war, and the more recently familiar marching along the Fiume harbour front.

Unlike her memories, she tells herself. Her memories, on the contrary, are erratic, and never announce themselves. Susceptible to sudden diversions, they attack when there is no defence.

The sky is the colour of wine-must, with grainy violet clouds piling up along the horizon's edge.

In the distance, beyond the grey pavilions of Fiume's insane asylum, a sea inlet seethes.

Standing still, Greta looks down at the ground. The gravel looks distant, her feet feel alien and indeterminate. At an appropriate distance, she tells herself. I must maintain an appropriate distance. Then she asks – from what?

She rubs one eye, dries one cheek. Eventually she continues on her way.

5 October 1919

To the Prime Minister of Italy
Francesco Saverio Nitti

For His Eyes Only

Entire army obsessed with idea of Fiume STOP Am barely able to restrain troops from going to Fiume by making Yugoslav attack appear imminent, which in fact cannot be ruled out, especially against this town STOP

Signed
General Pietro Badoglio

Fiume
October 1919

Giulio walks along the waterfront, hands plunged in pockets and eyes on the warships – the destroyers, the torpedo-boats, the E-boats – and on the row of warehouses, grey, shut down and deserted, as if derelict.

A seagull watches them from a stanchion. A glass bottle wallows in the waves, bobbing up.

"Wilson will never agree to Italy's annexing Fiume. And do you know why?"

Tullio, at his side, looks at him: "I'm about to find out. Or am I mistaken?"

Giulio stops, and he notices that the hollows under his eyes and cheeks are deeper. But his eyes are gleaming and vivid.

"Listen, Tullio. It's my friend I'm talking to now. But even if it were a journalist, you wouldn't find a soul who'd be willing to publish a word of what I'm just about to tell you."

Tullio studies him in silence, thoughtfully. He knows Giulio's been in this town since the first day of the enterprise and that he entered it at d'Annunzio's side – he's one of the few who are on familiar terms with him – in that same car at the head of the armoured column. He knows that he's always drawn to lost causes as a teenager is drawn to brothels, but that he has inside knowledge of everything that goes on in Fiume. And he knows that he would never pimp for his ideas.

"Carry on," is all he says.

They sit down on a low wall. For a moment they stay silent. Then Giulio resumes. "Fiume is an enormous powder-keg, which could blow up at any moment. The American President, Wilson, won't let Italy have it. The official reason is the risk of another war which would start in Fiume but might spread to the Balkans. But the real reasons are different."

Now the evening dusk blurs the outlines of things nearby, turning shapes into dark fluid patches.

"Circles in high finance are urging against Italy annexing Fiume. Vital interests are at stake. The peace treaties in Paris are being dictated by arguments that are far from idealistic, my friend."

Tullio gazes at him without responding, he waits for Giulio to carry on.

"Wilson's attempt to export a *new freedom* – that's his election slogan – is based on pretty concrete interests. Wilson refuses to recognize any secret treaty such as the 1915 London Pact signed by Italy as a premise to its entry into the war. Agreements of that sort, in his opinion, are among the strategies of decrepit European diplomacy: they're just the ruses of that old whore-monger. He proclaims self-determination. But wherever other interests are at stake – American interests above all – the music suddenly changes and the old rules are okay. In fact his approach to Asia Minor is quite different. There's talk of an American mandate over a good part of the Asian territories, including Turkish Armenia: the carcase of the Ottoman Empire."

"A swap at the top, then? The United States taking the place of Britain and France in control of countries and capitals?"

"You've got it in one, my old mate."

"But if what you're telling me is true, and I don't at all discount it, what can we do about it? And is d'Annunzio really the right man to carry out an act of... what can one call it? An act of anti-imperialism?"

"Today what's happening in Fiume looks like the work of a handful of crackpots, but it might even trigger a chain reaction. As for d'Annunzio, he may be a visionary lunatic, but in effect he's also making a bid to lay bare the rot underlying the lush carpets, moving strategic pawns like Istria and Fiume on the larger European chequer-board. And I personally prefer his titanic, crazy bravado to that of the tuxedo-clad dwarfs in Rome or Paris who use nations and peoples in a game of chequers."

He's spoken with gusto, without pausing for breath. Tullio observes the ships riding at anchor, the dockside cranes looking like embalmed giraffes, the crates of merchandise stacked up against a long warehouse wall: the bustle of a seaport that's always lived by trade is now forced to a standstill that's bound to become total. A town that seems to have been spawned from a writer's nightmare: somehow

94

governed by a poet, opposed by the president of a great liberal nation, overrun by adventurers – frontline nationalists – and by an ill-assorted bunch of idealists tainted by a deadly sin: disrespect for the mighty. And inhabited by a population that has really always lived together peacefully: Italians, Croats, Slovenes – and also Germans. Hungarians – who perhaps no longer see themselves as people of Fiume but as conflicting and ethnically divided groups, suddenly distrustful, torn apart.

Sea-mist swathes the harbour and the pier like ghostly ectoplasm.

Tullio feels he's groping among disconnected, unreal ideas. Produced by fatigue, he tells himself, or by the stress he's under. By the echo of a verse by Verlaine. By listening to Giulio.

An incisor of brilliant whiteness with a corner chipped off. He's noticed that she sometimes, when laughing, covers it with her hand. She's too young still to realize that little defects only make beauty more authentic, and perhaps more human.

Giulio's voice comes to him now as if from afar.

"And what about you, Tullio, tell me, what do you think?"

The lighthouse has just begun to slash its chill alphabet of light across the sea.

His tone is low-key. "Lots of things. I'm not much interested in annexation…"

"But you're mad! Or an imbecile…"

"… Just listen… Only a miracle will give Fiume to Italy. And I can't stand certain fanatics – the most diehard, you know – who march under a flag which up to a few months ago sent them out to be slaughtered. We've already paid dearly to the god of flags, don't you think? But here there are other challenges. David and Goliath. And possibly a way to defy the world…"

The look in Giulio's eyes now goes hard.

"… a world that's almost committed suicide."

He doesn't feel there's any more to be said. He recalls a wasteland, hears the wind.

A bird – a moorhen, he thinks it is – flies down to skim the water and flies off again.

6 October 1919

To General Pietro Badoglio
For His Eyes Only

Top Secret

Absolute secret. In strict confidence I inform your excellency that Wilson refuses to accept the proposal that Italy annex Fiume.
Signed
The Prime Minister
Francesco Saverio Nitti.

Abbazia
October 1919

On a day in late autumn they stroll along slowly, close together, Greta's auburn hair gathered in a long bunch, some of Edith's black curls escaping from her chignon.

They're good-looking, dressed in the bright clothes of adolescents who have turned into women, elbows touching in swing with their stride and hands coming up from time to time – out of the shade into the light – to shield against the sunshine. The intimacy which they've always shared makes the rare moments of silence between them simple and natural.

"But why are you staying away for three whole months, Edith?"

"I haven't seen my grandparents for years. And I won't be at all sorry, Greta, to spend some time with them in Vienna."

"And… what do you have to tell me about that cousin of yours?"

"It's years since I last met him, but who cares? Last time we met he seemed so stiff and wooden that you could have used him as a compass. And his personality is boiled würstel."

"With sauerkraut or without?"

"Without, without. At most with mustard or potato."

Greta grins, brushes aside a long bough. They proceed slowly down the path that winds its way among the rocks along the bay and the parks that slope down towards the sea.

"And when are you leaving?" she asks, a touch anxiously.

"Immediately after Sukkot."

"… the feast of hovels."

"… of tabernacles, Greta. Of tabernacles."

"Forgive me. Of tabernacles."

"But what will you do for three months in Vienna? Pick violets in the Prater? Play Bach? Or will you stay cooped up indoors among Prague knick-knacks and porcelain ware?"

Edith stops, stares at her. "Why are you being so sardonic, Greta? Are you, by any chance, feeling… jealous?"

An instant's silence.

"Spot on."

They've known each other since they took their first steps. Their neighbouring gardens are divided only by a low stone wall with a box-hedge, neither of which, obviously, has ever kept them apart. They played together as children and joined forces against Arturo who would pursue them with his catapult. They shinned up fig-trees and apple-trees together when those parks still comprised the world and everything else around didn't count. They had so many quarrels and even more peace-makings, swapping books and questions to which nobody had the answers and opinions about life, although they barely know what it is.

Greta kicks a stone towards the sea, hears it bounce off a rock, observes a seagull flying low. Then she looks at Edith again. "Will you build the tabernacle again this year?"

"Sure, same as ever, naturally."

"In the usual place?"

"Of course."

And Greta finds herself thinking that though she's now an adult, she is as fascinated and captivated by that rite as when she was a child. Sure, now she understands all the symbols, and the hut erected at the bottom of the park has lost its aura of mystery although it retains all the connections which have always entranced her: the exodus and the flight from Egypt, the Hebrews' long march, the memory of a precariousness that must never be forgotten: no solid roof over one's head, no fixed and secure shelter in which one can feel safe.

But once, when they were children, the hut was for her and for Edith just a hiding-place all of their own where they could escape from the world of adults and converse as if garbed in mystery: light filtered through the boughs, noises came muffled by the stiff jute fabric, the scent of resin and earth seemed to stick to the palate along with pungent, unfamiliar odours which were impossible to decipher. Up above, fruit and golden corn cobs hung festooned.

In there, everything receded into the background: school, their earliest misgivings, their fears. There, even Arturo's unforgivable malady receded into the background, though only for a while, when the onset of adolescence had not yet robbed Greta of the refuges of a childhood so richly endowed.

They stop. They've arrived. Edith is about to open the

gate. Greta takes out of her bag a small parcel with a white ribbon and passes it to her in silence.

She waits for Edith to open it for her to see the little things of which she suddenly feels ashamed because they're so obvious: a Bach score, a novel by Ada Negri which she had just read, a little tin of aniseed balls, her friend's favourites.

They exchange a quick farewell embrace.

As she makes her way home, Greta follows the flight of a flock of birds, compactly arrayed over the sea like a line of music, and she wonders why certain moments leave you with the impression that you're teetering on the brink: between a before which is already giving way beneath your feet, even if it hasn't always been pleasant, and an after that attracts and alarms at the same time.

Like the urge to be happy and the terror of not being able.

As when one suddenly comes of age and all at once feels afraid but doesn't exactly know what one is afraid of.

Fiume
October 1919

The boy is nude, standing on the prow, his long, dark arms stretched forward, his legs straight and poised for the dive, his shoulders catching the sun.

Then, just an instant, one step back, a short run-up barefooted: and if it's not quite a perfect dive, nevertheless it's well-judged and vigorous. He disappears through the smack on the water, remains submerged for a few instants, re-emerges amid spray and foam: then his arm rises, he disappears again, reappears, waves his mates a greeting and an invitation.

Then the lad swims to shore: with a few strokes he reaches the quay. Behind him, from the bridge of a ship lying at anchor along with the others, there in the docks, a bare-chested shipmate shows up.

Shading his eyes with his hand, Tullio observes the scene from the pier: he sees him toss something into the sea, yelling with throaty Tuscan consonants: "he who fishes it up again gets a litre!"

One after another dive in with laughs and belly-flops, splashing and shouting. Tullio watches one boy's movements: he disappears under water, vanishes from sight. When he re-surfaces, he's got his fist clenched, he raises his arm in sign of victory, waves to his mates and yells out: "It be mine!" Then he climbs slowly out of the water, his skinny body dripping wet, a little boy's smile on his face. And only now that he's close up does Tullio notice that his right arm is nothing but a stump. As his mates press round him, the lad opens his fist and says, bemused, in his lilting Venetian with its incredible consonants: "A medal? A war-time medal? Why, if I'd of known what it war, I'd of left it at the bottom of the sea, I swear it!"

Some of them laugh, elbow him.

He, however, goes on looking thoughtfully into the palm of his hand, a sour look on his face, which has suddenly gone hollow, lke that of a saint in a Byzantine mosaic.

Tullio is standing on the quay beside Paul and Giulio, who's come along with them over there, to the Fiume shipyards, which, on account of the blockade, are standing idle, like almost everything else in the town.

"But who are they?" Paul asks him, with a glance at the boys, who have moved off along the pier.

"Aspiring legionaries," Giulio explains. "And they come from most parts of Italy. But they haven't brought any papers, and headquarters hasn't enlisted them."

All at once the words of a song sneak upon them.

"… *Oh, Gorizia town be damned…*"

All three of them look upwards.

"You bastards lying in your woollen beds, you and your wives…"

A small group of them have shinned up the raised jib of a crane.

"You mockers of us human fodder, this war teaches us to smite…"

From up aloft, the chorus comes in a blur of sound. The lads, bodies wet, arms interlocked, sway in time with their chant. Their voices die down, and now the notes can be heard: hesitant at first, slightly unsteady, then stronger and more assured, a pizzicato from the throat that swells into true music.

The three of them remain like that, motionless, noses in the air, gazing at the boy who's playing his little mouth-organ, his mates around him silent, dangling their legs up there, their bodies occupied by an anarchy of sentiments that sting like nettles.

Giulio resumes pensively: "I was talking to them yesterday. Nearly all of them have seen combat. They came back home when the war was over, thinking they could make a fresh start. They thought they could do it with head held high, having risked their skin for the sake of a *patria* that promised them so much: gratitude, employment, land. But gratitude is in short supply, employment we know is lacking, the land stays in the same hands as before. They don't deserve this peace-time. And they didn't expect it to be like this while they were wriggling through the mud with brandy inside them to dull their consciousness and the military police behind them to induce them in their own way to leap out under a storm of shrapnel."

Tullio lights himself a cigarette, passes a couple to his friends. For an instant or two they smoke in silence, with their eyes on those lads up on the crane.

"They told me that they're not leaving this place. Fiume's become a symbol to them."

A symbol, and a challenge, Tullio repeats to himself.

But he senses that that's not all, that Giulio's thoughts are elsewhere.

"You've something else in mind. Go on, fire away."

Giulio grins. "You're right, old chap. There is something else. I've now got them sized up. Daredevils, almost untameable, resistant to rules and hierarchies. But tough, and straight, brave. Capable of facing real risks, if they believe in what they're doing. And in spite of being allergic to discipline, they're willing to accept new rules, as long as they're *anti* rules."

"Anti what?" The question comes from Paul.

"Anti war dressed up as peace: back to the same old order. The privileged against the poor devils."

"Go on."

"I would turn them into an elite corps."

"What?!"

"I'd turn those outcast lads into a crack militia. Top-notch. D'Annunzio's bodyguard. And there's already a name for them. I'd call them *La Disperata*."

There's a moment's silence, then Paul speaks again: "You said they're willing to accept new rules as long as they believe in a new goal."

"Right."

"What is it, then?"

Tullio can feel it in the air, this new tension between them. Ever since they met, Giulio and Paul have often fronted up on a purely verbal level of words and ideas, but nevertheless sharply: Giulio, the radical, always going to extremes, ready to do battle at the very edge of the absurd as if that were his natural space; Paul, the pragmatist, who always subjects an idea to the test of reality.

Tullio studies those bodies, those profiles: Giulio's aquiline nose, his sharply marked features, his as always unkempt beard and whiskers, so black as to seem almost blue, his gladiator's shoulders; and Paul's ascetic figure, his disarming blue eyes, his Protestant choir-boy's blond hair.

"So, then, will you tell us what it is, or won't you?"

"I really think I will, my friend. I shall put in command of these men someone very special whom they would never have accepted in any other situation."

"My God, do you really mean it?" exclaims Paul. "A painter or a musician, to match the poet-commandant? A blind veteran? A de-mobbed German?"

Giulio smiles. "No. A woman."

"A woman?!"

"And I already know her name. Want a bet? Give us your hand!"

★ ★ ★

Now they've climbed down off the crane and picked up their clothes and shoes which they'd left inside an old warehouse. Some have bare feet, some wear boots. The boy they noticed earlier is walking ahead of his mates. His mouth-organ peeps out of a pocket. His left-hand sleeve hangs empty, pinned back neatly to the shoulder. And Tullio suddenly asks himself whether there is a solution, here in Fiume, to the whole tangle of all those – too many – unresolved issues: a population that's being ignored, an army of disillusioned ex-

105

combatants and of nationalists who are ready for anything, a group of idealists and rebels up in arms against the order of the powers-that-be.

And possibly international intrigues that mingle politics and finance in an explosive mix.

8 October 1919
To General Pietro Badoglio
For His Eyes Only

Top Secret

Mussolini has gone to Fiume with idea of mediating STOP

Signed
Francesco Saverio Nitti
Prime Minister of Italy

Fiume
October 1919

This year the start of the school year has a completely different flavour: that must be why, she tells herself, not only does it not bother her in the least, but she's actually pleased.

She's well aware of the real reason.

So Greta has appreciated every moment, as if she were an outside observer of the otherwise ritual acts, the familiar spaces, the well-known faces: the half-lit entrance to the school, the starched expressions of the nuns, the smell of dust and mould that snaps at you as you go up the stairs and that of incense and candle-wax that billows out as you pass in front of the chapel beneath the low arcades of the cloister whose frescoes are gradually fading in the red of distant lands, depicted through palm-trees and olive-groves and beneath the footwear of saints who have all the air of Istrian country folk and fisher-folk from the Carnaro. That's where Greta meets up with her fellow pupils and exchanges hugs with those she is really close to.

They size each other up, eager to spot each person's bodily changes, as some fill out beneath their black cotton pinafores. Then they exchange the big news, which, for the first time ever, doesn't consist in mere personal snippets but involves the wider world: Fiume. And it's all that much more amazing when viewed from their convent school, with its simple daily rituals which, until only a few days earlier, seemed destined to stretch on for ever, like the cycle of the seasons: instead of which, everything has now gone topsy-turvy, and nothing seems to have stayed in its place. They find themselves all talking at once, telling each other things they already know: d'Annunzio's speeches delivered from the balcony of Government Palace, the night patrols in the streets, the public assemblies and the marches and torchlight vigils, often with military bands or fanfares, articles in every newspaper.

And the young fellows that Lucia's seen diving off the ships' prows in the harbour or off the cranes in the dockyards.

"And do you know how they were? Naked!"

All the girls turn towards her. The enormity of it requires an instant's silence to be taken in in all its petrifying absurdity. Then the incident takes shape, coalesces, becomes an authentic image.

"Naked? What d'you mean?"

Lucia strings them along, allows herself a deliberate pause as she arranges her books on her desk. Then, seraphically, she pronounces: "Just as mamma made them. Just that. And their bums were firmer," she adds, lowering her voice a little, "than that of the discobolus of Myron."

Greta gazes at her resignedly. Lucia has put on that new manner, half brazen and half blasé, which she now knows all too well but just can't swallow.

But there is a reason for the change in her friend: given the extraordinary new situation which Fiume is experiencing during these days, her status as a day student free to go home after lessons are over at one o'clock has suddenly turned her into a top-ranking spectator compared to the boarders like Greta who are confined to living and sleeping in the convent from Monday to Saturday morning.

So Lucia's taken upon herself a new role: that of tacking together two worlds – the real world in revolt out there and the rigidly cloistered school. And add to this the fact that her father, an advocate and the son of an advocate is a member by hereditary title of the Town Council, which has not been challenged since the olden times of Empress Maria Teresa. So she gets previews of the latest news right there at home.

The sudden sound of the school bell and the shuffling on the stairs catapults them back into their adolescence, on the benches precisely lined up beneath the authority of the crucifix, the throne of Sister Teresa, the Golgotha of the dais.

Only then does Lucia glance at her and slip a note between her fingers, with just a wink.

Greta opens it out and reads it curiously. And she feels her legs turn to jelly and her cheeks to flame.

She looks at Lucia for an instant. She thought she'd always known her on account of those years they'd sat on the same bench as little girls hiding their lips with their knuckles as they exchanged confidences, conspiratorial secrets.

But perhaps not, perhaps she doesn't know her. Certainly, she knows her to be freer and more grown-up than the other convent girls, if only on account of her unusual family and the wife barely out of childhood which her father has married recently, twenty years his junior and only a few months after his first wife had died.

That must be why, she admits, her friend has been behaving so strangely of late: she acts like a woman while still showing the enthusiasms of a child.

Greta is still holding the note in her hand.

As the lesson starts in silence she hides it deftly beneath a handkerchief, deep in one of the pockets of her pinafore.

9 October 1919

To the Prime Minister of Italy
Francesco Saverio Nitti
For His Eyes Only

Top Secret

Mussolini back from Fiume landed today Ajello airstrip STOP Has told me he will vigorously support projected solution STOP Appears convinced that d'Annunzio adamant on annexation STOP

Signed
General Pietro Badoglio

Fiume
October 1919

ESCAPE

The word is pencilled in at the centre of a sheet of squared paper, as though this would make it slightly less serious. Then comes the itemized list divided in two columns:

Risks

Benefits

1 Being discovered
2 Getting hurt
3 Serious punishment
4 Expulsion from school
5 Report to my family
6 Even more serious punishment
7 Suspension of my studies
8 Goodbye to Fiume
9???

1 Seeing
2 Taking part
3 Understanding for myself

Greta knows that this is an old dodge, and a naïve one. And it won't help her, in this instance.

But she fondly recalls that it was her nonna that had taught her it when she was still a child: just a way to rationalize the pros and cons of a decision in moments of doubt and crisis. A book-keeping dodge, admittedly: but there have been times when it did help her.

She gets up, goes to the window. She draws the curtains slightly and looks out.

She knows by heart the wall of the building opposite: the long array of windows looking out over the ledges, the tiny balconies in white Istrian stone and the mullioned windows of the top storey which makes the building less ponderous and less austere. And besides that building, she now sees, alive in her memory, the other buildings, the park of Villa Leopoldo, the prospect of the central streets that open downwards against the azure to debouch suddenly upon the sea.

A whole world unscrolls before her. And what she can't see, she divines.

The seafront drenched in sunshine, the shapes of the distant islands, shrouded in haze. She has never so sharply felt the longing for a freedom that perhaps she doesn't even know, that she has never really possessed.

But now her thoughts are on another Fiume, more fought over, more sombre.

Annexation by Italy, immediately. That's what d'Annunzio has demanded, rejecting any further compromise and any deferment of the issue. In a few days' time he will address the people of Fiume: the assembly he has announced is eagerly awaited. So Lucia told her. For now it's no holds barred: the legionaries will stay on only if the town backs them up, only if Fiume declares itself in agreement with the intention of not giving way, of continuing its protest so as to get itself heard.

She thinks back to the march of a month ago, on that hot September afternoon.

She had felt herself united with all the others by a new and unknown energy which was capable of sweeping aside every barrier between people: no more the rich and the poverty-stricken in Fiume, old and young, men and women, students with smooth hands and dockers with calloused fingers.

As if every diaphragm between herself and the world around had dissolved, every restraint crumbled.

She picks up that list. There's no doubt: the risks of escape outweigh the advantages by about three to one. And there may be other aspects she hasn't yet thought of: what are the streets like at night? Will it be safe for her to walk alone? Can her plan really succeed?

Almost in a rage, she strikes out the risks set out on the left with a black line and then traces a great ring over and over again around *understanding for myself*.

Then she rolls the sheet into a pellet, weighs it for a moment between her fingers.

The assembly will be held on the 24th of October at the Teatro Verdi.

She calmly tosses the paper into the waste bin, intending to be there.

On her way down to the convent's ground floor and the great library, her mind returns to the note. She again experiences the empty feeling in her stomach which she had when she read the message and the signature at the end, his name.

No rhetorical flourish, no fulsome compliment in an attempt to impress her. Few words. And she liked them. She found them honest and straightforward and, to her nose, sincere.

She had seen him there before her: his eyes, his features, his hands. That book between them, that voice.

And he was asking to see her again. It was at that point in the message that the world had turned to jelly: floor, walls, everything wobbly and ready to fall apart. Everything out of control, quite suddenly. Embarrassment, pleasure, pure joy. And a churning of sensations that started at the oesophagus and got lost in unknown meanderings. She'd felt all sorts of everything and summed up that everything in a single No. No, she could not meet him: it wasn't even to be thought of.

End of story. And she'd sent him her answer by word of mouth, via Lucia, the messenger.

Only now he returns to her mind along with harmless images which press themselves on her – the colourful stall of a pipe-seller, the sweetness of buttered *pinze*, red sunsets over the bay – as if the recollection of that man availed itself of every kind of innocence to blaze a trail and gain a purchase.

Now in the library what brings her round is a new, embarrassed silence, and the privacy of her classmates gathering round Maria, who's tormenting the hem of her skirt.

Greta, joining the group with an enquiring glance, finally understands.

Maria's leaving school. Hearing her concluding words – the school fees she can no longer afford, her three other siblings that have to be supported, her family that needs a helping hand – Greta gets everything into focus as in a sudden awakening: the blockade by land and sea has brought Fiume to its knees.

Its economy is in ruins. Middlemen have no work, shipowners are going broke, seamen have gone for weeks without sailing and thousands are unemployed because of the shutdown of the dockyards, the seafront warehouses, the torpedo factory. And the same has now befallen to several city centre stores, shipping companies, the Smith and Meynier paper factory. Fiume is a trading port. Fiume is Fiume. It's always lived by trade across the Adriatic and the Mouths of Cattaro.

Greta reflects that Maria's father, a seasoned sea-captain, is merely one of the first to lose his job, with no idea of how to making a living. Many others will be affected now. Hunger will haunt them all.

Silently, she leaves her classmates.

Now more than ever she feels them calling her, the happenings out there, beyond that barred window, beyond the books stacked against the walls, in chests right up to the ceiling – a bookworms' paradise – and beyond the enclosed space of the great library that seems to contain all the girls as in a reliquary or in a showcase: the air catches at your throat, nothing but mildew spores and dampness.

As it waited to know its future, the town up to now had seemed to her to be in a continual state of euphoria, as if it had abolished any past and any hypothetical future, after the long night of war, to plunge entirely into the present. And so as to make its voice heard by the great who were gathered in

Paris and seated around the peace tables, it had flared in a changed climate of trance and utopia: she had seen that delirious crowd turn suddenly into a river in full spate, advancing like a sea-swell amid the singing, clinging to the railings outside the palace where d'Annunzio resides so as to hear him speak, so as to shake off all fear and recognize itself in him.

But, all at once, she has a child's eyes.

And to her child's eyes Fiume is like the naked emperor in the fairy tale whose suit of clothes is tailored out of thin air.

A palm tree at the far end of the convent cloister is being buffeted by the sea breeze.

She observes it with a sense of shame, because though the present feels like a painful reawakening, she keeps thinking of herself: of the plan she has to hatch, of the risks she'll be running on her own, of all she's about to set up. Not to speak of the consequences if something goes awry.

Greta knows she has little time left and she's got to make the most of it.

Fiume, Government Palace
October 1919

The room would be fairly nondescript, were it not for the grand piano and the end wall, draped all over with flags.

But to get here, to enter the Palace's Holy of Holies, set in the heart of its first floor, one has to get through three relays of guards and thorough checking by two staff officers as well as further questioning (though more easy-going, more tactful) by a special secretary who is as solicitous as a Latin mother and as punctilious as an English tutor. And before that, one will have had to traverse the marble double staircase, the grand glassed-in foyer, and the severe hall with its three loggias overlooked by dozens of portraits which condense at least two centuries of Fiume's history in the faces of its magnates.

The door is closed. The music score on the Steinway is by Debussy.

On a small corner table, as upon a tabernacle, are

displayed several rare incunabula and an edition of Petrarch's *Canzoniere* bound in dark Morocco. To the left, in between two armchairs, are a fern in a brass pot, a sagging archive cabinet, and a large window opening on to the balcony facing the sea.

At the desk submerged by papers, a glass-shaded lamp casts an almost livid light on the man's shiny cranium.

The tapping of typewriters, repeated trilling of telephones, orders given and received, telegrams being read out and other noises caused by the continual coming and going in that score of offices housed in Fiume's grand palace manage to filter into the room from beneath the locked door.

But the man sitting there hears none of this hubbub. He is immersed in his reading.

My faithful Friend,

I understand perfectly the necessity in which you find yourself to postpone our meeting until Tuesday next. Since it is a matter of taking decisions that involve not only Italy but also the people of Fiume, it stands to reason that you, as guardian of their rights and guarantor of justice, must want to hear the precise expression of their desires...

He briefly raises his head. His gaze wanders into empty space. Yes, a plebiscite is necessary. And the public assembly that he's just about to conduct, the messages and attestations that keep on coming...

The people of Fiume are with him. And, like him, they do not intend to give in. They will not delegate to anyone else the future of their town: not to the great who are gathered in Paris – Woodrow Wilson, Lloyd George, Clemenceau – not to anyone who has never set foot in Fiume and does not know its spirit and its features, its language, its culture. Who does not know its expectations. Not to one who yet bandies about the principle and the right of all peoples to decide their own destiny.

… I open by facing the key issue, that is, by examining the issue of the annexation of Fiume. I have told you that shortly after my arrival in Julian Venetia I had telegraphed to the government a proposal for the annexation of the town. The government felt unable to take this step. It summoned the Royal Council, and all those present, including Salandra, Barzilai, Federzoni, expressed their opposition to annexation, since Italy could not run the risk of finding itself completely isolated in moments as serious as these…

There's a knock at the door. The man looks up. An attendant looks in: "Commandant, there's a…"

"Not now, not now. Later."

The door slowly closes. The man looks down again at the pages in his hands.

Now… that it's absolutely certain that a government which has been properly set up in accordance with our laws will never resolve to declare the annexation of Fiume, I have made up my mind to come to you and say: Faithful Friend, what is your decision? There are but two possible solutions. We shall examine them together…One of these solutions would be to overthrow – I won't say the government (which would only be replaced by another which would be unable to act any other way) – but the State as currently organized. Would you, my comrade in arms, feel ready to lead the Nation down this path? Would you feel ready to drive our Country towards revolution? I say not…

That leaves only the way which I have followed and which I have pointed out to you. That is, to apply every possible pressure on the Allies, setting certain essential conditions on which we declare we will not yield. In this way, while leaving America the satisfaction of not seeing her position completely scuppered, we actually save the substance of the matter…

He lays the letter down on the desk and passes his hand over it, as if to absorb by touch the meaning of every line, the very urgency of the decision. He's written at length, has Badoglio. He's written to him as never before. He picks up a sheet of notepaper, takes up his pen, pauses.

It seems to him ever more difficult to remain consistent with his intentions, to find a balance in things. He doesn't trust the government there in Rome. And he doesn't trust Mussolini. The annexation of Fiume is far away, its isolation ever more complete.

And ever more difficult and extreme has his own position become.

★ ★ ★

He goes up to the window, looks outside. The sea is barely discernible in the darkness beyond the balcony, beyond the street that leads down from his Palace as far as the seafront and harbour.

On that sea's horizon, a few hours earlier, an American vessel sailed past. He had watched it for a few minutes, thoughtfully: its bulk was evident and impressive, its navigation decisive, it steered a clear and steady route, well defined.

Nothing seemed to compare with that steel colossus, with its self-assured sea-faring.

But now his thoughts go to the E-boats – the MAS, the small craft at anchor in Fiume's contested harbour.

And all at once the acronym – Motoscafi Anti Sommergibili – Motor Anti-Submarine Sloops – comes to his lips in a different version of the name and its meaning: Memento Audere Semper – Remember Dare Always.

He's about to turn fifty-seven. But that's always been his creed, ever since his days at boarding school in Prato, when during the night he stealthily filched the oil out of the lamps of the other boys who were sleeping around him so as to keep his wick alight and carry on reading in the dark.

More than forty years have gone by, but something within him hasn't changed.

Memento Audere Semper. Remember Dare Always.

Then in an instant he knows what answer he will give Badoglio, and through him, to the entire world.

Fiume
October 1919

Her strategy is so simple that it might even work: banal as it is, it doesn't raise suspicion.

Suddenly she feels calm, and moderately confident: but she still crosses her fingers and wishes herself luck, while she crosses the convent cloister to access the most secluded hallway, the one that leads beyond the chapel towards the great library and by which, going up the stairs, one gets to the nuns' rooms.

She sees her at once, as she enters the library. She was sure she'd find her there.

Sister Teresa's profile is distinct, bent over a book and silhouetted against the light, and the outline of the starched veil that falls down on to her hand looks like a wing: she is so absorbed that she doesn't even seem to notice the new presence by her side.

Greta sits down silently. She lays out on the oak table the volumes of Hegel, Fichte and Kant.

Only then does the woman raise her head and, as if coming to herself, smile. Greta responds with a respectful nod, her pencil poised in mid-air, hesitancy and the anxiety of the moment making her doubtful. But she knows that every decision – every logistical move, in there – has always been made by her, by Sister Teresa.

Certainly the most cultivated of the nuns, brilliant in argument, impassioned in communicating.

Her philosophy teacher. And Greta has long sensed that for that still young woman, open-minded and generous of spirit, it's not just a subject but a continuous challenge of understanding and rigour, a sort of intellectual voluptuousness which might perhaps take the place of weaker, all too human passions.

Greta is not averse to those studies, but never as in recent times has she plunged almost headlong into them, with the fastidiousness of an apprentice and the rigour of a Franciscan.

So now she gets herself in hand, she takes the plunge.

"Forgive my disturbing you, Sister Teresa, but if you could give me a couple of minutes… I'm not absolutely clear about this point in Hegel's *Phenomenology*: *truth is the movement of truth itself.* Could you help me understand?"

Greta couldn't really say how long that explanation lasted, which she strove to follow, taking notes on key points: she knows only that this is the right moment and that she must make the most of it. So she blurts out her request, justifies it as she has prepared herself to do: her difficulty in concentrating, the noise interfering with her studies.

It's important for her to get a yes. The nun smiles, she's favourably disposed. "Certainly you can have that room. Maria used to sleep there, as you know, and she's left school.

You're right, it's quieter than yours: in there you won't be disturbed any more by the hubbub from the street."

Then she adds, glancing at the window: "It's pandemonium in Fiume, and the Lord only knows when it will end… *the world's prose*, Hegel called it. You can move in right away tomorrow, Greta."

Suddenly relieved, she decides to go the whole hog: "Couldn't I move in right now? Tomorrow I have Latin translation, and I'd like to settle down and study…"

Sister Teresa closes her books. "Right. If that's what you want, that's fine by me."

Blissful naivety, thinks Greta. More like a philosopher, really, than a nun.

But suddenly the nun gives her a sharp look. "*Non scholae sed vitae discimur.* You have no problem in translating that, have you, Greta?"

Greta feels herself swallowing hard, her voice trembling. *"We learn not for school but for life."*

The nun remains still for an instant, then nods slowly and, looking deep into her eyes, adds in a lower voice: "I was sure that you knew that, Greta."

Greta goes down the corridor feeling weak at the knees and with pounding heart.

Has the nun guessed something, or were hers merely chance words? She goes down the stairs, stops at the end of the hall, goes up to the wall.

How many times previously has she brushed past that fresco? Yet she's never really looked at it.

The expression on the face of that folk Madonna she now finds gentle, the hues of the paintwork restful, familiar the slightly faded landscape that forms a backdrop to the Annunciation scene.

It's a familiar scene, she knows it well. Conventional is the curly-headed angel with one arm raised and his foot barely touching the ground amid the fluid drapery of his garment that is still moving from his flight. And Mary's pose is also the usual one, her unresisting compliance with her destiny, her gaze of serene acceptance which barely betrays a tremor of doubt, a lump of anxiety and dread.

But above the woman's head, above her face inclined within the veil, the white bird that hovers there is not a dove, the harbinger of peace, but a well-fed seagull just like all those in Fiume.

And in the background, beyond the stone arch that frames the scene, under a white cloud overfraught with chubby cherubs, the landscape is not one of whitewashed houses amid the palms of Galilee: instead, it's a little harbour watched over by a distant lighthouse, amid woods of oak and hornbeam and dazzling white Istrian crags like the cliffs of Cherso sheer above the sea: and looking at it as she does now, head and heart, Greta seems to hear a faint whine of cicadas and to feel the warmth of the earth beneath her feet and scent algae and flowers from the beach covered with anemones in an anchorage she'd seen as a child.

It's like life grafted within the cloister, the overwhelming inrush of the world, thanks to the paintbrush of an anonymous painter who lived centuries earlier.

And it strikes her as a good omen, that it augurs something positive: almost a sign that everything is possible, if one has the will to imagine it. Even the plan she now has in mind and which she does not intend to give up.

When she eventually gets to her room – her new room, from now on – she feels serene once more.

Then she looks out of the window and smiles at those cherry boughs that come almost up to the window sill and take over the whole space in that last strip of garden which is so secluded in shadow, squeezed in along the convent and besieged by clumps of bushes in between the left wing of the school and the enclosing stone wall.

Then Greta addresses a silent thank you to the athletic upbringing that she's received as a girl from an Austrian-born mother of Spartan habits.

Face resting on knuckles and elbows on the sill, she sees in memory the long swims across the bay along with her brother, the breathless racing and chasing down the park, the figs and apples and cherries picked by reaching out a hand and eaten just like that, she and Arturo, perched on a branch, fingers filthy with grass and earth and pitch, with pulps and juices ripened in the sun.

And all the dares between the two of them. Dangle from a branch. Count up to ten. And then go on counting. First to get to that rock. Climb on to it. It's slippery. Fall. Swoop from the bay so as to run up to a given point and scramble up beyond what's possible, wet all over, hair and body: she upon the tallest horse-chestnut in the garden, he on its oldest helianthus.

And risk your neck, even, trying to reach the ripe fruit which has survived intact through the summer months on the highest tips of the branches: then crawl along like pine-martens and, holding your breath, get to the fronds which only the birds can reach and contend with them, like thieves, for the plums and pears and apricots or for the figs dripping with juice and coating your fingers with sugar.

In memory she also suddenly hears the snapping of that persimmon bough beneath her feet: the sudden emptiness, the plunge, her heart leaping into her mouth, the new sensation of fear. Her chin has struck a stone wedged in between earth and roots. She's felt the blood spurting from her lip, and, putting her hand to her mouth, she's immediately discovered the damage: a corner of an incisor has been chipped off, sacrificed.

But no one had made a drama of it: it was just a foreseeable stage in the apprenticeship for a life of both seaside and countryside.

Her father did show his disapproval with looks of annoyance and harsh gestures. What games were these, what manners? Certainly not those of a well brought up girl. But often enough her father wasn't there.

And her mother, feelingly pronouncing *mens sana in corpore sano*, allowed her to bake in the sun and to transform her skinny body into firm muscles, strong arms, legs trained to endure, to move: a pagan girl's body.

A childhood so different, she reflects, from Elisa's muted childhood…

Greta's expert eye gauges the robustness of the branches, the small distance from the wall, the deep chinks between the blocks of stone caused by the climbing plants: perfect for a toe-hold or a finger-hold.

She studies the twinings of the wisteria – a gibbous old trunk – clinging like a handrail to hang on to and the opening masked by a hibiscus beside a mouldering garden bench.

She considers her route carefully, the time for lights out, the last nun patrol.

The days have grown shorter. The sky is already darkening. Two hours later, Greta is out.

23 October 1919

To the Prime Minister of Italy
Francesco Saverio Nitti
For His Eyes Only

Top Secret

On 22 October night expeditionary force led by Gabriele d'Annunzio consisting of one thousand commandos bersaglieri carabinieri infantry grenadiers and Dalmatian volunteers arrived aboard Royal Naval vessel Cortellazzo and Torpedo Boat Destroyer Nullo and Torpedo Boat 66 PN and MAS 22 STOP Complement disembarked Zara amid exulting Italian population STOP Given my word as soldier that Dalmatia in London Agreement will never be abandoned STOP

Signed
Admiral Millo
Military Commander in Zara

Fiume
October 1919

Squeezed behind the wall of people, Greta is now happily listening.

She's had a hard time getting in. Two hours ahead of the time set for d'Annunzio's public meeting, the theatre was already crammed, and is now overflowing with folk. Not only on the proscenium benches, in the gallery and theatre boxes: every inch of space has been taken and many people are sitting on the floor amid pushing and shoving, stumbling and swearing. But people made a bit of room for her and let her through, not minding too much the fleeting contact with her body amid the throng.

It quite suits her to be almost squashed against the wall in that far corner: that out-of-the-way nook is ideal. Still almost in disbelief, she can now look on.

On the stage, d'Annunzio, in spats and uniform, has begun to speak.

That voice of his is as she remembered it: precise and enthralling, clear and grave. Its inflection strikes her as musical and the flow of words, natural.

She shifts her weight for an instant, leans with her back against the wall and struggles to find an equilibrium that affords her a visual slice between a docker's back that hides half the scene and a woman with sculpted curls that hides the other half.

She even puts up with that elbow sticking into her sternum. What matters is that she's done it: she's here. What matters is being here, taking part. And trying to follow the long and fiery speech of that warrior poet:

The right of peoples to rule themselves, so frequently proclaimed, but always trampled underfoot, must in the end be consecrated... Fiume cannot be a free city but does want to be a city of a free Italy, with its entire territory, with its entire sea, with its entire archipelago...

The woman with curls like whipped cream vigorously nods her approval.

So does the lad next to her.

The crowd seems intent on listening and alternates concentrated silence with abrupt outbursts of enthusiasm: it's like an oyster that envelops a foreign body and mysteriously makes it its own.

Meanwhile, with the precision of a cartographer, d'Annunzio has begun to define what should be Italy's new border at its far north-eastern corner: Idria and Postumia, San Pietro, Castelnuovo... lines and sea-coasts, archipelagos and settlements take shape right there before their eyes, in the draft of a collective dream that has the colours of the land, the rocks, and the sea. And for each person there present those names have a profound meaning and mark loyalties and belonging: who is there that does not recognize in the name of an island or a village part of their roots or a happy summer memory?

The atmosphere grows more ardent as the voice rises in tone.

… from Ireland's indomitable Sinn Fein to Egypt's red flag which marries the Crescent and the Cross… all those rebels of every race will rally under our ensign. And the defenceless will be armed. And the new crusade of all the world's poor and impoverished nations, the new crusade of all the poor and the free against the nations who usurp and accumulate all wealth, against the predatory races and against the caste of the usurers who yesterday profited from the war in order to profit from the peace today, this newest crusade will re-establish true justice…

The attention of the crowded theatre is paroxystic.

D'Annunzio's voice is now in crescendo, from the chest, assured.

Greta senses that the speech is not just about Fiume, this evening. It's not just about annexation. There's something that still eludes her, a meaning she needs to grasp.

… People of Fiume, your cause is the greatest and finest to pit itself today against the insanity and the baseness of that world. It spans Ireland and Egypt, Russia and the United States, Romania and India. It unites the white races and the coloured; it reconciles the Gospel and the Koran, Christianity and Islam…

So that's it, muses Greta: Fiume is turning into a symbol, the emblem of freedom of some kind.

But in this political language, which is for her still so new and strange, Greta finds it hard to move, her novice's curiosity risking a stumble at every step.

And while d'Annunzio's voice fades and finally dies away amid the crowd's ovation, people get to their feet around her and the woman with whipped cream curls, applauding, somewhat dishevels her hair.

Greta slips outside.

She is met by a cloudless night. The violet sky is teeming with stars.

The wind twirls a few leaves, teases her ankles suddenly with a crumpled sheet of newspaper A nocturnal bird glides low, long shadows stick out sharply beyond the street-lamps' cones of light. Greta shivers slightly, wraps her mantle around her more tightly. She listens to the night noises, breathes in air that already speaks of winter, hurries along keeping close to the walls.

A couple brush past her with their voices. A passing patrol singing. From a first-floor window, a child's desperate sobbing. Ahead of her, a window shutter squeaks and a door shuts sharply down an alley, not far off.

A skinny cat is stripping clean some fish remnant beneath a partly opened blind: as Greta goes by, he raises his head and gives a slight wave of his tail, then resumes his meal. An odour of fish and mould wafts out of the walls and hangs in the air, along with a hint of tobacco.

All at once, the street is deserted, with its labyrinth of alleys – between higgledy-piggledy walls and closed doors –

within the heart of the old city, which she's always thought looked so like the Venice she'd seen as a child: a maze of dark lanes and sudden bends in the walls, of clothes-lines gently swaying in the empty air, of little crumbling shrines barely lit by little night-lights like lizard eyes, of nooks and crannies where cats improvise matings and retreats.

From far off, as if in dream, she catches the sound of tuneless singing and the barking of a dog quickly silenced by its owner.

Then a new sound creeps in. At first it's just an impression. She pricks up her ears: maybe it's just an echo.

But she is alarmed to realize that it's real: footsteps following her own and now – her heart misses a beat – getting closer.

Greta quickens her pace, her heart beating fast. The following footsteps also get faster. She can hardly overcome the instinct to run, the impulse to flee. She is aware of an already looming presence, the long shadow of a body upon her.

She'd like to scream, but her voice fails her. And, anyway, what good would it do, here? The street is deserted at this hour, there's not a soul around, the doors are bolted.

And, with her heart in her mouth, she feels that hand gripping her and a deep, ironic voice, that doesn't sound totally unfamiliar: "Easy, Greta. Don't be scared. I'm no cut-throat… "

She feels her body relaxing beneath her mantle's stifling weight. Finally she recovers her voice and snaps out: "But I could be one!"

Now she looks at him, furious. She's immediately recognized his face, his tuft of hair slanting across his forehead, the shadow of ill-shaven beard, that long lank body that he drags along like a cassock: something awkward and Spartan not to be too much bothered with.

Her instinct is to use her fists on him: she'd almost died of fright.

"You'd like to bash me, I know."

"You've said it."

"I read your mind."

"Anything else you can do, at dead of night, besides scaring girls and practising telepathy?"

"I can also walk back home convent girls who've slipped out of school."

Greta goes crimson. She'd like to sink into the ground. So that wasn't a chance meeting: he'd seen her and somehow tailed her, just as he did that other time. She's livid, looks at him with hatred. Meanwhile Tullio goes on talking. "You've never answered my messages. And I don't even know whether you enjoyed my book."

She senses that the alarm she's experienced comes out in her harsh tone and in her cutting words: "You used your book as an open sesame. And you well know what I mean."

Tullio looks at her for a moment, and then says quietly: "Is that really what you think?"

With the tip of her shoe she kicks at something invisible in the dark. Finally she looks up.

"I don't know."

A window shutter suddenly flies open, a woman leans out rearranging her dishevelled chignon: "... What's all this 'ullabaloo, you young'uns? Be off with you, some folks 'ere 'ave work tomorrer."

They move away noiselessly as the silence swallows their

footsteps. The unreality of her absurd escapade, of her walking at night in the company of a fellow she hardly knows: Greta feels she's tiptoeing on the brink of a dimension that allures her and at the same time scares her, like cliffs above the sea in some of her childhood memories.

"D'you often run away like that, scaling the walls?"

"No. This is the first time. I wanted to hear d'Annunzio. To understand what the guy who's dragged you to this place has to say."

"He hasn't dragged anybody. I think those who have followed him are certainly intolerant of lots of rules, but also of undeniable injustices. Angry, in a word, maybe fanatical: but passionate, too…" he pauses, studying her face. "And perhaps there's also a bit of idealism."

"You might explain it to me some other time. I've got to go now."

"I'll come with you."

"Believe me: it's not necessary. Nothing's going to happen to me this time. I don't need any guardian angels."

"Maybe I do."

"You kidding? To protect you from cut-throats?"

"Apart from snapping, can you talk as well?"

"I don't want to talk. I can't. Not at dead of night, and not to you."

"Liar."

"What d'you mean?"

"I mean that you're dying to talk. To talk and to understand, to know."

"I don't know you, hardly."

"That's easily dealt with."

"You're the persistent sort, aren't you?"

"Persistent and curious. Same as you."

She gives him a sidelong look, dubiously.

"Only I'm that way because of the work I do, while in your case it's because you're shut up inside there and that enclosing wall mortifies your intelligence as well as your freedom of movement."

She's struck by the sheer directness with which he always seems to attack the divide between form and content, between the way things appear and their reality.

Tullio holds out his hand, smiling. "What if we start again from scratch? Last time, if I remember right, we exchanged greetings in a bit of a rush. I'm Tullio Marchior. Aged twenty-six. Journalist. Former pilot. Shall we put on today's agenda just a touch of friendliness between us two?"

She returns the smile. "Just a touch."

Then she holds out her own hand in that solemn, slightly formal, greeting.

"I'm Greta Vidal. Student. I've turned eighteen."

And she feels a lump – interest? affection? – which conflicts with her brusque manner, dictated by a suspiciousness which she doesn't know whether to attribute to her character, to embarrassment, to upbringing: certainly, she ought not to be out here in the street with a young man she hardly knows.

But it's great to be out here in the street with a young man whom she already knows a little.

★ ★ ★

They're on the seafront.

A light breeze ruffles the water, wafts traces of salt on

their faces, raises whinings and creakings from the hulls of boats and lighters, dark shapes in the harbour. From somewhere – she can't tell where – comes the sound of distant music, which seems to roll along the alleys like a child's marbles.

From inside a tavern comes the rattle of dice.

Greta feels a magma of questions, the urgent need to clarify so many doubts. "Just now you were talking about ideals… but a lot of these legionaries look to me just like daredevils all too ready to use their musket or their fists."

"That's true of some of them. But don't trust in simple explanations: things are often more complex than we like to think. Many of the legionaries that have followed d'Annunzio are actually former commandos, the elite troops of the Great War: intractable, rebellious, ready for anything. Folk who have fought for years in the mud, full of lice, and who now can't fit in to normal, ordinary life. Folk who returned home only to find no work, none of the land promised to them by the government, not even social peace. Have you any idea what's going on in Italy?"

Greta hesitates, she's tempted to lie. Then decides to be sincere: "No newspapers get into the convent."

"There's unemployment, hardship. Unrest violently suppressed, protest demonstrations and strikes. Inflation hitting wages, workers' demands rejected. Not what the soldiers were expecting, after years of carnage. The peasants have occupied the great estates, the workers have taken over the factories in the North. And to protect them from the police they've organized defence forces: patrols and pickets armed with guns. The legacy of the war is devastating the peace as well. But if this is how it is in Italy, it's certainly not much better elsewhere. Not in the new Weimar Republic, not in Austria, not in Hungary. D'you understand what I'm saying? You can't send millions of men off to massacre one another for years and then hope to extract warlike habits and mindsets out of their heads as if they were just rotten teeth that you can pull out at one go."

Tullio pauses. Should he go on? She's little more than a girl… he might risk boring her, dazing her.

He looks at her, hesitating, then adds: "And now, I don't know whether you can understand… Fiume has become a symbol, an act of defiance."

They stroll along slowly, close together.

Their bodies barely touch, their eyes momentarily meet, their low voices are swamped every now and then by the sound of a breaking wave or by the wind gusting from the sea. Around them the world seems to shrink, the autumnal air is laced with woodsmoke.

In order to lower the emotional register, Greta puts in: "Fiume's a symbol, I've got that. But whose symbol, exactly? And symbol of what?"

He puts a cigarette in his mouth, strikes a match hard against a wall. "At the Paris peace conference, which has now been going on for months, many matters have been settled. The Great War has wiped out a world, but the powerful men sitting round those tables don't seem to have grasped the fact. And maybe they've made bad mistakes."

She asks, hesitantly: "What mistakes?"

"First, the way I see it, was the absolute refusal to negotiate with the defeated powers, humiliating them to no purpose. Germany has simply had the peace terms imposed on her. But the Germans are a proud people: I may be wrong, but I have the impression that they won't take things lying down. But above all what I believe is that in Paris the logic of annexation has won out over every other, and I see that as another mistake. It's a logic that belongs to the last century, and it no longer holds good. Its result is to aggravate the gulf between Nations. Wealthy nations with colonies on one side, and on the other side the starving and the subjugated: the former, in fact, get ever fatter, the latter ever more woebegone. That's why here today we have people coming from India and from Ireland, from Egypt, Albania, Montenegro… Fiume is now their symbol, Greta: a symbol of the nations that are harassed by the mighty."

She makes no response. She's reflecting. Suddenly everything seems clear, disarming in its enormity.

"But that's not all there is to it, is it Tullio?"

"Right, that's not all there is to it. This is only a part of reality. Of today's reality, in Fiume."

They seat themselves on a bench.

Greta looks up at the sky. The stars flicker white, the moon seems to slide over the sea.

"And what's the other part of reality?"

"Anarchists, nationalists. Socialists, syndicalists. Monarchists and republicans, imperialists and communists. But also poets, writers, assorted artists. They're arriving here from the most distant places. And d'you know what they're looking for in Fiume?"

"You tell me."

"A different society. A new world inside the old world. A free port as an experiment in a possible utopia."

"A utopia?!"

"D'Annunzio is the first poet to be at the head of a

government. Just think: an artist in power! For some people it's a sign: maybe here, in your town, a freer and more creative society will be born, based on wholly new principles and on revolutionary ideas."

"For instance?"

"For instance, anti-imperialism. D'you know what that is?"

"As a matter of fact, at school we've got up to Napoleon…"

He smiles.

"D'Annunzio intends to found a league of oppressed peoples so as to rescue them from the hegemony of the imperialist powers. There are those who think that Fiume is merely the necessary first stage on the way to a much vaster uprising that will set up a democratic government in the place of the ancient monarchy. This is what the republicans dream of. But the Fiume experiment might also give birth to new economic and social forms. And this, in varying gradations, is what the left-wing parties dream of. Then there are those who believe that even you women should go to war just like us so as, in this and in other ways, to bring about equality between the sexes. And this is what the futurists dream of. And there are those who talk of abolishing prisons, doing away with insane asylums…"

"… insane asylums?! D'you really mean it?"

And she listens eagerly, fascinated.

"There are those who want to promote a new primacy of the spirit – and of art, of imagination – over reason and materialism. And this is the dream of… "

"But your dream, tell me… What's yours?"

He looks at her intently, smiling. "Well, we'd need at least another entire night to talk that through. But for the time being, I'll tell you something: you can't choose the age you live in. You can only choose *how* to live in it. And it's so as to understand that *how* that I've turned up here."

She's not sleepy, and she doesn't feel tired. She could go on listening to him for hours.

A powerful fragrance wafts down an alley, of bread freshly baked. Together, they follow the scent until they get to the bakery, which is just a tiny room with a great wood oven against one wall: Greta raps repeatedly on the glass pane, presses her nose against it in an effort to peer inside. Then she makes a sign and smiles, and waits.

The fellow opens the door with floury hands which he cursorily wipes on his apron, eyes them uncertainly, reprovingly. Snorting at the unearthly hour, he eventually agrees to give them a stick of bread.

Between the two of them, they break it in half – it's hot, it burns their fingers – and they munch it slowly, in silence, resuming their walk. From time to time, but few and far between, there's some sign of life between the walls: a door or a window opening, the sound of footsteps on the stairs, a shutter creaking slightly, the tinkling of a coin rolling on the hard floor, maybe after slipping out of a pocket as someone gets into his trousers. The chilly white moonlight silhouettes the shapes of things.

They sit on the steps of a church flanked by a small cloister. A stray dog comes up to them, sniffs at them and wags his tail, gobbles up the piece of still warm bread that Greta holds in front of him. And so, as she pats him on the back, she finds herself talking.

About her father, about her sister Elisa, about her *zia*

Ingrid, who's been locked up for months. About a mother who's had her life scooped out by Arturo's death. And about Arturo.

About how he would climb up the helianthus, and how he'd flayed his wrist yelling to board the enemy vessel and hurling himself from a branch while wielding like a scimitar the bill-hook which he'd purloined from the gardener, about how he could recognize every different bird's call, both land-birds and sea-birds: wrens and warblers, little sparrows and seagulls, cuckoos and great tits. And as she talks about him, she can still see him, toasted by the sun by summer's end: small and swarthy like the coffee beans that their father would buy in Trieste, but with that blue-eyed gaze that seemed to pierce through.

Tullio listens to her intently. Appreciatively, she talks on.

She even manages to tell him about herself. The thorniest of all topics.

About what she's reading, about what she writes. About what she would like to do, if she had the freedom to do it.

A childhood tranquillity recovered, her soul scalded by shame because of words that pour out of their own accord and unembarrassedly depict a life's simple pattern.

Then the chiming of a bell takes her breath away for an instant. Greta looks at Tullio in terror.

It's five in the morning, and she's still out! That seems to suddenly throw into focus the enormity of all she's been up to in the course of this long, strange night, the number of rules she's broken, the gravity of her misdemeanour. And it's all at a measureless distance from this feeling of fulfilment, from this peace.

"Come on," says he. "I'll see you back."

They hurry along the remaining way in silence, but when they get to the convent they are immediately obliged to stop and dodge smartly round a corner. The lane – a short blind alley that branches off the main road – skirts the convent's right wing and leads to the niche in the wall which she climbed to get out, but now a group of men stands at the alley's mouth: some grasp an empty bottle, others are smoking as they lean against the wall. One is sitting on the ground, possibly laughing.

Getting through is out of the question.

Paul re-reads the last lines. The clock on his bedside table shows shortly after five.

He hasn't been able to sleep. The urgency of having another go had prevented him from shutting his eyes, relaxing on his pillow and letting himself finally fall asleep.

He *must* write to his father. Try to make him understand. Try once again to explain to him that if he's staying on it's not on a whim or a sudden tantrum. Nor is it to punish him – his father – as if he was going through, out of season, the teenage rebellion which he'd never gone through as a teenager.

So in the end he got up. He's been at his desk for quite a time, in the silence of that room, hunting for inspiration – or at least for the right tone – to dictate the words which would spell out a start to his thoughts.

Out of doors, it's a clear night. A dribble of wind, a few stars. A nearly full moon pours its pearly brilliance into the darkness of an icy sky. For an instant he considered making that image his starting-point: so peaceful was that nightscape that everything seemed possible, even stitching up the wounds and suturing the silences of years, stemming rancours and misunderstandings.

But then he guessed how his father would read those words.

He read in his face his usual astonishment, his disapproval at the way he lived his life. Right away, he changed his mind.

Then he tried starting off by explaining to him, as best he could, what it had meant to be in the war, to feel he was hanging from a thread that was giving way. And in his mind he went back there, to the French front first, then to the Italian one. He himself had never understood by what weird miracle he had managed to get out of it alive, but all at once it seemed important somehow to make his father aware of that miracle, to lay it before his intelligence as a man.

He hunted a long while for those words. They always seemed ready to come out, like mermaids just below the surface: but the moment he reached out for them they vanished like a mirage and left him feeling as humiliated as when he wet his bed as a child, after his mother had died, and his father would say nothing but unfurled over his body that long cold giant's gaze which looked him up and down from top to toes: an enormous anteater's tongue.

So he had another go, looking for another cue.

But instead of words, what came to him was images, memories.

His comrade, Henry, for instance, drowned one October night in that enormous inverted funnel, the pit blown out of the ground by a mortar shell. His hand stuck out of the mud like a root torn out, his head hanging loose on one shoulder like a broken spring. And there hadn't even been time to drag the body out of that mire, to squeeze out a prayer through gritted teeth.

That was how things were, those days, in the war. The rain that fell that summer was the worst in forty years: it poured down steadily, it seethed like pitch in the canals, it ate through leather soles, it rotted the skin and the clothes on your body. The drainage system had disintegrated under the bombardment and, during the rare lulls in the rain, the sun wasn't strong enough to dry out the sea of slime – yellow clay, a sticky, lethal trap – into which feet sank helplessly and bodies slumped unaided.

Meanwhile the shelling thoroughly pockmarked the terrain: huge cavities which you couldn't see in the dark, nor through the rain: and the cavities filled with mud and the mud filled with corpses, Dad. For if you ended up in those craters, you never got out again.

Shattered by the weight you were carrying – kilos and kilos, would you believe? – crushed by the pack on your back, your uniform and your boots waterlogged, hand-grenades in your haversack, your cartridge belt around your waist and rifle and bayonet and gas-mask, too, on your back, with bursting shells blotting out your hearing and splinters raining down around you, if you plunged into one of those potholes you'd end up dead, sinking to the bottom.

You drowned in mud. And that was it.

And it's sheer chance that it happened to Henry and that it didn't also happen to me.

But if you weren't drowned, you went on. You'd cross that empty space they called no-man's-land. And if you made it across, then came the fighting, medieval style: not a rifle's length between bodies, but a duel with dagger or bayonet or rifle-butt, or shovel: anything you could kill with, you could smash a skull with, you could rip flesh and nerves and life with. And if you only had your bare hands, then that's what you used, your fingers clutching at the other's throat and squeezing, digging, strangling.

Then Paul saw his father wearing his double-breasted grey suit sitting on the armchair beside the window, with a glass of whisky in one hand and a newspaper spread out in the other.

But still he tried again, using different words this time.

He wrote that he'd lived in that inferno for nearly a year and a half, and that he's carrying that war inside him like pus that hasn't yet erupted.

He wrote that he can't come back home until he's worked out whether that vast slaughter made any sense.

He wrote that in war – not earlier – he's learnt to pray, and that for months he begged only to be able to go on living until he could feel his knees being devoured by the pain of arthritis, his eyes being invaded by cataracts. He begged for the blessing of growing old.

But now that it's all over, he doesn't yet feel up to returning, to living among briefs and law-courts and looking out on affairs and on the world from there, sitting behind that desk that seemed to him as a boy like a wall which could separate away all that was important and that took place at school or at home, down on the football field or out on the street. All that marked out the distance between their lives that were already so far apart.

Finally, Paul laid down his pen. He re-read those pages from the start, and discovered regrets which he didn't recognize between the lines, new rebellions, strange heartaches. And possibly something great, or at least powerful, among them, that he can't put into words.

So he said: no, he won't understand.

And he picked up the letter and crumpled it up: methodically, calmly, without anger.

Almost like a misguided caress.

Greta stood and watched him – holding her breath, her body tensed – as Tullio went up to the legionaries huddled together in a noisy group and addressed them. Her room inside the convent, at the end of that alley, suddenly seemed to her, not so much far away, as remote.

Then she saw the men become animated, while Tullio raised an arm and pointed towards the sea.

She watched them move off amid singing, laughter and back-slapping. Only when he's beside her again does she manage, still tensed up, to ask him: "What did you say to get them to leave?"

"I set them an irresistible goal." Tullio looks amused. "The best brothel in Fiume." And he laughs as he sees her expression as his words sink in.

"Only, I made it all up," he hastens to add, "from the street names to the… to the house of pleasure. So now you'd better get a move on before they come back. And I don't think it will be to thank me."

Then he gently holds her face between his hands. Greta seems to linger an instant, draws back slowly, frees herself.

As he watches her move off, Tullio nods a faint yes.

Before she climbs up the wall – her hands moving confidently along the handholds – he stands out of the way, on the look-out.

Then he catches that sharp thud, the moment's silence that follows it, the footsteps padding away as a night bird takes flight out of the garden's shadow.

Tullio hesitates, then goes on his way.

In his pocket – now he realizes – he still has a small hunk of bread.

Winter

In reality they're only details, yet she finds them necessary.
The frosty landscapes on the window-panes, the crackling ice in
the fountains, the plumes of smoke rising from the white and red
roofs of the houses.
The wind combing through the reeds, the flight of a marsh bird,
the crinkling skin of one's hands as one blows misty breath on
them.

She looks at the world from the outside, sometimes, through panes
tinted yellow and green and blue.
She shuts her eyes, letting herself go.
She might recount what she sees: just like that, to keep herself
company.
A ship crossing the sea.
The flames dancing in the fireplace.
The sun dying in the distance, behind a violet cloud, and a crow
gliding in the garden like a falling accent.
The world becomes voiced: each thing answers to its name and
every name has a thing all to itself.
It's hard, to say all those names, to find the right sounds and put
life into them.
Yet she senses a great peace. She feels at home, inside words.

21 December 1919

To Lieutenant Colonel Gabriele d'Annunzio
For His Eyes Only

Ultimatum

If by eleven hours tomorrow Gabriele d'Annunzio and the representatives of the Fiume National Council do not appear at Cantrida, in the usual house, to sign the proposal put forward by the Italian Government, and the attached protocols, General Badoglio, in the name of the Government, will declare that all negotiations are at an end.

The aforementioned General must receive a reply by twenty hours this evening.

Signed
General Pietro Badoglio
Military Commissioner Extraordinary for Julian Venetia

Fiume
January 1920

How far can he venture, he wonders? How far can he go?

Tullio has always believed in the meaning of his work, in the need to be honest, in the responsibility for what he writes, which descends upon him like a cassock the moment he sits at his desk and takes up his trade: journalism. And it doesn't really matter whether he's writing just for a provincial newspaper, if the articles he writes won't do much to shift national opinion. What matters is to do the job well.

To report with maximum courage and with the fullest possible sincerity, without ever falling short of the imperatives of conscience. Yet now he is doubtful.

He re-reads that page full of notes, the words marked in pencil, the marginal notes.

A delegation from Fiume has arrived in Paris on an official diplomatic mission assigned to it by the citizens of Fiume. Considering the exceptional nature of the situation, the representatives of Fiume have requested permission to attend the peace negotiations regarding the town's future.

Clemenceau, who chairs the Conference, has denied any such right.

It's no small matter, the indignation he feels.

It seems to him that there's an ever more blatant contrast between the ideals proclaimed – officially publicized, and loudly – and the shabbiness of actual events, and of the real interests pursued in this seaway on to which the heart of Europe looks out. That's what he's been coming to think for some time.

He races through his notes. He crosses out his personal comments. Just outbursts, he admits to himself: weaknesses to be eliminated.

He's well aware that censorship operates and that Fiume is also cut off by a postal blockade as by a gag and hood so as to stop its voice being heard outside, but they've even managed to overcome this.

The idea came from Ludovico Toeplitz.

Tullio has just met him and has conceived an instinctive admiration for that open-minded and cultivated young man, the son of a Polish banker, who supported the cause from the start and was appointed by d'Annunzio Foreign Minister of the little Republic of Fiume. Paul's been working with him for some time. It must have been the two of them that thought up that plan to get round the censors: to organize a courier service that's beyond any suspicion.

And they really succeeded: the Fiume correspondence is

secretly entrusted to the chief guard on the Orient Express.

The Paris-bound for Europe, the Istanbul-bound for the Balkans. And no diplomatic courier has ever been more reliable and more punctual, more free from restrictions, than this de luxe service which goes through the Simplon tunnel, leaving Switzerland behind, and, passing through Milan and Venice and then through nearby Trieste, crosses the whole of the old continent to emerge finally on the shores of the Black Sea.

Tullio slips the cap back on to his fountain pen and then puts it into its leather case, which he sticks into a pocket of his jacket: it's his only orderly action in days of febrile chaos, of meetings with all sorts of people, of assignments which are now coming thick and fast, of articles dashed off in a rush to make way for urgent new priorities.

It's his one and only ritual action which he's perhaps hung on to since middle school, since a time that sometimes seems to him quite remote: like certain flavours, and memories, and life before the war.

★ ★ ★

Greta observes her own footsteps over the cobbles: she feels them to be detached, almost alien, distant from her.

It's just fear, she tells herself. It's my misgivings, it's tension. It's the knowledge that this time I'm running a big risk.

Instinctively, she's almost propping herself up against the wall, then she looks up at the trees that border the street: boughs are swaying in the wind, a few remaining leaves flutter away.

Then for an instant she relives the carefree light-heartedness which she used to experience as a child when she was swinging on a hammock in the shade of an acacia. It was the best place, she thought, for surveying the sky from the earth: a sky unveiled in arabesques between leaves so tiny and tousled that the merest breath of wind will variegate their outlines: everything then is in movement, all frilly, so you can't pinpoint the divide between the fringe of green and the airy gap, between what quivers and moves and what stays steady and clearcut, true to its placement.

Now nothing but leaves, now sky. Now shapeless patches, now nothing.

And that's the way she feels now. No definite bounds between things. No longer any clarity of outlook capable of distinguishing between what is right and what shouldn't be done, between what still makes sense and balances out and what might only have the appeal of emptiness and really amounts to nothing more than a vision. So for an instant she pauses, unsure whether to turn back or to press on.

A window shutter banging in the wind amplifies the silence around her. From the spacious garden of a house nearby comes the resinous odour of recently cut firewood.

Greta stands there stock still, undecided, with a shiver down her spine.

Then her thoughts are lit up by that deft and distinct final brush-stroke which *zia* Ingrid used to paint on the canvas: her farewell to tarrying, her setting an end-point to otherwise interminable journeyings bound to entwine themselves within her. So she abruptly pulls herself together, looks ahead and walks on.

Tullio picks up from his desk the article he's dashed off and starts slowly re-reading it. He's suddenly overtaken by some doubts. Whether to mention for instance that d'Annunzio has coined for Prime Minister Nitti – the present head of government whom he accuses of faint-heartedness and hypocrisy – the contemptuous designation *Shitbag* and the description *vile guzzler*?

Whether to report the infectious enthusiasm that his oratorical vehemence is arousing amongst Fiume's exasperated population? Or whether to confine himself to current happenings without raising the tension?

He pulls out his cigarettes from one of the pockets of his jacket slung over the back of a chair, searches for his matches, lights up. He sits there for a moment, gazing at the cloud of smoke, savouring his *Nazionale* to the full. In the end, he does insert that *Shitbag*. Yes, he includes that, too.

And all at once Tullio asks himself where are the most intractable dividing lines. Between integrity and conscience? Duty and ideals? Between his personal morality as a man and his duty as a journalist?

Everything has been tried against this town, now cut off: embargo, threats, censorship.

Italian and foreign newspapers, obeying directives from above, have for some time been painting a dark picture of life in Fiume: a town in the hands of scoundrels and anarchist-leaning inventors of utopias and practitioners of free love.

This view is shared, it appears, by the *Times* and the *Corriere della Sera*, by *Homme Libre* and the *Chicago Tribune*. And they've made up all sorts of rumours and tall stories.

They claim that d'Annunzio is held hostage by officers who bend him to their will. That he's cut loose like a coward, slipping away aboard a Greek schooner. That he's ready to abandon Fiume in return for a bribe. But those who know him, muses Tullio, know that only a successful outcome would get him to depart the town.

He goes to the window and looks out: facing him is the sea, the Gulf of Carnaro, the hypnotic scything of the lighthouse beam. He hears the throb of an engine, a draught of air sneaks through the window joins. He senses a sick electricity in the air and a frayed anxiety in things, as when rain is imminent before summer storms, when everything awaits the water that might pour down.

Greta looks up at the dark sky, which seems to promise rain: the branches of the plane-tree overhead are shaken by a gust of wind.

She wraps her mantle around her more tightly and quickens her pace keeping close to the wall.

For an instant she's dazzled by the headlights of a passing car, then everything is plunged once more in darkness and unreal obscurity. She thrusts her hands into her pockets, realizes that they're sweating. But how could she, she asks, two weeks after her escapade, be again so irresponsible as to run such a risk? A clap of thunder surprises her, making her start. She hurries faster and then breaks into a run, as the first hard drops bounce off the cobbles, drawing out of the street and things around an odour that speaks strong and live.

He hears the first drops against the window. He taps on the sheet of paper with his finger. He's not convinced by what he's written. In reality, he was distracted, and he knows it.

Tullio looks up away from his work. His room is a

simple, Spartan space, its perimeter drawn with a set-square as if on a child's copybook: bed, unsteady bedside table, a great, dark-coloured wardrobe set against the wall, two straight-backed unmatched chairs, a small table which it takes courage to call a desk, though at times he slips – but only from ingrained habit – into thinking of it, indeed, as a desk, like the one in his newspaper's editorial office.

Beside a shaded lamp that has seen better days, piles and piles of books, and various newspapers. Books on the floor also, stacked against the wall.

In one corner, the one nearest the bed, a bowl and wash-hand basin set on a tripod, with a soggy towel hanging from it.

Further along, atop an old chest, the second-hand gramophone which he had managed to unearth with difficulty from among daguerreotype plates and a wire birdcage in a pawnbroker shop. The only luxury he's allowed himself, and which he does not in the least regret.

He shuts his eyes the better to take in a passage of the *Histoire du soldat*: he loves this work of Stravinsky's – the broad sweep of the woodwind, the hardness of the percussion. He loves that strange score – the consorting of waltz and chorale, the merging of tango and ragtime. It's a music that even makes his surrounding space less bare.

The little hotel right from the start promised no more than a discreet welcome and hospitable cleanliness. Anyway, he had virtually no choice.

When Tullio had arrived, along with Paul, the town was already thronged with people and seemed close to collapse: it was an act of faith – and one well rewarded – to find on that very first night a decent place in which to sleep.

158

But Fiume has changed, just lately. Fresh foreigners are turning up, including the most sordid types: hashish dealers, adventurers, individuals pressing interests all of their own: agents of big business, of the political parties, of the Rome government itself. And each has a specific aim of his own, though it's not always so obvious that you can immediately grasp what it is.

Yet something about d'Annunzio's enterprise still deserves attention, of this he remains convinced.

Something still deserves attention.

It's no good cheating, he's got to admit it: his re-reading news reports and notes, that review of all the facts as for a school test... it's really a dodge on his part to anchor himself to concrete logic and weighty issues, in an effort not to keep thinking of her, of Greta. He recalls her proud outbursts, seeing them as the sudden rearing of a colt. He sees her smile, half shy, half cheeky, her gaze, alive and steady. And he recalls in amazement the sound of her voice, her laughter.

He feels he sees into her mind, divines her dreams and her dreads: he sees she's drawn by light-heartedness, hindered by an innate sobriety.

But what disorients him most is Greta's effect upon himself, the desire she instils in him to be the first to guess her needs, to apprehend her wishes before she herself does so. And the urge that has welled up in him to learn somehow to be worthy of her: but not as a trophy, not as a prize to be won. As the meaning of an experience, as a reason.

From out in the still clear night he hears a dull and distant rumble, a deep roll of thunder.

And all at once, barely audible, a persistent knocking at the door.

Greta is pale and erect before him: her gaze firm, her breathing hurried, her arms crossed over her breast.

She is the first to speak: "You've no idea how cold it is out here tonight…"

He manages to overcome his astonishment and find his voice: "But that's not what's making you tremble…"

There's a sudden flash in Greta's eyes, an unexpected spasm of tension which is also annoyance with herself and anxiety at being there. "Seeing how you always know everything about me, I may as well go away again."

"I don't know everything." He speaks to her firmly. "I know only enough to guess… well, what you're feeling." He doesn't add that her face has always seemed to him an open book, that that straightforward and transparent gaze of hers is easy for him to decipher.

"I know for instance that you've already used up all your courage to come here. And possibly now you have none left."

Greta gives a start, looks at him: that's exactly what she's feeling. Her strength gone, and a fear upon her barely under control, just a shade short of terror.

Amid the silence which weighs down on them, there's a sudden sound of rain, an abrupt downpour. He stands aside from the doorway. "Come on in."

But Greta doesn't budge. "No, I can't. But you could step outside."

"D'you find double pneumonia romantic in itself, or the idea of doubling it between us?"

She doesn't want it to happen, and hates herself when it does: but she still blushes in spite of herself.

"Well, then, have you made up your mind, convent girl?"

"I detest being called that."

"Of course, otherwise why would I do it?" He shuts the door, leads her in. "There's not much choice, but it's your call: where will you sit?"

She glances round the room, moves towards a chair: "This'll do."

And she swallows, tensing, while Tullio comes up close.

"Just as you like. I prefer the bed."

Greta is flustered, looks away from him. "I know what you're thinking about me."

He goes on looking at her for a moment.

"No, that's exclusive to me. You need more training: you're too young, still. You don't know what I think of you. But I'll tell you myself, that way we'll do away with any embarrassment."

"I'm not... not embarrassed."

"Agreed. But I'm talking now. I think various things about you. The first is that you've come here because you've been won over by the free Greta. Which I believe is the better one."

"Meaning what?"

"That side of you which at the moment is not fully domesticated, not fully submissive. Not to the convent conventions, not to those imposed by your family, not to the rules of good breeding which often means – especially for you girls – no more than good form and façade: hypocrisy."

She looks hard at him without speaking. She unclenches her hands on her lap, relaxes somewhat against the chair-back.

"I think a lot of other things about you, mind. And perhaps I don't yet want to tell you what. The only thing that

161

really counts this evening, I think, is that you've come here because your really want to talk, to understand certain things a bit better. And I'm glad to think that in your search for understanding you've chosen me. Do I think wrong?"

She shakes her head. She's grateful for that calm, clear voice that succeeds in finding the right inflexions so as to make her presence in that room a little less absurd and her heart feel less guilty.

She feels the tension slacken, the contraction down her frozen spine slowly melt. Finally her courage comes back, too, and her voice in its natural timbre: "Do you give lectures at all?"

"What about?"

"Telepathy. Mind-reading, reading thoughts."

He smiles. "You already have that gift. It's pure instinct."

"What makes you say that? I don't know a thing. In fact I haven't guessed anything at all either about you or about… about what goes through your mind."

"You've guessed that you can be here at night alone with me in my bedroom without having anything to fear. At worst you'd have to put up with being called a convent girl. Wouldn't you call that pure instinct?"

Momentarily, Greta lowers her gaze. That's true: that is how she feels.

Suddenly, she's at her ease, she feels safe.

Risking nothing but the reality, of which he's unaware, or pretends to be, that she can't trust herself, her own feelings and desires.

Fiume, Government Palace
January 1920

He observes the small hourglass at the corner of his desk. He's always loved hourglasses, the way they measure time in grains: he has a whole collection of them. Then he checks the time on his fob-watch, pulling it out of his breast pocket. It's already after one o'clock.

Now the silence is absolute, behind the closed door to his study, in the great slumbering Palace.

He enjoys writing like this, when the world outside seems dormant.

But tonight the endeavour is demanding. And he is not helped by the certainty that all agreements have now collapsed.

He's read and re-read the latest proposal put forward for Fiume: diplomatic acrobatics which marry Eastern subtleties with wholly Western domineering.

The air is fragrant with the incense which he's burning in a little brazier.

D'Annunzio takes a sheet of paper out of a drawer, dips his pen in the inkwell. He feels as if his anger is dripping black ink.

… There is no denying a certain courteous intention in this trinitarian ferocity.

In the court of Byzantium it was the custom for three Palace officials ceremoniously to present on a shining gold platter the well-twined silken noose or the waxed bowstring to the man who was to strangle himself with his own hands.

It must be acknowledged that this halter is being offered to us by our doughty Allies in a style even more exquisite than that of the Byzantines. There are those who prostrate themselves on our behalf, there are those who force a smile on our behalf, as they receive it.

The Italy of the Other Shore, west of the Adriatic, has not learnt… to hold its head high and its gaze firm and its neck upright.

But what of the Italy of this shore, east of the Adriatic?

Man – especially the Italian – is expected to be the most accommodating animal in the universe.

Let us meanwhile… wait at ease.

And, like the good Aesop, let us leave the talking to the beasts.

He folds the sheet. Does not re-read it.

With a weary hand he strokes the head of the greyhound that's sleeping at the foot of the great desk.

Abbazia
January 1920

In the room's half-dark Greta opens and shuts wardrobes, checks inside all the drawers of the writing bureau, ducks swiftly beneath the bed, peeps behind the cretonne curtains, lifts up a picture, a lamp, a rug.

After having searched every nook and cranny, she chants to her sister Elisa, who is huddled under her blankets: "Inside a drawer is Hansel and Gretel's witch…"

"In a corner of the big chest Cinderella's stepmother was hiding…"

"Underneath the carpet I've found Bluebeard…"

"Look, a seven-headed monster's crept into the wardrobe. Goodness, he's really hungry! But don't worry, Elisa: Snow-White's witch is feeding him the Seven Dwarfs…"

Then she ruffles her sister's hair, plants a big kiss on her forehead. Then she adds with a wink, as she tucks her in:

"They're all here with you, just like every night, keen to keep you company…"

This has become their evening ritual, invented by Greta: laughter overcomes fear.

And though at times she still wants to have her bedside lamp lit, still Elisa has learned not to be afraid any longer of being on her own when the dark comes with nightfall and it's time for her to go to sleep.

But her little sister isn't smiling tonight. The teddy bear beside her pokes out his balding snout in between the pillow and the sheet hem. As Greta turns to leave, Elisa grabs her arm and holds her back, lifting herself up into a sitting position.

Her wide-open, serious eyes hold back a hint of tears. Greta sits down beside her. She suddenly feels somewhat guilty with regard to her little sister who is growing up alone and neglected, with a father who is often away and a mother who, even when she's there, is really absent: a fragile, shrewd child who tiptoes through life and plays without making any noise, who always thinks before she speaks and then says nothing or else eats her words. A strangely adult child, who's had something taken from her that no one can ever give back to her.

Greta strokes her forehead, taps her nose with a finger.

"What's wrong, Elisa, is someone missing? Hasn't Tom Thumb's ogre turned up this evening? Or is it the big bad wolf?"

Elisa shakes her head. "I miss Arturo. Just him."

She wasn't expecting this. She looks at Elisa, in silence. The child's fist is clenched, she herself holding her breath, the balding teddy bear between them. Then she bends down

166

and hugs her tight to her chest: they stay like that, without speaking, close together as they rock each other, which may not console them but at least unites them in their grief.

Then Elisa draws away and looks at her, hesitating before she speaks. "Greta, may I ask you something?"

"Sure. Otherwise what's the use of an elder sister?"

"D'you think Arturo can see us? What I mean is… is he still interested in us? And does he ever… think of us still?"

That's a long question, coming from Elisa.

So he lands there between them, unexpectedly but naturally after evening playtime, like those fairy-tale presences that are more real than the whole world of actuality: fifteen years old, an infectious laugh, diving off the boat into the water, long swims.

But with the passing of time his features grow fainter: Greta starts, as the thought registers. His face is no longer in such sharp focus: his profile, his hands, appear less vivid, so also the brightness of his eyes, and his smile. There are still glimpses, instants. There's still the memory of his enthusiasms.

The tiny coloured flags that he moved punctiliously on the map during the opening months of the war, marking advances and retreats on the battle-fronts that were as fluid and mobile as globules of mercury. The novels by Verne and Salgari, the cars, the warplanes. And the collection of which he was so proud, hundreds of toy soldiers in resplendently colourful uniforms: hussars wearing jackboots, Bohemian uhlans and dragoons, Prussian infantrymen, Bavarian lancers, Cossacks with kolbaks on their heads and Tyrolean mountain troops with mountain boots and tiny pointed skis on their feet.

Greta suddenly recalls their swift inglorious end – in the fireplace. It was evening. Outside, it was raining.

She relives that scene distinctly, feels that same chill in her body: the flames that blaze up higher, the rivulets of molten tin glinting in their coloured bubbling. They had only just heard. Egon was dead, killed in battle. Their cousin – *zia* Ingrid's boy – wouldn't be coming back.

She clutches the edge of a pillow. She forces herself to keep her mind on her brother.

Arturo, beloved by all, the only son, his father's pride, the perfect likeness of his mother. Sunny temperament, promising, generous. Then wasted in fevered delirium, his eyes sunken and distant, his lips cracked and parched as they mouthed meaningless syllables.

Nothing had done him any good: not the healthy air of the Carnaro and of Abbazia, not medical advice from as far afield as Vienna, not any of those treatments. At the end of what was called the Great War, it was tuberculosis that had been the victor. Nor had his mother survived, except as that empty, ethereal husk: a pod enclosing nothing. A mere shadow of her former self: of that strong, energetic, vital woman she had once been.

Now Elisa's voice is a whisper that obliges her to surface back to the present. "Well, Greta? Can he still see us?"

She thumps the pillow in rage, then smooths it back with a smile: "It was rumpled."

She turns to face the child, looks at her intently, brushes back a lock of her hair. How long had she been nursing that question before managing to blurt it out?

"I think so," she replies at last. "I think he can hear us, Elisa. I think Arturo is somewhere peaceful. From where he is, everything must look tiny, just like the miniature cardboard theatre which Santa Claus brought you in December. Abbazia in miniature, Monte Maggiore in miniature, a miniature sea beneath the sky. But his eyes have special binoculars and he sees us as though we were close up. So I'll bet he was one of the first to notice that you've lost another tooth, little missy, and that that wee window lets the air through even though you don't want it to and makes you hiss your esses as if you were a sssssserpent."

At last she sees her smile, one hand masking her mouth, one finger exploring her gum.

"But I think at times he gets bored with all the peacefulness, and then he misses our squabbles and your wilfulness."

"I'm not wilful. Hardly ever."

"Well, you ought to be. I was, at your age."

"Really?"

"Sure. Lots of times. You're much better than I was."

"Seriously?"

"Absolutely. You're even much too good. And children who are too good, like yourself, end up being wilful later on when they've grown up or even when they're old. Because everyone really needs to be a bit rebellious, at least at some time in their life. Disobeying, if it's for the right reason, can help us grow up, and understand."

Elisa looks at her hard, concentrating, taking care to catch every word.

Out of doors, the rain comes down in heavy squalls, and gusts of chilly air blow in between the window frames causing the long bright cretonne curtains to billow gently.

She turns her gaze away from the night and looks at Elisa

again. What would her father say if he heard her preach that heretical behaviour, that sermon of dissidence against respectable upbringing?

"So don't be afraid to speak out about your desires or your fears. Those who love you need to know the things that are hidden away inside your head, under your ribbons and tresses and hairpins. Promise me you will."

But Elisa pins her down. "Do you?"

Greta looks at that adult little child who's so earnestly interrogating her. "I try to," she says, lying even to herself.

"Well, then, I'll try to, too."

And she snuggles back under the blankets, small and white in the bedsheets, beside the teddy bear missing an eye who peeps out on the pillow.

Greta gets up, goes to the bedside table. There, beside the lamp, stands the little musical box which had long been her own: it had been a present from her father on his return from a trip to Vienna, and she well remembered her astonishment as she held that object which magically, as it seemed, released the strains of an organ and a violin.

Perhaps that was exactly what had started her passion for music as she handled those metal disks with their circular grooves which were instantly able to deliver lullabies or heavenly waltzes: and she was entranced by the chubby little cherubs embossed in relief on the wooden lid that were playing on lyres and violins, hovering amid vine fronds and puffs of bright clouds: strange vineyards rooted clinging to the sky that flowed with musical notes instead of wine.

And the mysterious word, writ large above – that looming black Leipzig – was perhaps a foreign term that spelled happiness.

Now she looks at these and smiles: mere mass-produced ugly lithographs, an irreparable triumph of kitsch and an assault on children's aesthetic taste.

But no matter, she tells herself: at the time it meant peeping into paradise. She picks up a disk, starts up the music, lingers an instant listening to it.

Finally she tiptoes out of the room, shutting the door behind her, to the strains of a Strauss waltz.

This year's Christmas holidays have seemed to her to be long-drawn-out and strange, the rituals proceeding by inertia, now that Arturo's gone: the Christmas tree to be listlessly adorned, the Christmas Eve dinner eaten in silence, the visits to elderly relatives who have to be called *signorina* and who, in between brandishing their missals or reciting the rosary, relay the local gossip spiked with cyanide.

And long hours reading on her own, the occasional fairy tale for her sister, letters to Edith, her writing.

Greta silently goes downstairs and enters the little study at the rear of the house. The grandfather clock shows ten to nine. That's not late, she can still play. She sits at the grand piano which used to belong to her *nonna* and to her *zia*.

For a moment she pricks up her ears to the sounds from outside: the heavy downpour has dwindled to a bare drizzle, and the fragrance in the air is that which has risen from moisture and moss, from berries, from rain-sodden roots drinking life.

Then her fingers descend on to the keyboard.

She chooses Auguste Franck's *Prelude, chorale and fugue*. That's the mood, this evening. The music fills the room with a new, unknown passion: and, under her closed eyelids, she sees that face and those hands. She sees them in a pleasing light, in expressive gestures she has often recalled. And she lets them flow into the music, as if entrusting them to it.

Fiume, Government Palace
January 1920

Paul leans back in his chair, folds back and lays aside the newspaper. Through the large window on his left the cold grey light of a wan winter's day.

He has read the news item twice over, and has registered the risks and implications which it conveys.

> The Honourable Alceste De Ambris as from today takes up office as Cabinet Head in Fiume. A pioneer of socialism, driven into long years of exile in Brazil and in France, erstwhile Secretary of the Chamber of Labour in Savona, a Socialist Youth leader in Rome as well as an active trade unionist, the Hon. De Ambris has given numerous proofs of his political nous, consistency and strong discipline. The cooperation of this comrade is a valuable prize for Fiume's cause, which today sees evidence of a wholly new life as part of a profound social renewal.

Since he started on his new job at the Office of Foreign Relations, Paul has been in a position to comprehend affairs by observing them from a much closer vantage point. And now he has no difficulty in realizing the corollaries that lie behind the choice of a new name: Alceste de Ambris. A syndicalist, a political exile, a foundational socialist.

A man who organized a robust protest movement in the Parma area and who has openly aligned himself with radical reform, envisioning new solutions for the world which had just emerged from the war. A man who will soon set his hand on Fiume's Constitution.

Such is De Ambris in the eyes of the legionaries.

But for Paul it has become natural to look at events through other people's eyes also, as if he were now split between different and obligatory identities: one inside and one outside Fiume, both observer and actor. Perhaps this is what it really means, he told himself, to be still and always an outsider. American, of course – he's well aware of it, nor will he or others ever forget it – but now also adopted inescapably by this odd corner of Europe, and involved in its every problem.

Alceste De Ambris... he reflects. From the outside, merely a revolutionary, a dangerous subversive seen in a bad light by too many circles in Italy itself, an exile from his own country. They say he's an able man, but in the short run all Fiume gains is a surge of new enemies, of which it felt no need.

Paul picks up a pamphlet and opens it, attempting to regain his lost concentration.

Through the half-open door he hears the constant coming and going between the other offices on the second floor. He looks up for a moment at the little wooden chest standing on his desk in front of him, locked and with its corners reinforced with metal.

That chest has been getting heavy. He reaches out to touch it. Somehow he has to get it out of Fiume and deliver it swiftly he knows to whom.

He feels anxiety gripping him, the urgency of deciding and acting. There are no few spies in town, and his own name has already been mentioned. He won't have much time, he tells himself.

He opens the envelope which he's taken out of a drawer. The letterhead has a solemn air: *United States Embassy, Rome.*

He's already read and re-read that letter, but his annoyance is undiminished: the sense of having had a violence done to him, a feeling of impotence and frustration. He's received three injunctions at once, in a sharp, lapidary style: to hand in his personal documents, to leave Fiume at once, to return immediately to his own country.

He folds up the letter, slips it into the chest.

He has made his decision without further misgivings.

Quite simply, he will disobey.

Fiume
February 1920

The rain seems to have eased.

Through that single window only a subdued dripping sound can be heard.

Tullio re-reads the last poem, then closes the copybook with the stiff black cover that Greta left in his hands before leaving him on the evening when they had seen each other.

"I've never shown them to anyone," she had said matter-of-factly. "I'm glad you're the first to read them." He found himself amid those pages as if he were embarked on a journey into her past, into her present, into her memories and her dreams and her flights: a journey into Greta's soul.

For he has found everything of her in those tormented and musical verses which have ruptured all rhyme to carve open free and troubled pathways.

The anarchy of a distant childhood, the contemplation of the sky and the sea, the enigma of a father and a mother defeated and sought after, lost and loved. The absence of a face – several faces – and the emptiness they've left behind.

The simple suffering of children and the already guilty suffering of adults. Regret over what one has not been, over life not lived, over all the life that will not be lived. Passages that moved him, details that touched him: the notes of a wooden whistle carved some time back by her brother, the arabesque of acacia leaves, music bursting every boundary and becoming a Noah's Ark on which to load every cargo – every possible anxiety – so as to transport it afar.

He's even found there the poets they both love: the French.

He's found the six-year-old Greta – heady and filthy, faint and happy – and the Greta of a time still to come.

He's found death and life and above all the feeling of going forward, of a journeying with teeth gritted to make it one's own and not imposed.

And all at once he feels he knows that free young woman as perhaps up to now he has known no one else.

Now Tullio knows what he will do.

Spring

Fragrances, maybe: fragrances above all.
They tussle together, at times.
The sweet warm fragrance of resin with the cool perfume of mint,
the intenser tang of lilac with the salt air from the sea, the more
pungent overtones of sage with the youthful breath of lavender
which circulates around the fountain, lays siege to the walls.
The Easter currant cake has a mild, golden fragrance, while the
mussel broth always has a sharp and piquant flavour.

Smells like these need new words, so Elisa reflects.
Words she hasn't been able to find.
So she's tried drawing them.

Resin shows up as orange and yellow dots, sage as spirals of green
and blue.
Mint has long, pointed spikes, the fragrance of pinza currant cake
has golden flounces.
Colours have filled whole sheets, have smeared her cheeks and
fingers.
For other people they're just daubs.
They aren't. They're springtime.

Fiume
April 1920

I n the small square of light shimmers a patch of sea.
A woman's slightly bowed profile is outlined against the
window, little more than a convent peephole through the
thick wall.

She looks motionless and deep in meditation, swathed
in the smoke of candles in the little funeral chamber, her
face veiled, a single large ring on her ring finger, a wisp of
hair hanging down over her forehead. Strangely, she's
dressed in white: she certainly had not expected to be in
mourning, and this was certainly no time to purchase
garments, in Fiume.

Standing slightly to one side, Giulio watches her in
silence. It was he who had escorted here – to where lay the
boy's lifeless body – that illustrious and unexpected guest:
the Duchessa d'Aosta, no less. A representative of Italian
royalty.

A woman who has come all the way to Fiume defying fancy protocol so as to judge freely for herself: but, rather than transform her visit into a formal ritual, she has immediately decided, upon arrival, to pay her respects to the dead boy. A legionary who had just been killed by the blockading forces, a lad who had believed in the enterprise and who had deserted for the sake of the cause, but who had ended up dying in Fiume, the victim of a history that was too complicated and larger by far than he.

Giulio looks down at the corpse: an adolescent's body and face, a uniform which has not had time to get moth-eaten in some old trunk.

He feels a rage suddenly rising in him such as he has not experienced for a while.

He catches the cries of a seagull, running footsteps, the shrill call of a child. The air smells of incense.

And as the Duchess takes her leave – the aspergillum traces the outline of a cross in the air with drops of holy water – he tells himself that it's not a matter of chance that the only person in Italy today to have dared make the defiant act of coming as far as Fiume to visit the rebels is a woman.

Her gesture – her independence of mind – will smart like a slap full in the face, will bury the government in embarrassment: hers is the homage to an Italian killed by Italian troops, in what appears to be the start of a real civil conflict.

It's a body blow to the brokers of Machiavellism and of power politics dressed in their double-breasted suits.

Only once he's outside once more – the daylight seems to explode mercilessly – does he feel a tap on his shoulder: he turns round, to see Paul.

"I must talk to you. It's important."

Unwillingly, he follows him some way along.

★ ★ ★

"What d'you mean, you're coming with me? This isn't some school outing!"

Giulio's voice shows his anger and his expression is cold and hard. But Paul doesn't look astonished, as if he'd expected that reaction: "I repeat: I'm coming with you."

"It'll be a long flight, and a risky one."

"If I were after pretend risks I'd have stayed home playing bridge."

"Just listen to me one moment, *americano*. I can't guarantee you… "

"I've been through the war just as you have. I'm not in the habit of having guarantees. However, look here: keep this. I hoped it wouldn't be necessary, but…"

Giulio looks at him in silence, snatches the envelope from him, tears open the edge, reads. He utters an oath, looking into the distance. The letterhead is the one he's familiar with, the message beneath is brief and clear.

At the bottom is d'Annunzio's signature, with the usual sharp black line underscoring it like a flourish.

Gabriele d'Annunzio

Which now puts an end to any argument.

Giulio turns and looks Paul up and down: still standing still beside him, unshaven for the first time since they met, two violet shadows under his aging seraph's eyes, he suddenly strikes him as a changed person.

He realizes that this Fiume rebel experience is leaving its marks on all of them, who had already been tested by war, marks which all at once seem to him destined never to heal.

"Right," he says, handing back the letter. "It'll be two days from now. Be ready."

And as he moves away, hands in pocket, he wonders what kind of mission might have been entrusted to that lad who's always struck him as a Bohemian chasing after powerful emotions to take back home with him when the game's over.

For the time being, all he knows is that he'll really have to take Paul with him on his protest flight.

Fiume
April 1920

They walk into the nearly dark hangar.

In front of them the biplane seems waiting to fly off, its winged black emblem merely a darker patch along one side of the fuselage.

Ardisco non ordisco – 'I dare, I don't plot' – reads the Latin motto painted in red just below the emblem and borrowed by Giulio from among the many coined by d'Annunzio: but in the darkness there it's just a sludge of characters that might be anything: a pictogram, a curse. Or possibly a bloody smudge.

Giulio feels uneasy.

His map is folded in his pocket. He's studied the distances and the route, possible stopping places, range.

"There's something you must see," he says without turning to Paul, as he finishes checking the engine, pouring in more lubricant and watching it pour down like the gilded piddle of a child: he's always preferred to be the one to have a final look at everything before climbing up into the sky, amid the ribs of emptiness. "And we can have a look at it right now. It will be a trial for tomorrow. Come along, hop in."

Paul has never flown before.

Now the sudden emptiness in his stomach drains into his head, into his thoughts: and down below, in the broad sweeping curve that makes of the SVP a twirl resembling the great tail of a beast determined to get rid of a horsefly, he sees a different world that looks rinsed in light. He feels the cold hit him in the face, but beneath his jerkin and sweater he suddenly notices he's perspiring.

Giulio's question is unexpected: "Have you used me for your initiation? To prove you're a real man?"

"I've used you because you're the craziest. Apart from d'Annunzio, of course. But between the two of you it's a tough contest."

Their voices are loud, almost yells: otherwise they couldn't be heard. Yet it's just there, in the middle of nothingness, with the wind whistling in their ears and the sun's disc blazing with a light that takes your breath away, it's just there that Paul suddenly realizes that he can be completely honest, that sincerity there is not a burden: "I've used you so as to understand certain things."

"Such as?"

"The list's a pretty long one."

"As long as you have the voice to yell, I'm listening."

"Who are you, and what are you up to in Fiume. I want to understand whether you're the last of the romantics or a madman playing politics during his exercise hour."

But he receives no answer. Could Giulio not have heard him? Paul leans out, he peers out of the cockpit: all at once the town seems to be slapped against the side of the mountain behind it, as if it were slipping towards the sea after having picked up momentum on its slopes.

Beneath the sun, the glinting sea is a shimmering of living needles, the ceaseless sizzling of scales on the azure surface of the waves,

For an instant he shuts his eyes. There are so many other things he would still like to say. About himself, about his motives, about what the devil he himself is up to in Fiume.

So he tries speaking first: "If you like, I might as well go first. I'm from New York, I was born there. I have a stepmother my own age and my father is a penologist who's been threatening to disown me since he tracked me down to this corner of the world."

But he stops short, awkwardly, suddenly feeling an idiot.

How does one really tell one's story? How does one really open up?

One can't do it even up in the air, not even in that light so pure that it makes you forgive the past itself. Not even up there can he explain that he's been in the war, that damned war, that it's left its mark on him and that he doesn't intend to go back home until he's understood this poisoned old continent, what it is and how the devil it thinks, this continent which, God knows how, has robbed him of a year and a half of his existence: a year and a half in a slaughterhouse, which really had nothing to do with him. Not directly, at least. But to admit all this to oneself, that can't be done.

Giulio must have already understood as much. Maybe

he's been the first to grasp the powerlessness of words and that's why he hasn't yet answered. Even when you get close to that truth you're chasing, you never quite catch it.

Like a starving fellow who gazes at pastries with his nose pressed against the shop-window.

Or like making love in a hurry, only to find that you've missed something.

The broad sweeping curve is complete and down below the outer streets of Fiume, now close by, take shape.

Paul feels as though the air is sucked back down his throat and into his lungs and an emptiness around his stomach, which suddenly closes in, contracts.

A single white cloud, far off in the sky, seems to nibble away the horizon into that one cottonwoolly strip. Then everything closes in: the mountain over the sea, the long road network sliced by the river, the streets clambering up to the hilltop suburbs. And beyond, the white finger of the lighthouse, the outline of the great inlet: and in the middle of the harbour, facing Piazza Dante and lined up along the quay, the warships at anchor among steamers, torpedo boats, E-boats. As the aircraft descends sharply, lines fall into shape, details regain their meaning, showing themselves for what they are: cranes with arms outstretched, the little sentry-box at the end of the bridge that links the Croatian suburb of Sussak to the heart of the city, the sentry who pops out, and looks up, shading his eyes, searching in their direction, amazed at the engine noise suddenly zooming out of the sky.

The plane is now so low that nothing seems more likely to Paul than a crash into that mountainside, their little biplane – and themselves included – reduced to an inglorious monument of wreckage and sludge.

Then he sees them. Under the port wing.

They're trudging along a mule-track that climbs uphill northward from the outermost edge of Fiume: a regiment in formation marching down those slopes towards Fiume, rifles shouldered, with long sprays stuck in the barrels and swaying in step. Little by little the figure leading them takes shape and also gets closer and now looks up and spots them, waves them a greeting, orders the soldiers to halt.

Then Paul realizes. And when his intuition is confirmed, he merely looks on for a moment. Then, throwing himself back, he has a long laugh, as if liberated.

He is almost sure he knows the smile that is now on Giulio's face, under his Rasputin beard and his card-sharper profile.

From above, he's still staring at that figure: the slim physique, the khaki skirt, the close-cropped hair, tomboy-style. A woman. A woman leading a bunch of desperadoes.

And Giulio's voice bursts into a somewhat jocular announcement: "I present to you lieutenant… Isa… Di… Camerana!"

The syllables scatter in the air and seem to suspend faint echoes on the mountain slope that looms close by. And it all, suddenly, seems a dream, or possibly a hallucination.

But it's all really happening, Paul tells himself, though he can't yet work out whether it's an ironical pantomime or a final plummeting into the totally absurd.

He knows only that he feels he himself is a part – unexpectedly, and without effort – of what is happening there.

The SVA is now climbing again, gaining altitude, banks in a wide curve between mountain and sea.

And when it straightens out again, Paul catches Giulio's voice, suddenly different, remote. "I never answered your question, old boy. I reckon I'm a lunatic who's able to enjoy too many flying hours."

Then everything is so unexpected that he hardly has time to register his terror: the plane begins to corkscrew in a nightmarish spiral and straight after, like a nail struck by a hammer, hurtles down in a nose-dive. Paul plunges in a world turned upside down without anything to cling to, twisting, senseless: sea in the sky, sky in the sea, and the whole town slopping around like a giant hodge-podge which at the last moment rearranges itself, becomes recognizable again, makes peace with itself, with the sky, with the sea.

A few instants longer, and they would have been smashed.

At least, he tells himself, he's left his lunch and supper behind that tree-trunk, but his stomach hasn't yet found its way back to its proper place.

When he recovers his dignity, Paul is pale, but he holds himself up straight before his friend's gaze.

"Okay?" says Giulio, puffing on his cigarette. "Ready for tomorrow's flight, then?"

Paul looks at him in thoughtful silence. A buzzard has settled on a branch. He knows it sometimes feeds on carrion. Suddenly, he likes that idea.

"Okay." His stomach's burning. "What time do we leave tomorrow?"

He can't be sure – he wouldn't swear to it – but just now he seems to read in Giulio's eyes a hint of insecurity and dismay, plus something he can't identify.

Fiume
May 1920

The two SVAs stand motionless, side by side.

Before climbing into the biplane, Tullio makes sure that his packet is still there, where it should be, held tight between his three woollen sweaters and the leather jerkin that he's wearing, with the muffler wound round his neck and the double gloves to protect him from the biting cold which in flight always slashes one's skin and one's breath. He runs his fingers over the package as if to adjust its shape and weight: it's rectangular, and light. Touching it makes him cheerful. That air-drop will be a surprise.

He's had thirty copies printed for her, not one more nor one less than he could afford with his little nest-egg. But now he smiles at the thought of that little book – eighty pages – straight off the press: Greta's collected poems. Tullio has wrapped the first copy in stiff waxed paper and has tied it up tightly, and written on top, in black, simply *Greta*.

He'll back up Giulio and Paul shortly for the first leg of their flight. He'll carry fuel to supply them with at the halfway stage. He's set only that one condition: straight after take-off, a brief deviation over Abbazia.

"Abbazia? And why the devil Abbazia?" expostulated Giulio, belligerently, tucking his map back into his pocket and looking at him suspiciously.

"Some day or other I might explain," he replied evasively.

Now beneath them the sea is calm with depths of dark violet which shade into azure transparencies around the edges of the larger islands and near the coast.

Tullio savours to the full the unexpected sensation of this novel flight, so unlike the many he's done before: his hands respond obediently to a natural familiarity with the control movements on the instrument panel, but he detects a lightness in his thoughts and a new freedom from the world – or at least from the world's worst – which he now feels he can experience.

There's no more war, down there. He does not sense the anguish that devours, the jaws clenched in anxiety, the eyes burning with the strain of watching every little thing: the horizon ahead and on each side, ambushes and surprises from the clouds, fire from the trenches.

The bay, intense cobalt blue, shimmers amber with slate-grey flakes. Abbazia reaches towards the sea, between thick woodland at its rear and cliffs jagging the coast, jutting inland in a rocky elbow which, digging in deeper, carves out a sharp hollow.

On his left, level with him, Giulio's SVA casts a long shadow on him, intermittently shielding him from the sun.

Tullio turns towards his friend, makes an agreed signal

with his hand. The other man nods, continuing on his flight path. Then Tullio splits off from him: he starts descending, resets his course, flies lower over the bay of Abbazia.

He can now make out the large villas squatting in their parks that slope down to the sea: helianthus, boxwood, great palm-trees, recently fashionable and still exotic and strange with their touch of the Orient. Then the jagged coastline emerges amid rock-spray, as if tracing an alphabet of its own in some mysterious ancient tongue.

Eventually he spots the house, the garden's red-and-green anarchy, the space that opens out towards the south, the inlet that fans out to the sea. He banks slightly, flies lower.

And all at once he sees her, sitting there. At the spot which he knows to be her favourite.

He watches her raise her face towards the sky, prop herself with one hand on the ground and with the other hand shade her eyes to search in his direction.

Tullio retrieves the package tucked in between his sweater and his jerkin, feels its weight for a moment with his fingers: it seems light enough to get lost in some crevice among the rocks or in the bushes if the wind carries it too far. So he unwinds his muffler and ties it round the packet. Finally, after reaching out his arm and waving his hand in greeting, he tosses down the little cargo.

He watches the red muffler wind whirling down, tracing a trajectory that daubs the azure air with colour: and that spiral seems to him to be a point of union and understanding, a way of bridging and annulling the distance and the void that separates them.

He flutters the biplane's wings a few times with a brief, measured roll.

He sees Greta answer his greeting by waving her hand in reply.

Before banking to rejoin Giulio, he catches a last glimpse of her: running fast on tip-toe with bounds that fill him with fondness.

At that point, Tullio climbs and flies off.

Greta picks up the package carefully and for some moments eyes it, feeling its weight. On the outside, with some astonishment, she reads her own name, inked in large letters leaning slightly to the left. She starts undoing the first knot, to unwrap the paper, to ease out its contents cautiously.

Eventually the package is stripped bare, between her fingers. For an instant her gaze sharpens in an expression of disbelief and joy and in the tense craning of her neck as she searches as far as the horizon, getting everything into focus.

Then, standing among the rocks, Greta looks up at the sky, and laughs.

★ ★ ★

Paul feels the cold like pins pricking the most exposed skin of his face: it penetrates at the edges of his helmet and pierces like a blade into his fingers, getting through the silk gloves which he's worn underneath his much thicker woollen ones. They've been flying for nearly three hours.

It's two madmen flying, Paul knows. And that their flight itself is crazy is proved by the worrisome stuff they're carrying. The small chest is there at his feet, wedged in such a tight space that it looks like a nesting box.

Paul has been looking down at the world, feeling the

emptiness in his stomach grow gradually familiar and then recede, disappear, like the sea that opened out beyond the gulf, the green of the coast on the horizon, the chain of the Appennines in its tangle of crests and ridges: the route traced on the map which now assumed its real form. Then the flattened cones of mountains scored by gullies and broad tufa plateaux gradually turned into rolling pastures and forests and countryside. Now the SVA banks gently. Beneath them, hump-backed hills like ancient animals: the shadows stand out sharply, like shearing-blades.

The biplane, gauging its speed, descends on to a broad clearing. In the distance, a watercourse, a patch of woodland, a slight slope eroded over time, starved even of colour. A flock of grazing sheep dots the meadow's green.

Paul feels the plane labouring as it seems to fly against the wind, its steadying in the air as it prepares to glide in.

Then they are struck by the silence, while they remain like that for a moment, still a part of the biplane: around them is only an unwrathful wind, the slight bending of the grass, the distant bleating of a goat which seems to tickle the air with its insistent, guttural cry. The day, still cloudless and limpid, is warm, announcing the coming of summer.

Paul clambers out of the cockpit and scans the surrounding countryside: bramble bushes, clumps of grass, the occasional olive tree with gnarled trunks and cracked bark. Not far off, under the shelter of a tree, a little heap of grey dust is the last remaining trace of a fire lit perhaps by some herdsman.

Then he spots the waiting car, at the far edge of the meadow, on the verge of a country road that looks little better than a track. The agreement he's made is precise and the time scheduled for the flight has been strictly adhered to.

His journey from here on to Rome will take less than an hour.

So he retrieves the chest, exchanging farewells with Giulio. They'll meet up here again at the same place, as already agreed.

Before heading for the car, Paul steps in front of the biplane and gives a great shove to the propeller on the biplane's nose: then stands by to watch the plane run forward, bumping along the ground, and then take off.

Then he strides quickly towards the waiting car.

Piazza Montecitorio at this hour is thronged with people. The little girl holding her mother's hand looks up, stops, tugs at her mother. The white ribbon on her hair tickles the back of her hand.

The bird that has emerged from the clouds flies with great and strange power: then it descends over the palace roof.

The girl points to it, bracing her feet against the travertine, her lace socks neatly pulled up over her black patent leather shoes, but in her mother's eyes she reads her own astonishment. The woman's voice hesitates slightly as she stops beside her daughter, the weight of the shopping bag suddenly encumbering her.

"What's that, mamma?"

"It's an aeroplane."

"And is that a present for the people who live there that it's dropping on that house? And would you say that it's brought something for us, too?"

The woman, bemused, follows the biplane's sudden nose-dive and the trajectory of the object tossed on to the palace. Then she instinctively clutches her daughter in a grip that binds them together, as she runs with her child in her arms expecting to hear the blast.

The driver is a man of few words.

Paul knows only that he's an ex-officer, an old comrade-in-arms of d'Annunzio's. Contrary to what he expected, he's hardly asked him any questions. Paul feels grateful for his gift of simple silence which allows him to recall what he wrote last night.

He'd stayed awake almost until dawn, chewing over his words, trying to fit in his misgivings and his protests, his passions and ideals and the lurking threats. Shards of phrases and reflections are still straying through his head even now, but they're like disjointed limbs.

He wonders whether what he's written will manage to chip a vertebra or two of dogmatism, to shatter the assurance of being always in the right, of always holding in our hands the torch of some truth or other.

Will his fellow-countrymen take heed?

The first amendment to our Constitution guarantees, besides freedom of religion, freedom of speech and freedom of the press…also the right to appeal to the government to right wrongs.

Only wrongs that affect us American citizens, or also those that affect other peoples, other injustices, other inequities?

It is to this right that I, Paul Forst – an American citizen – now forcefully appeal: so that a voice may be heard that for months has been lost in a void.

So that the plea of the people of Fiume may be pondered and debated, recognized as legitimate or else discredited.

But not simply dismissed – as has been happening for too long – by the Paris Conference, where the victorious Nations sit.

He gazes out of the car window.

The landscape looks gentle and mild: green hills, small townships, distant patches of woodland. Then undulating expanses of tufa scored by erosion: deep gullies, broad dark hollows. On the horizon, an azure expanse gleaming with light.

Among the trees lining the road, the car's projected shadow flits as precise and alive as a pike amid the rocks in a watercourse.

He concentrates anew on what he's written to send to Ben and Rose.

… It's a beautiful and awesomely new dream, this great American dream that is being proposed to the peace negotiations: the principle of self-determination. Every people contained within boundaries of language, nationality and culture. A geography made of common history, land and roots, of a belonging derived from a single shared past.

Every people free, in the end, to dispose of itself and its future, following the end of a long war which has had devastating consequences. It's a dream that speaks of justice, of courage, and of truth.

Let's not allow it to go adrift.

Let's not allow it to be applied inequitably and, ultimately, hypocritically and arbitrarily.

Let's not let it be guaranteed only when it really coincides with the interests of the mighty, with the aims of the victors, of those who have the means to redraw the planet's geography.

Here he's let himself be carried away.

But how do you build walls around ideals you believe in, around real passions which you grip between your teeth – and which you turn into clumsy words – to prevent them from going adrift?

…The Germans of East Prussia and of Alsace-Lorraine cut off from their motherland, those of the South Tyrol summarily assigned to Italy, the Albanians in Kosovo in effect subjected to a Serb kingdom, along with Croats and Slovenes, Macedonians and Montenegrans. And Dalmatia destined for sacrifice, Istria deeply violated, and hypocritical mandates enabling the holders to act as guardians of peoples held by the hand and treated as eternal children or on a par with lunatics or criminals.

How long will this ancient, huge, patched-up body hang together without plunging the world into another war? And how much can Fiume mean if the cause that now bears its name becomes the voice of ideals which are not exclusive to Fiume, but belong to every nation and every person and become universal values?

The car is now coming into Rome. Ben and Rose, lifelong friends, will soon be leaving for Boston. He'll entrust what he's written to them, and to their unwavering moral principles for which he's always esteemed them he'll entrust the mission of delivering that letter – an open letter, from the heart – to the American press.

… Italy is the only Nation whose victory in the war was instantly pronounced "mutilated": a victory that hasn't brought the changes people longed for.

A Nation rent but vital, seeking wholly new horizons, between

visionary imagination and overweening individualism.It's from here,
I'm convinced, that the most unexpected shifts will come.

To ignore this reality is not simply short-sighted and unjust.

It is, above all, dangerous.

He finds himself looking afar, beyond that slightly blurred town. He doesn't know what will become of what he has written, whether it will ever be accepted for publication, whether in this delicate moment there might be room for words that are hard, unwelcome, a nuisance. Words in which he's bared his soul. He knows only that he had no choice: he just had to try.

Peace is far too important to be left only to the victors.

The impact was sharp and sudden, but in striking the roof tiles it gives out a metallic clang, a noise both high-pitched and hollow, not the boom of an explosion.

The knot of passers-by that have stopped to stare look dumbfounded rather than alarmed as they follow the flight of the biplane away from the scene.

Further along, some parliamentarians stand apart, tense, at the entrance to Montecitorio Palace.

Then all look up again towards the roof of the *Hotel Milan*, close by the Parliament, which is where the device dropped from the plane appears to have landed.

Then the silence is broken and a medley of voices arises, each advancing its own hypothesis and contesting a dozen others.

★ ★ ★

Climbing out of the dormer window with one last thrust of his hips, he feels his jacket ripping between elbow and shoulder.

And now that he's out there on the roof, out of reach of clients and managers, at long last he lets loose all the imprecations which he's kept bottled up since that moment when they foisted on him that job which has next to nothing to do with his duties as bell-boy for that floor.

He inches forward gingerly on all fours, taking good care not to slither on the somewhat slippery slope of the roof tiles, resting his feet and the palms of his hands on the more secure flat surface of the imbricating tiles. At the same time he searches for the object which he's been detailed to retrieve.

An explosive device? he wonders. Or a piece of the fuselage or undercarriage or some other damn bit of the biplane that has just swooped down over that roof and across the piazza?

Then at last he sees it, its white enamel glinting. It looks as if it's upside down, but intact.

And as he slowly approaches, getting a clearer view of its shape – edged in black or blue piping – he murmurs under his breath that, no, it can't be right. Then he reaches it, picks it up, turns it about in his hands, without yet knowing whether to laugh or feel humiliated at the thought of getting back down among other people – everyone there waiting for him on the top floor – clutching that trophy which he'd know who to give it to.

Even better: why not go right up to the manager and hand it to him in person as the fittest recipient, with a meaningful bow?

Inside that white container is a bunch of turnips and carrots with a card addressed: *To the Italian Parliament, For Its Eyes Only.*.

The fellow looks up: the chimney conceals him from view. As long as he keeps huddled there, no one can see him. His curiosity aroused, he glances at those lines.

Giulio Kepler
Bestows upon the Parliament and the Government
Which have long relied on falsehood and fear
The tangible allegory of their valour
Fiume – Rome, May 1920

And he instantly sees it all: the mockery of that protest, the meaning of what he holds in his hands, the town that is the talk of all the newspapers. And the strange destiny of the aerial drop which only missed by a few metres the building which was its intended target: the seat of Parliament. The Montecitorio Palace.

So he laughs aloud, in relief, lingering to take in the view of the city outspread beneath his feet: the forest of churches and palaces, a bend of the distant Tiber, the long shadow of the obelisk which traces its spike across the cobbles of the piazza.

How long has it been, he asks himself, since he was able to enjoy such a moment of peace, unhurried and free of immediate objectives, a moment just to stand and stare?

Then, managing to look serious again, he climbs down again to join his colleagues who are gathered in a corner of the loft, and solemnly advances, with the oblique rent in his black jacket and the chamber-pot which had come to rest upon the roof firmly held in his hands, enthroned with its turnips and carrots as if on the Papal palanquin.

The car has set off again, raising a light cloud of dust: Paul senses it in his mouth, on his palate.

He's alighted, and is walking over. The warm, level evening light now seems to enfold things. The insistent call of a cuckoo is suspended for a moment as he goes by, then resumes more loudly than before. The SVA can barely be made out among the foliage, crouching amid shrubs and brambles.

Giulio is sitting a little farther off, resting his back against the trunk of an olive tree.

Paul squats beside him, taking a puff at his lighted cigarette. "Pleased with your flight, airman?"

"I've seen better, old chap. But one needs grandeur when leaving and… well, humility when arriving."

"Might a chamber-pot be humble enough?"

Giulio winks, hints at a smile. "It might be enough even off-target."

He's really done it, Paul tells himself. He's taken his defiance to the limit. But, given that the weapon used was irony, it's left behind the melancholy of a theatre when the show is over. No relief or satisfaction, not the slightest hint of mirth.

To succeed in sneaking into history, through the creases and false mends: and with the patience of a clothes-moth, to devour the toughest fibres, the tautest threads of jute, the buttonholes that strangle the buttons. To unstitch the basting of geographies ordained by the mighty.

Wasn't that the delusion? The persistence of an insect and the fantasy of a child.

To leave a mark on the course of events, to set up a new mode of counting. But suddenly there they are, stationary, in silence, with no certainties to haul to glory. They share only their doubting, and the misgivings that will not be uttered. The mighty will never hearken. That's the heart of their might, the kernel of their hardihood, the impassive ability to transmit themselves through the endurance of an order that replicates always and only itself, even when it furthers new forms.

Paul suddenly manages to view himself as from a distance: from a remote nook of the future the enormity of dreams with no escape.

Gazing at his hands, he hears Giulio's voice, as the latter is rummaging in a pocket: "Today it's on me. You thirsty?"

"A vintage Scotch wouldn't come amiss. But I guess I'll try alternatives."

"So try an eighty-proof."

And he holds out a small flask that despite its military appearance contains a triumphant grappa flavoured with the ripest Fiume plums. Paul sips away at it slowly, holds the first gulp a moment or two, allowing his palate to absorb it and his tongue to start burning, then swallows, and feels the fiery alcohol hit his empty stomach and spread in a wave of warmth. Then he passes the flask back to Giulio, who imbibes a bit more grappa before speaking.

"The Colosseum, the gondolas, Vesuvius… A few museums, grand ancient ruins, the marvels of the Renaissance. That's as far as the foreigners go, when they come here to Italy… You'll have come to know not just the clichés but also the crazy rebels of Fiume. A novel perspective to display like a flower in your buttonhole upon your return to New York. That's what I used to think about you. Sometimes one's thoughts are crap."

Paul makes no reply. He smiles. He imagines that's as near to saying sorry that Giulio knows and perhaps has ever uttered. And he realizes something which suddenly seems to him to be really important. He's long found this man fanciful as few are, radical. An extremist out of love of arguing, a fanatic determined to amaze.

Yet now what matters is just one thing: they're both there for the self-same reason.

Life gives back no change, nor certainties. And they will gamble everything away – the dreams it allows, its challenges.

It's just then that something in the air round about changes, immediately alarming them: a cloud of smoke slightly thicker than the creeping evening haze, its approach from a distance, the birds' sudden silence. Then they perceive the noise which becomes more definite, nearer. Shaking themselves suddenly out of that sensation of unreality, they both leap to their feet and race towards the biplane so frantically as to dispel in a few seconds all trace of alcohol or fatigue. Then everything takes place at lightning speed, feverishly: turning the propeller, rocking the plane, the hand movements on the starter, the juddering of the aircraft along the ground, the spray of foliage that gets caught in the undercarriage and goes aloft with them and seems to brush a bush at the far edge of the paddock.

It's not the best of take-offs.

But it's only when they're flying at a height of a few dozen metres that they can see clearly through the cloud of smoke that's settled down below.

Even from this height they can make out the armoured cars and military transports. The late afternoon light strikes the barrels of the 91mm cannon with unexpected brilliance, but at the height which they've reached the shots fired at them seem little more than a nuisance.

Then they become aware of the darkness, of the threatening clouds piling up on the horizon, of the wind that already at this altitude seems to toss the biplane about as if it were a tin toy.

The feeling of helplessness that assails them takes them both back to earlier times.

Crossing their fingers, silent, their hearts in their mouths and their stomach turning over, in their different tongues they both wish themselves the same good luck.

Il Piccolo

5th May 1920

ROME-... Towards midday yesterday an aeroplane was seen flying low in the sky over Rome. It was later found to have taken off from Fiume... The target was evidently the piazza, but the air-drop landed on the roof of the Hotel Milan... Several parliamentarians and journalists were then standing beside the porch of Montecitorio Palace, and gave the alarm: first thoughts were of a bomb, of an assassination attempt... The pilot – ex-airman Giulio Kepler – is now charged with terrorism and subversive activity. He is being sought by the police.

From our own correspondent

PARIS – On 5th May, in response to the refusal to receive the Fiume delegation at the Paris Peace Conference, an aircraft from Fiume piloted by the airman Cesare Carminiani, after flying over the Alps, dropped over the Opera in Paris hundreds of leaflets containing a message from d'Annunzio to the French people.

The flight took 7 hours and 20 minutes.

Landing at Bourget airport, the pilot from Fiume was given a cordial and warm reception by French airmen and by the representatives of the press.

The French dailies have published articles and interviews which, among other things, also illustrate the details of a flight which was by no means without its dangers.

The attempts by the Italian Prime Minister, Francesco Saverio Nitti, to obtain from the French authorities the seizure of the aircraft and the immediate repatriation of the airman have so far proved vain…

Abbazia
May 1920

"*Scum. Criminal louts.Real bastards, that's what they are. Real slobs!*"

The newspaper is almost touching her face, before it thuds into a corner of the wall behind her. Greta hesitates to pick it off the floor as her father yells his outbursts of imprecations.

The table has not yet been cleared, Elisa shrinks back on her chair, her mother, having finished eating, is folding her serviette: her movements measured as ever, not a single hair escaping the perfect symmetry of her chignon.

Greta looks at her father in silence. She well knows what's coming over him. The end of a dream, that's all.

For him – as for many other people in Fiume – d'Annunzio and his legionaries, at least at the beginning, had been vindicators of the rights of the Italians of Istria and Dalmatia, heroes who had come from afar to become the champions and spokespersons for demands hitherto unheeded. But then everything changed little by little in that isolated little republic into which Fiume had turned.

D'Annunzio began to speak a disturbingly subversive language: a new political and social order, the rejection of capitalism, dialogue with socialism and with the rebel anarchist fringe, and even with the newborn left-wing governments that had arisen out of what her father considered to be the end of an era and of a world, the crash-bang-wallop of the collapse of Austria-Hungary.

But d'Annunzio hasn't yet called a halt, he's gone as far as seeking radical options: he's talking now of abolishing the law-courts and even the prisons, the bastard. And standing armies, why not? Reform them, rethink them anew, broaden the democratic foundations even for those who pick up a rifle and before they use it have to learn to say yes-sir.

He'll give him democratic foundations. In the shape of a good blast of buck-shot. And legalize divorce! Which had already been passed in Hungary… And why not give the vote to women, why not even send them out to fight, why not send them off to be governors as the English have already done with their Lady Astor, Holy God?!

And so on and so forth about what d'Annunzio is calling for: a whole rigmarole of blasphemies and heresies which to hear just the half of could send even a saint stark raving mad, bellows her father pacing the length of the room around them with great strides hawking out fresh imprecations.

"Damned rogues and blithering idiots, holy sacrament of sacraments. Brigands and pirates. Proper slobs!"

This wasn't what her father had been expecting, and with him the Fiume bourgeoisie: not the toppling of a nice solid world, not the proclamation of a revolution away from a free port which had always minded its own business first and foremost.

And the town swarming with people, low life of every breed and every kind: spies, traffickers, adventurers. And – Godsaveusandprotectus – all sorts of artists. Poets. Writers. Dreadfuls. Who – with time – become magnets.

Bound to – just give them enough time – bound to bring on more trouble.

And now this. These flights. Over Paris, over the Italian Parliament Palace of Montecitorio. Subversive acts of provocation, the newspaper had called them: carried out in the name of Fiume.

She translates for herself, in silence: publicity protest flights, or carnival pranks.

Her thoughts suddenly go back to Maria, forced to give up school, whom she hasn't seen for months, and her father, a sea-captain, one of the first to lose his job in the crisis that hit the town and paralyzed all its sectors: and it's said that their sacrifices must have a meaning, a reason, that maybe Fiume deserves something which, however, not even she can define. Respect? Simply to be heard? Greater attention?

Or perhaps new visions, a new history?

Meanwhile she's poured a few drops into half a glass of cold water – *Drink this and calm yourself, papa* – then watched her father get up and trip on the carpet and leave the room with head hanging down, his frock-coat flapping loosely like a Roman toga on his suddenly shrunken body.

She was sorry to see him looking like that.

Sure, he's a boorish and distant man – more distant since the loss of Arturo – but in his own way he's always treated her with respect, and he probably loves her: she doesn't remember him ever beating her, he's let her go to school, and he must have moved mountains to get her all the permits that enable her to keep going into Fiume and complete this school year.

She picks up the newspaper that her father flung against the wall.

The account of the return flight reminds her of the storybook adventures that her brother loved: the storm on the way back, engine trouble over the open sea, the emergency landing at San Marino.

For an instant she again sees the two biplanes flying over the bay beyond the bottom of the park, the Y of the diverging flight, the red spiral of the muffler.

Now she knows where they had been heading, what their objectives were.

With one hand she hides the smile that comes to her lips. From the next room she hears her father coughing, then senses someone's gaze upon her.

She looks up anxiously, and sees her: her mother is gazing at her, mute, as if reading a new book.

Fiume
May 1920

Huddled on the floor beside her, Greta suddenly looks at her as perhaps she has never done before.

She knows why she's come here today. For the first time, she's not here for Ingrid, but for herself, as she admits: she's here because she needs support for something on which she's really already made up her mind.

She silently repeats her name, retrieving for a few moments the flavour it had for her as a child, when merely pronouncing it – cool and crisp – made her feel as if she were sucking a mint: Ingrid is her name. *Zia* Ingrid. Sister to Else, her mother.

Ingrid, three years older than Else, and twenty-four years older than Greta. Ingrid, a slender brunette, instinctual, broad-minded and big-hearted. Else, blonde and gentle, rational, steady and precise in her way of being in the world like a compass drawing a circle. But both of them once full of energy and life. Sisters. Different from the start, and now united by a grief so alike.

Greta knows that she's not pursuing a reasoned argument: it's emotion pure and simple, first aid medicament, an attempt at self-defence to keep her mind busy and fend off further suffering, for tonight, at least.

Not in this room so bare and sad, before an Ingrid lost inside herself, imprisoned within her mute body, transformed into an exhausted pendulum: her legs as if fused with the chair, her upper body pitching endlessly: forwards and backwards, still forwards and backwards, desiring to be elsewhere and doomed to stay put where she is.

And Greta suddenly understands. Ingrid isn't moving through space, but through time. It is through time that she keeps up that perpetual sleepless movement of hers, that continual floundering in the net: yesterday and today, past and present, memory and zero memory. Only the future no longer exists. Expelled, denied.

And with equal violence Greta senses that she herself needs that – a new alliance with time. Out of a drawer she takes a hairbrush and begins to brush her *zia*'s still lovely hair slowly back, as she's so often done before.

I've decided, zia Ingrid. I've decided. I'll live all this to the full.

How many years does life allow before calling us to account? And how many years have gone by since that flawless plenitude which then may have been happiness?

She sees herself as a child, her fingers streaked with coloured paints, under the vibrant light of the patio which stamps the shadows on the wall. Seated on a wicker chair, with a little white carton on her knees and the invaluable treasure of a handful of sultanas in her pocket. Her gestures passionately mirror the gestures she has observed in *zia* Ingrid: and Ingrid stands before the easel, the paint dripping from her brush, her gaze fixed on the canvas and the magic of the images which come to life, fermenting. A horse on the seashore. A red flower. The portrait of her mother smiling.

Greta herself – the excitement! – with Arturo, dangling from a branch on the canvas.

And while Greta also is painting, her cousin Egon pops up just there holding a slice of bread which he breaks in two to give half to her: it's the half with more butter on.

How many years ago? she asks herself.

She continues to brush that hair, works the tresses into a braid and gathers them behind the neck.

She hazards a guess: ten years? Maybe less.

The brush back in the drawer, the drawer pushed back in, the hairpins carefully in place.

And yet that world no longer exists. She's seen it vanish little by little like an ink drawing under a downpour. The figures become smudges, the smudges dissolve into visions: there goes Egon with his slice of bread, there goes Arturo on the branch with his sling, there goes her mother's smiling face, there goes, too, Ingrid's hand that gives definite shape to them all, that combines them all like a winning hand of aces, with her brushes and her cheerfulness breaking out in romantic arias which everyone in the family bears like the stench of turpentine in the rooms. Just minuscule daily disasters.

And all at once she realizes she's trembling. For a brush has suddenly appeared in Ingrid's hand, perhaps just extracted from a pocket, and now – but gently – her *zia* is using it to stroke her hand: a bristly caress, quite unexpected.

And following Ingrid's gaze – which, just for a moment, is alive and present – Greta only now notices, on the wall, a small canvas. A *painted* canvas.

She catches her breath, goes up to the picture, lifts it off and looks at it closely.

Low down, amid clots of paint – at times seemingly thickened into berries, at others rarefied almost into air – there's a woman's face, slightly tilted, like a mushroom sprung up at random: violet looming all around, white bursting over the face, grey in two eyes – deep pools – which pierce hard into every grief.

But the mouth is missing from that oval. A face which is all gaze, all eyes, all high, very high forehead for thought. Yet no lips, she tells herself, able to voice its thought.

Greta bends down over Ingrid and runs her fingers lightly over her mouth which is shut tight and which is denied to that woman painted on the canvas: it's a very light touch, really not more than a breath. But for Ingrid it has the force of a shock: her body almost goes off balance, her neck darts back in alarm.

However, their glances meet as if they were both off course on a wire suspended in the void.

And within that space and that moment the two of them recognize each other all over again, both realize who they are.

Greta is aware of a great sense of peace, of calm suddenly recovered.

She kisses Ingrid lightly, silently. Then she shuts the door behind her and walks slowly away, knowing what she will do.

Fiume
May 1920

S he feels Tullio's arm on one shoulder, Paul's body on the other side, the shadow of the biplane behind her.

Today's light – its brutal transparency – is of the sort that seems capable of making everything easier, and not merely more distinct and brighter.

Greta looks ahead at their friend, a strange piratical type straight out of a Salgari thriller, beard carefully unkempt and hair gathered into a pigtail.

In that instant of precarious expectation – all suddenly seized in the moment, motionless before the camera – she notices the harbingers of summer in the noises she knows so well: a hustling of insects in the air and on the ground, the persistent drone of a bee, a slight rustling in the grass, possibly that of a lizard running off.

An old bottle abandoned at the edge of a nearby field seems almost to be sailing amid the furrows, as if it had gone off course as a result of a shipwreck.

"Smile!" yells the pirate.

But Greta was already smiling.

Further away, behind the photographer, a bird has just taken flight out of a rustling clump of cane: she follows it with her eyes, keeping it company, then lets it disappear in the distance. She reflects on how magical it must be to view the world from above. To look at things from on high, to enjoy that freedom.

She hears the click of the snapshot.

"Immortalized!"

Giulio now passes her the Zeiss and takes his place among his friends, casting a lover's glance at his waiting biplane. "And now let's all go and celebrate!" he announces gaily, looking at Greta.

"Celebrate what?" she asks.

Giulio gives Paul a wink, looks at her, and laughs.

"That we're all still alive, old girl!"

In the distance, amid the cane stems, a duck keeps quacking.

Abbazia
May 1920

It's a dark, though cloudless, night. The brilliant white sliver of moon looks like a small rip in the sky. The sea is barely ruffled by a light mild wind that traverses its surface like the hand of a blind man. In the distance, a dog barks furiously.

Greta has crept out on tip-toes and has gone down the gravel path that leads to the bay: only once has she looked behind her at the sleeping house, the veranda giving on to the garden, the white steps among the palms: and everything seemed to be in its place, familiar to her even in the dark of the night, obedient to its allotted space.

Only her own steps signify defiance, going against the current as she walks secretly, alone.

Then she turned her gaze further afield, beyond the garden and the house, where the darker shadow of the mountain rises from the sea. The occasional gleam of an isolated light seemed to make a living thing out of the wooded mountain-sides, the slopes, a courtyard flanking the road.

Now she senses the sea, just ahead of her. Moisture cool and strong on her skin, salt smell in her nose. She takes off her shoes and stockings. Her first foot in the water is sheer freeze, but she immediately senses the pleasure of the waves frothing around her ankles as she goes forward slowly and finally seats herself on a rock, her feet dangling into the water and an unreal calm descending on her, which even dislodges her fears.

Her father's away for a few days. His business trips to Trieste have grown more frequent and prolonged, turning into habitual absences. Her mother has fallen asleep early. The laudanum in the little bottle has lately been disappearing more quickly. There's no more movement in the house: every room deep in silence, lights out, every door closed. But her fears are of another kind, she well knows: not the unlikely and banal fear of being found out: it's rather the sensation of a turning-point which now becomes definitive – leaving a well-worn track – and which she has taken in shutting the back door behind her, leaving her home and sallying out for that nocturnal appointment.

As from now – this she does not hide from herself – nothing perhaps will ever be the same again.

For a moment she thinks of her mother, and, straight after, of her aunt. Were she ever to get to their age, she would want to have only one regret: for her bones bruised and smashed, not for lacking the courage to somehow attempt to fly for herself.

She hears the chimes from a church belfry: she's well aware of the hour, but she keeps count as if to seek a final confirmation of her novel dimension.

And it's just then that she hears it: at first it's a distant lapping of water, then the rhythmic cadence of oars, a shadow that emerges out of the night and now draws slowly nearer.

She doesn't get up, but sits and watches: even when the boat draws up, when he steps into the water and sees her, when he anchors the small craft behind a more sheltered spit, where the shore is grassier.

Only then does she leave the rock and stand there, waiting, as if to imprint for ever the picture she's taking in with her eyes, linked to the sea air: Tullio coming towards her, his long trousers rolled up over his thin friarish ankles, his shirt and his hair slightly wet.

For an instant they remain almost in disbelief of themselves, of the moment.

It's she who takes his hand, guides him amid the rocks and leads him up taking care not to slip on the stones wet with night moisture, seaweed and moss and shingle: the stepping-stones, then the footpath, towards the clump of cane now grown so tall and thick as to create a natural windbreak. They go forward slowly amid the boles, Greta pushing them aside. Eventually they reach the glade, under the darker shadow of the walls.

Now Tullio, too, can see it: a house so tiny that it seems to have sprung up all on its own. He has heard from Greta that when she was a child the gardener lived in it, and he senses the childhood atmosphere which that place must have for her. Without speaking, they go in close together.

A small square entrance leads into one more room, a

window looks out on to the sea. A jasmine vine clings to the wall. A chair and a bedside table in one corner beneath a dappled wall where a bunch of dry stems dangle head down from a nail. On the floor, a folded blanket.

Greta huddles in her bright-coloured shawl, uncertain as to whether or not to move. Then they seek out each other's faces. Their breathing becomes convulsive, mingling as one.

She feels his cracked lips pressing against hers, the delicate force of his tongue, the warmth of his hands on her shoulders and then on her neck.

She breathes in Tullio's odour, keeping her eyes shut for a moment or two: it seems to her to be charged with the sea breeze, hints of tobacco and sweat, the moist freshness of the sea. His fingers quiver slightly as he slowly undresses her. The blouse slipping to her feet causes her a sudden tremor. Tullio grasps her hand and opens out her fingers one by one, and once her palm is outspread he lifts it slowly to his chest, beneath his unbuttoned shirt, and Greta feels the throb of his heart-beat. Then she slips his shirt off him, rests her head on his chest, running her fingers along it, and then her tongue, slowly, while Tullio loosens her hair and she feels her locks tumble down on to her shoulders and along the small of her back.

She sees him bent over her corset and smiles at his look of frustration over buttons and ties.

So she starts undoing them herself, but Tullio's hand stops her, taking over from hers.

Tullio watches that body emerge: the line of her shoulders, her naked breast, the yielding amphora of her hips. Desire rises imperiously in him like a sudden pain.

Greta knows she can never forget the details of this

moment, the expression she catches on his face as he bends down in front of her, brushes his mouth over her skin, starts gently caressing her.

Then she sees him draw himself up sharply and senses the burden of an uneasiness which suddenly strikes her as despairing, and she has no need to ask any questions, but understands his hesitancy, reads his conscience like a familiar book. To his man's eyes, she knows, she is really little more than a child, and her future might depend on what they are doing now. So she touches his lips to intimate silence.

"I've only loved once before. I lost him before we'd exchanged a kiss. I don't know how he'd have handled me, how we'd have made love. I won't make the same mistake again, Tullio.I know how much it means, what we're feeling. If we're here now, it's because I want it, too."

She takes his hand and puts it on her breast. Her nipple swells on contact with his fingers.

Tullio feels at that moment relieved of a nameless weight, and that he is free to enjoy happiness.

Outside, the murmur of the sea seems to ordain an ancient calm.

She feels she knows that body, she's always been waiting for it, its movements are part of her.

She feels she's plunging gently into a rhythm in which they join, and everything seems to her to reach unimaginable heights – unreachable, extreme – and then plummet and somehow dissolve in achieved bliss.

Then they slump like infants, but still cleave together.

A stronger breath or two of wind finds its way through the

cane thicket, buffeting it: now and then producing a high-pitched sound, a note drawn from hollow fibres.

Words now flow unbidden, as if after an over-long wait: and for the first time it's Tullio that bares his being to her. Greta listens, snuggled up to that body which keeps her warm. Projects and reminiscences, grand designs and tiny details well up in total anarchy: the first book he read as a child, his favourite food, his life-changing experiences, his earliest memory. "Once, when I was little, my father took me to see Buffalo Bill's circus, which was touring Europe. They performed in a *piazza*, Zardin Grant. I can still remember the war-whoops of the Indians who re-enacted for us the battle of Little Big Horn. After the attack on that stage coach I decided what I'd do when I grew up: I'd be a cowboy."

"Well, you've lived up to your ambition. You live the life of an adventurer and an outlaw in dangerous territory, on the frontier."

"But I only have a fountain-pen instead of a Winchester, don't you see? And at times I have the impression that it's not enough."

She keeps silent for an instant, then turns to face him. "You know, there's something I want to tell you. One day, while visiting *zia* Ingrid – and you know where she is – I met a fellow in the corridor. He was a harmless patient, or else he wouldn't have been there. He was elderly, and tottered as he walked, with a vacant look in his eyes. But he held out one hand, and, as if he were holding a pen which existed only in his head, he made a distinct gesture in the air, which he kept repeating persistently, like a woodpecker on a tree-trunk, never changing it. And he did it with meticulous precision, with every atom of his remaining strength. He was acting out the motions of writing, and it seemed as though that motion was what somehow still kept him going, kept him from plunging into the dementia that was waiting to waylay him. D'you get my meaning? Even when our memory really loses every other thing, even its own dignity, it can't quite sever the link it has with language. Perhaps that's the umbilical cord which we still carry into adulthood. So do you think your pen is some small matter?"

Then he sees her: in spite of the dark. He sees the woman in that young girl. The woman she will turn into and the woman she already is. And, in the dark, unseen, he smiles.

He knows, he's found out at his own expense: the present is always a little beneath what we expected and yet always a little above the way we recall it later, the way we consign it to memory: prettified to be laid aside, so that its permanence has meaning and purpose.

But this moment is perfect. It is the way he wanted it to be, and he feels that this is the way it will remain.

And he realizes that all at once even talking about them becomes easy.

He has never done so, since it happened.

Since that stony waste ground. Since the rubble of three years previously.

And they all appear, slowly: as though shy, self-effacing as ever.

His father, at work late into the night, among presses in the print room, fingers black with ink, whiskers stained with tobacco, spectacles raised on to his forehead, where he would never find them, searching for them in the gaps between the printing machinery and towering piles of paper.

His mother off to school, a crooked hat on her head and Spartan shoes on her feet, carrying a basket of coal for the great stove in the classroom which on the cold winter days – of which there were a fair number – kept her young pupils from freezing.

His sister, still a child, born many years after him, when he was already almost a grown man.

A precious present, unexpected. A grain of sugar and pepper. Merry and irrepressible, vital.

And, lastly, Elia, who's always adored him. Enlisted as a volunteer in the war in emulation of him, the elder brother, his life-long beacon.

And that's where his voice breaks. Because everything is so alive in memory that merely to touch it hurts.

Or perhaps it's impossible to touch. To touch is at once to plunge into the darkest depths, the images are so powerful and alive that you can smell them, and the fear. And the features eagerly exhumed give hell distinct outlines, carve into its chiaroscuros.

He'd seen Elia for the last time at Christmas in the second year of the war.

Both of them at home, which hadn't happened for months, to enjoy a few days leave.

The Nativity crib was set up, as it always was, on a mat of moss with a shingle track marked out on it: little plaster statues, chipped with long usage, cuddly sheep under the palm-trees, an angel hanging by a thread over the roof of the stable, one wing missing a half and a miniature lyre in his arms looking like a round of cheese.

On seeing each other again, they had embraced with

almost desperate fervour, and while sitting all together for dinner – their mother vainly forcing a show of merriment which she did not feel – Tullio had wondered what made his brother look so different, a changed person. And he had suddenly thought that it had always been hard for him to act the elder brother to Elia, stretching out impossibly the few years that separated them, to endow him with the guiding role which had always been a burden to him.

Elia had followed in his footsteps from as far back as he could remember, taking Tullio as his model, as a beacon to light up the way. In play, in books, in life. In boyish acts of disobedience and in forays up the Torre, slithering over the stones, knees covered in scabs and in their hands the slings which they had fashioned together.

His brother had imitated him in his choice of school also: the Jacopo Stellini Royal Gymnasium and Lyceum. It had an elevated outlook, beyond the sluice, on the broad platform called the Zardin Grant, or Great Garden, which lies at the foot of the castle, as if to recover its breath before taking a run up the hill.

Shaky at Greek and Latin, virtually laconic in his essay-writing, Elia made good strides in mathematics and had a passion for chemistry, which Tullio had never been able to understand.

Then the war had broken out. Elia was just a boy.

But once again he had taken the path which his brother had already taken. And all in vain were the shadows under his mother's swollen eyes, his father's expostulations, Tullio's own words of attempted dissuasion, seeking to root out that intention as in the past he had prised a billhook or a knife out of his fingers: anything which might injure him.

Elia had joined up as a volunteer – just after turning eighteen – following the tracks of a brother whom he had not ceased to worship.

So on that Christmas day – the second of the war – Tullio had spotted on a chair, between the kneading bowl and the crib, the mask allotted to Elia.

It was in a tin container which looked like a harmless biscuit tin, except that instead of the brand name there ran a bold legend in black which read: *If you remove your mask you die. Keep it always with you.*

Tullio had glanced at the large, thick lenses – owl-eyes – the strap to be fastened at the back of the neck, the multiple layers of gauze, looking like a clumsy baby's napkin.

Why Elia had brought it with him on leave, he couldn't understand. But he had for some time ceased to think that everything made sense, that everything sported a reason.

It wasn't until later, when their parents and sister had gone to bed, that Elia had picked up the mask and shown it to his brother. His voice had taken on a light and casual tone, but Tullio had sensed the strain that underlay his words: "You know, they keep telling us that this is the best mask that soldiers can dream of… Actually, I dream of other things," and here Elia had winked at him, "but what do you think, Tullio?"

He had felt something hard and dry in his throat which certainly was not the turkey which had been immolated for their dinner.

"I really don't know what to say to you, Elia. You know I'm more expert about planes… But you just clap on that gadget at the slightest sign of danger, got it?"

"…they say that if you use it properly it protects you from

229

those damned gases. I really mean from all types. And that it's effective for over twenty-four hours. All we need now is to be told that it even cures asthma and the common cold. And syphilis, while we're about it…"

He seemed to be speaking for himself, with an intelligent boy's look, as if immersed in school memories, in chemical formulae from long ago.

"… you've just got to pour the alkaline solution on the gauze to protect you from the chlorine…"

"And what if we poured another drop of wine instead?"

Tullio had tried joking, handing him the wineglass. But suddenly he felt anguish come over him, and a subtle nausea.

Elia had knocked back his wine in one gulp, against his inclination. The bells of the church in the *piazza* had started ringing.

They'd gone upstairs, to their beds, without managing to look each other in the eye.

★ ★ ★

Tullio squeezes Greta's hand. The contact fortifies and reassures him: but it does not erase what he sees. She strokes his face with a finger and feels that it's chill and sweaty at once. Her body hugs his, but with delicacy and modesty.

Just to tell him, I'm here, and I won't let you go adrift.

It had been in October '17.

The successful use of gas in Flanders deserved to be repeated, on the Carso, Italy's eastern front. As the previous year, in spring, around Monte San Michele.

But this time the Austrians had studied every detail

punctiliously with extreme precision as the war had become more cruel and they had completed their apprenticeship. Wind direction, ground contours, optimum position for the chemical weapons battalion – broad alluvial terraces. Then nine hundred gas grenades – Tullio now knows the number – had burst simultaneously over the Plezzo depression and, from above, the toxic cloud had begun to descend with its smell of mouldy hay into the gullies and valleys, into the depressions in the ground, into the guts of the trench system, and then into throats and lungs: with no bursts of gunfire, without any booming, with the extreme discreetness of death creeping on its serpent belly and drifting in noiselessly. Then, out of those gas clouds – out of that slime-yellow blanket – shapes had slowly emerged, wielding spiked maces like those of feudal knights, as though spewed out of the Middle Ages: and those maces had come down on bodies already stunned – mere wraiths – to destroy any remnant of life.

How many had perished in those few seconds – never a scream nor the strength to react, no time to pray, or to curse – in the most absurd and total silence? Two and a half thousand, in the spring. Hundreds, in that second attack.

Tullio knows only that among them was his brother Elia, and that his gas-mask hadn't protected him from the phosgene.

Then everything crumbles in memory like crusts of dry bread: past and present, errors and faults, the delusions of the *maybes* and the *ifs*, the emptiness left over from then. Tullio feels such an urge to cry as has not come over him for a long time.

He reaches out to embrace Greta, finds confort in her warmth.

Then that unease, a bitter taste in his mouth. His has been a lengthy confession, memory flooding in while she listened: and with every image, with every word, the weight he has been carrying for so long became less absurd and less painful in being shared with Greta.

But all of a sudden he finds himself asking how he could speak to her of war and death, of horror, after making love. After their first time together.

Yet he seems to understand: whether it's a feeling of inescapable guilt or grief exploding like a grenade as soon as his defences were down, telling her now was no chance matter.

His brother will never experience what he has experienced today with Greta.

Perhaps his body sensed it: pleasure and pain go together, like the sense of life in its fulness and that of its fragility.

And after years of emptiness he senses that in him now there is peacefulness, as if his every grief – father and mother, brother and sister – had at last found a place which can contain it all and which perhaps is called forgiveness.

Greta is still there, beside him, breathing calmly, waiting.

She hasn't spoken, has asked no questions. She has sensed that it would be meaningless to offer words of comfort, that griefs so great cannot be dammed up.

Now she reaches out to him, strokes him. And at once they seek each other out once more, with an almost overwhelming urgency, and they make love as if their bodies have always known each other: warmly, simply. Like young spouses accustomed to sharing a bed, as well as pleasure.

For one instant – one instant only – he sees before him

again the huge expanse of stony rubble which was once his home, his district, his entire past.

But he senses that the wind has stopped, that at last it's no longer blowing.

And he wonders if this is how, as if muted, without grand gestures, one makes one's peace with God.

Summer

When it arrives, she feels it on her skin.
That's how summer announces itself.
Maybe she's cold-blooded, like a lizard, and needs the sun's rays.
Then she enjoys raising her face towards the sky and feeling the
warmth swathing her like soft fleeces whilst it makes the distant
outlines of things shimmer in bright gauze.

The stars at night atop the magnolia, resin seething on the tree-
trunks, the cicadas hidden in the fissures.
The smell of rotten seaweed.
The earth's relief when rain comes.

Even strength quivers, like the sultriness.
Thoughts become dust, scatter like swarms of bees.
She thinks of the leaps of grasshoppers, of the flight of bumble-
bees and hornets who seem to be seeking fresh water, pockets of
shade to rest in.

Even shadows sweat in August.
But it's easy to surrender to summer.

La Nazione

24 June 1920

Marconi's day in Fiume

At 15.30, welcomed by the siren of the Dante Alighieri, Guglielmo Marconi's magnificent yacht Elettra enters Fiume harbour and moors at the Cristoforo Colombo quay... His meeting with Commandant d'Annunzio is of the warmest... later on, during the afternoon, a crowd gathers in the square and there are loud calls for Senator Marconi, who then appears with the Commandant on the historic balcony, from where he delivers a speech addressing the people of Fiume... Subsequently, the Commandant and some of his officers forgather on board the Elettra as guests of Senator Marconi, who displays to them the ultra-powerful radio-telegraph equipment which enables Senator Marconi to converse with his friends in Paris, London and New York...

Using that equipment, news of the provisional government and of the historic moment which Fiume is going through with indomitable spirit and unyielding faith was transmitted. The illustrious scientist and his party listened with profound emotion to the words which d'Annunzio delivered over the world's airwaves.

Fiume
June 1920

"That's Corsica, isn't it?" asks the young lady, whom several bystanders turn to look at: she's standing on the pier in Fiume and pointing her finger towards the horizon out on to the azure Gulf of Carnaro.

Paul swings round and stares at her in astonishment. "You mean Cherso, don't you?"

She returns his stare, peevishly: "No, I mean Corsica. Napoleon's island."

For a moment, Paul is uncertain: should he explain to her that in between Fiume and Corsica, besides the Carnaro and the Adriatic, there lies the Italian mainland, including the regions of Emilia-Romagna and Tuscany and the Apennine peaks and then the Isle of Elba and a stretch of the Tyrrhenian sea?

In the end, he gives her an amiable smile: "Exactly right. It is Corsica. Well done."

She's good-looking, is the young woman. Even that ridiculous little hat that looks like icing on a cake can't ruin her profile, as of a slightly suspicious, a slightly pouting, cameo.

Standing beside her on the quay, Paul lingeringly observes her: hair gathered behind with a few blond curls escaping, red lips slightly pursed, that skimpy dress that seems to cling to her body and reveals with a touch of sauciness a hint of slender calf-muscle between skirt's frill and shoes.

Claire's her name, and she's a journalist. But what counts most is that she's French. And French, besides Latin and Italian, is the third language, in addition to his own, that he's had to learn.

And that's why Paul has been assigned the task of taking her on an exploratory tour of Fiume. After all, it's Paul who shares with the Belgian, Kochnitzky, the role of foreign minister in Fiume's *Bureau des Relations Extérieures*.

Paul looks away from the woman.

He has already given her an interview on the hows and the whys and wheres, on the initial objectives of the enterprise and on the significance of its evolution into something broader and more universal, and Claire struck him as being interested. Sceptical, and occasionally hostile, that's true, but also unquestionably interested.

At times the questions she asks are almost isolated details, like splinters that have escaped the system, fragments on which she dwells, composing a mosaic all of her own.

Why in your opinion has the Berlin Dada Club thrown its support behind d'Annunzio?

Is it true that Lenin has defined your poet commandant as

being the only Italian today who is capable of sparking off a revolution?

Who planned the flight over Paris? And what purpose have you achieved?

Then she looks at him more sharply: "I know that you, Dr Forst, are American. Can you explain to me what it is that you're doing here?"

He feels he's in the dock: the accused. But he's keen to explain, to try to make her understand.

"The United States are the only nation whose constitution declares the right to happiness. Everybody's right, not just its own. That's how I interpret that point."

"And, tell me, what does your government think about that?"

"I'd distinguish, if I may, between the American government and the American people. I'm not saying anything yet about the former, but as regards the latter I believe it thinks – or anyway respects – exactly what I think."

"You're a real optimist, aren't you?"

"I'm a person who has thought through his dreams."

"Are you perhaps referring to those chemico-neuro-cerebral phenomena, the nocturnal expressions of the unconscious, that have been investigated by Dr Freud?"

For a moment or two Paul doesn't reply. He gazes into the distance, towards the island of Cherso, towards the haze that hangs over the sea.

"I'm referring to something that knows how to forgive life even for its mortality."

Now it's her turn to stay silent. She winds a ringlet of hair around a finger.

"You amaze me, Dr Forst. I am standing in front of a

candid soul: you believe in destiny and progress and a human race that will march, a little bit at a time, straight towards happiness."

"On the contrary. I think too many countries – too many outcast peoples – are being excluded by diktat from that march towards happiness."

"And what has Fiume got to do with all that?"

"Fiume has lots to do with it. Shall I list the reasons alphabetically or shall I expand on them freely?"

"I'm sure that you'll find the latter style most congenial."

"In Fiume people are planning absolutely new projects, which could revolutionize the entire set-up of society: an international organization opposed to imperialism, full equality for women, a form of direct democracy based on productive labour, the reform of the prison system, schooling open to many languages and to all religions. And a modern constitution, based on principles so new as to scare more than the dyed-in-the-wool conservatives: divorce, the vote for women, job protection with the right to a minimum wage. But there are other issues: Fiume is a Latin city, a western city on the threshold to the Orient, to the Balkans. And it's a city that demands – and has been demanding for several months – to be heard. So don't you think it's a good point, since there has to be one, to start from?"

The woman looks at him in silence, then shifts her gaze towards the horizon, towards the furthest reaches of the Gulf of Carnaro. Her voice now is low, almost husky.

An unexpected flash of mischievousness suddenly lights up her entire face. "That's not Corsica, is it?"

Paul looks her in the eye, smiling. "No, it's not Corsica.

But it's nice to be able to think, occasionally, that one can see so far."

The Elettra, Marconi's yacht, is sailing out of the harbour.

Remaining silent, close together, the two of them walk off.

Abbazia
July 1920

It's been a dinner like many others, no less formal, not more strange. Elisa is in bed with a slight fever, her father's been away for a week.

So Greta's dined with her mother, just the two of them in the grand dining-room, sitting close together with elbows almost touching along the side of the table, but each immersed in her own thoughts.

They've only exchanged a few phrases, the clatter of their cutlery on the dishes seemingly amplified by the silence, the darkness marking out shadows as it gathered slowly around them, the cat curled up as ever in her nook beside the fireplace.

But, when dinner was over, harrying some apple peel with the knife she still held in her hand, her mother suddenly murmured: "Greta, I must talk to you."

Greta kept silent, feeling a subtle unease. She's noticed

that her mother is pale. And that announcement sounded strange, she felt a troubled atmosphere. The pendulum clock on the wall has struck nine.

Then her mother uttered that phrase that sounded different in timbre – infinitely sad – even more than in the words themselves: "At times one has to learn to make a little peace with oneself. With oneself and with one's life."

Why does she feel embarrassed, why is she now watching her mother and swallowing, already alarmed?

"Mamma, what's wrong? What do you mean?"

Then Else lifts up her face and at last looks at her. In her flushed eyes Greta reads everything which for so long – uncaringly, she thinks, or selfishly: because she refused to see – she has preferred not to grasp. And she struggles to meet that gaze. All she can do is get a little bit closer, and not only with her body and her face, in the simplest and most obvious way.

Then the words flow with assurance, as if they'd been often rehearsed: "I'll ask your father for a divorce."

For a moment Greta fails to understand, but feels her cheeks are burning. She doesn't manage to utter a sound. She listens to her mother as she ends: "I'll grant your father his freedom and myself a little dignity."

Greta feels a knot of pain that seems to catch at her throat.

So her mother could see. She noticed everything, and put up with it. So her detachment from all emotion wasn't so extreme. And she is also following what's happening in Fiume: couples arriving, sometimes after travelling from afar, so as to be able to get a legal divorce.

She'd like now to express her distress, and bring everything out into the open: her pain at this new ending, her unspoken love for her mother, her solidarity with her decision, her feeling of blank helplessness.

And at the same time she'd like to ask, to understand: is it one woman? Several women? Since when? And how long have you known, mamma?

But then, what does it matter, she asks herself. Numbers, names, length of time... What does it matter, if it's all over now?

As perhaps never before, she feels bound to her mother by a secret, invisible bond that has no need of words.

She just raises a hand to stroke that hand beside her. Her palm upon the back of the hand, squeezing gently. She feels a tremor, gives a start, shrinks back.

She feels a sudden temptation to open up in return, to speak out. It would be lovely to be sincere, to confide her own story at last, to feel for the first time perhaps that she's no longer merely her mother's daughter but a woman facing another woman: each capable of listening to the other, of understanding. Of sharing misgivings and fears, of letting their burdens be dissolved by an untried intimacy.

But she is stopped in time by her own good sense.

That's not the way life goes, in reality. Not for her, not right now. Not here.

So they stay, as darkness slowly gathers: feeling no further need to talk, or to move, or to turn on a light.

Abbazia
July 1920

It sticks out brightly coloured from a crack in the earth. It must have resurfaced after last night's storm.

The lower part of its body is still stuck in a fissure between the edge of the fountain with the putto statue in the middle and a boxwood border. Greta stoops and extracts it from the ground, then looks at it for a moment, the tin shiny with rain, on the open palm of her hand.

A tiny hussar standing to attention, rifle pointing up. One of her brother Arturo's toy soldiers, lost who knows how long before in some game.

Probably the last one left standing, the only one to have escaped the pyre that consumed the entire collection amid the flames in the fireplace, one now distant evening during the war which she still so well remembers.

She studies the uniform, the chevrons, the moustaches painted on to the face like two dark commas, the plume on his hat, the legs rigidly lined up above the minute boots: and she is moved and touched and seized by fierce nostalgia.

She dips the soldier in the water, scrapes off the clotted earth, wipes it dry on her skirt and then slips it into her pocket.

She can't tarry, she must be off now. A new task awaits her, which she herself has requested and wanted.

Closing the gate behind her, for a moment she takes in the beauty of this July day: the scent of jasmine that covers the stone wall, the air rinsed clean by the night's rain, two turtle-doves that spread their wings and fly together on to the same branch to resume the amorous ritual which has been interrupted by her footsteps crunching on the gravel of the footpath.

Out of an open window come the words of a song: *Blackcap they called her for her lovely black curls...*

Though the voice is out of tune, it sounds nice to her. Then someone shuts the window and the song tails off suddenly.

She notices a ladybird that's alighted on her bare arm and is now moving towards her wrist and on to the back of her hand.

Watching its progress over her skin, she wonders whether it will bring her luck.

Fiume
July 1920

" *The* Egyptians will greet with joy the hour in which your
... *just* demands are ratified... and let it also be equally soon
that the hour strikes in which the whole of Egypt can be free and
independent...

This war that has racked the world has not brought to everybody
the just and reparatory peace which was so eagerly awaited. Egypt is
the chiefest among its victims...But we shall prevail. British
imperialism must yield. It must yield, for the sake of historical morality,
of the happiness of nations, and of worldwide security.

We shall prevail. The drama unfolding in Egypt is but one
episode, though a highly significant one, of the intense drama that is
being enacted in the secret recesses of political consciousness between
the selfish theories of the past and the principles which must guide
humanity's march towards a future of ever more perfect justice.

We shall prevail. Brute force fails with time, but the law of the
spirit is eternal...

We have noted, with profound consolation, that Italy alone has up to this day refused to recognize the British protectorate over Egypt.

…To you, who have in your poet's heart found such moving accents of sympathy for our cause, I can assure the deepest friendship and gratitude of all my compatriots."

Paul has read the document carefully, underlined some passages, jotted down some reflections and scribbled some notes in the margin in his spiky hand-writing. Then he adds a memorandum at the foot of the page.

The signature at the bottom is bold and terse, black: Saad Pasha Zaghloul. The man who has put himself at the head of the movement for Egyptian independence, and who is living in exile in Paris. The League of Oppressed Peoples – Paul is working at it energetically along with some fellow thinkers – must now become a reality. The list of peoples that they aim to weld into an Anti-League of Nations is a long one, an organization of national groups who do not have seats at the victors' table: from the Germans within Poland to those within Czechoslovakia, from the Egyptians to the Afghans, from the Irish to the Flemings. And then the Indians, the Albanians, the Croats…

It is such an ambitious list that he himself at times is startled at the scale of the undertaking, at the grandeur of the dream which he refuses to renounce. Sure, there's hard work to be done, but that has never scared him.

Yet, for some weeks now, he's had the impression that they need to speed things up, as if time itself – not the difficulties he's been encountering – is his worst enemy. Then the memory suddenly hits him, with a shudder redolent of desire which seems to go right through him. He recalls the heat of the night, the delight that lasted till daybreak, the tangle of bedclothes.

He sat up and gazed at her. It gave him pleasure to watch her sleeping. Her bare shoulder, her neck, her profile. The weight of her breast. When his lips touched hers, she scratched her cheek and slightly wrinkled her nose in her sleep, suddenly kicking away the sheets and huddling up away from them.

He got up, went over to the window, rested his forehead against the pane to stare at the old everyday world which has now become familiar to him and yet now looked so new: the deserted pier in the dawn light, the pearly brightness out at sea, the town shaking itself out of its slumber with the precise sensation of having lost its entire past without gaining any glimpse of a future.

He forced himself to think of the morning ahead and its pressing business and engagements. Of his colleagues already at their posts up at the Palace, and the scurrying in the various offices.

And he felt strong yet light, exhausted yet full of energy.

The sky was clear and cloudless: it promised to be a beautiful day.

Fiume
July 1920

The little girl walks boldly, her over-size checked pinafore hanging loosely around her knees, her hair a tousled mop right over her blue eyes, an immaculate large bow on her head sitting slightly askew and failing to discipline her boisterous curls.

She could be aged eight or nine – one gathers from her set gaze and certain serious glances – but she's pale and slender, diminutive, and is struggling to keep up with her friends' fast pace in the file.

All her energy seems to go into the firm grasp with which she holds her younger brother, three or four years her junior, by the hand, towing him behind her: his little face streaked with tears, his mouth and chin smeared with mucus which he keeps wiping over his face as he vainly tries to clean himself with his soiled sleeve and with his fingers.

They don't have far to go, but the little ones' gait slows

them down. Reaching the final crossroads, the long line of children turns off to the left.

From here Greta can see that entire crocodile of children heading slowly towards Fiume's railway station along the avenue running parallel to the waterside, holding hands in pairs.

The youngest children – no older than three or four – are in front and strike her as little chicks: heads turning round curiously, drawn by tiny details – a cat, a canary at a window, a soldier going past, a fisherman with a full basket dripping a trail of water – and looking out all around as if pecking out of the air something visible only to themselves. Some of the little boys wear caps of coarse dark canvas which don't make them look any more grown-up, the girls have long tresses held by smart bows: as if they were the last strongholds of dignity which they were hanging on to with no intention of giving up.

Shoes, on the other hand, are a disaster. Some are even without: several in carpet-slippers, and wooden clogs that make a shuffling noise, sharp and soft under those feet.

In fact, clothing and footwear have been among the first things to run out.

They walk strangely silent. Hardly any child says anything, not one – Greta observes – is smiling.

This is not an outing, not a trip to the countryside: even the smallest children have no difficulty in understanding that, as they march hand in hand. Their mothers have been requested not to accompany them to the station, but to entrust them to the organizers and to display confidence: better avoid embraces and long-drawn-out laments which would sound like final farewells and would certainly spread dismay.

They are led by a corpulent, severely garbed lady wearing school-ma'amish shoes who walks at the head of the file in conversation with an officer. She has organized the whole thing: the journey into Italy, hospitality with families that have volunteered, the required documents for the over two hundred children now setting out for Milan. And five hundred more will be leaving, to be received in Florence and Bologna and rescued from the hardships being endured in Fiume.

The town has been short of food since March.

So, in Italy, some women have launched this initiative: out – get the children out. Assure them for a few weeks of regular, reliable, hot meals: feed and clothe them for a while. At least the ones most in need, of which indeed there are not a few.

Greta insisted on joining in and helping. And Else in the end gave in to her headstrong daughter, giving her permission, maybe sensing that in any case she couldn't have stopped her.

Since her father left home, the atmosphere hasn't greatly improved: Greta sees her mother suffer, though, she thinks, differently: with a somewhat relieved reserve, with a dignity and a silence that seem to her the fruit of reflection and not of desperate solitude, not of self-effacement. She would like to grasp what she could do to get closer to her, but she hasn't been able to recapture the magic of that single instance in which her mother had bared her soul and accepted her comradeship.

And it has been such a job seeing to the children's transfer: Greta has found herself involved in the weirdest and most diverse tasks. Processing data, compiling charts, relieving many women already hard-pressed from inescapable guilt feelings, as if they were abandoning their children rather than saving them from hunger in an emergency. And collecting items of clothing, cleaning their hair with paraffin – the children squirming like eels under the soaked cloth – to get rid of even the slightest hint of head-lice, of nits, of neglect and penury.

But she still had some misgivings, thoughts of possible alternatives: "Are you sure it's a good idea to send them away from home?" she had asked Tullio yet again, in the thick of that distressing transfer. For some time, their exchanges had been ever more focused on the emergencies of the moment, on some concrete problem.

"I think it's better this way," he'd replied, deep in thought. "You yourself know how things are going in Fiume. The Red Cross is doing all it can, but there's only a trickle of foodstuffs coming into the town. Food is getting scarcer all the time and it's the kids more than anyone that pay the price of penury, delays, gaps. The kids and the elderly, as always. A few less mouths to feed will give breathing-space to their families."

That was true, as she well knew. Pasta and rice, oats and flour... not to mention milk or meat. Everything now was really in short supply. The National Town Council had issued strict regulations: no confectionery was to be produced or sold, no cakes, chocolate, goodies. Meat consumption reduced to the minimum, many food items rationed in eating-houses. But it was a very hard choice.

"But some of these tots have never left home. And they're so tiny, you should see them..."

"Listen. The government wants to bring this business to

an end. You realize this occupation of Fiume is an ever-growing embarrassment for Rome. Perhaps they've decided, I don't know… to starve the city into surrender."

"But they can't do that! It would be inhuman!"

"In fact they're playing for time, you can see that. But for how long, Greta? For how much longer? Nitti has even tried to stop the children from leaving Fiume and being hosted in Italy. What do those kids mean to him? Propaganda in favour of the rebel subversives, negative publicity for Rome."

Greta knew that, too.

There had been more stonewalling on both sides. She had felt humiliated – as if personally discomfited – by that rebuff to good sense: in the end the clash had been resolved by the threat of force, not by dialogue, which is what she believed in. *The children will get through at any cost*: so the commandos had sworn.

And they had added a promise: they would put them on board a steamer and ship them to Venice under the escort of a destroyer with orders to open fire on anyone preventing the young refugees from disembarking in the lagoon.

★ ★ ★

Then the sudden downpour and the march turns into a rout: the line wavers and scatters, the smallest kids scooped up by troopers and carried shoulder-high amid yelling and laughter, the bigger children rushing off and needing to be kept close together.

She finds herself carrying a little boy and holding a girl by the hand amid the general helter-skelter. But the station is only a few steps further on. Within a few minutes, they're there. She dries off wet hair as best she can, picks up lost clogs, comforts some muffled weeping.

She herself is wet through, and chilled. Then that curious, unfamiliar environment – the waiting trains, the hurrying and scurrying, the station-master's whistle – cheers up and diverts the children. But not the toddler she's been carrying and has now set down again just close by: digging his heels in and bursting into tears, he clings on to a bench. His sister tugs at his arm and proffers him a morsel of bread which she's fished out of the pocket of her pinafore.

For an instant the toddler stops crying, greedily snatches the small hunk and gobbles it up whole. Then starts sobbing desperately again.

Greta goes and squats beside him. She slips her hand into her pocket and brings out Arturo's toy soldier and presents it to him with a wink. His eyes popping, he clutches it. He turns it around admiringly.

Meanwhile Greta talks to him quietly. Little by little he begins to listen: "…so, this train, you see, is going to be taken by storm by a heap of kids from Abbazia who want to take your places and go away instead of you."

The little boy is still shaken by his sobbing, but he goes on gazing at the toy soldier, noting the details in the metal, while his nose sniffs up his misery, his desperate sobs.

"But now you and this soldier will fight off even the worst foes from your wagon, you'll see. You kids are made of the right stuff, don't you agree? You're the ones who deserve to go on this holiday in Milano. D'you feel up to defending your train along with your brave buddies?"

Now the little fellow is looking at her. She takes her

handkerchief from her pocket and gives his nose a wipe. "Well, then, tell me, do you feel up to it?"

He glances down again at the soldier. The idea is tempting, but he won't give in. Then, after another moment, he nods, serious and tight-lipped: an understated manly signal.

She nods back: "Report back in one month, general."

Then, with his sister once more holding him by the hand, she watches him board the train.

As he gets to the top step, the little boy turns for a moment seeking out Greta amid the station's hustle and bustle. His pout doesn't yet spell peace, and is certainly not a smile, but is the least unconsolable she's been able to get out of him.

Then – just as the train is moving off – Greta sees him, contrite, standing up against a window. It's just an instant, a fleeting gesture: probably he's on tip-toe to reach the window-glass as he lifts one hand to his brow in a brisk military salute.

Relieved, she responds, standing to attention. Then winks at his sister.

La Nazione
10 September 1920

The Commandant's Oath

… In the evening, over thirty-five thousand townspeople gathered in Piazza Roma. Gabriele d'Annunzio, appearing at the balcony of the Government Palace, delivered one of his memorable speeches…: "Devoutly interpreting the freely expressed will of the majority of the sovereign people of Fiume gathered in Parliament, from this balcony where… the will of the people has been reconfirmed several times… I, Gabriele d'Annunzio, first of the legionaries of Ronchi, proclaim the Regency of Carnaro…"

The delirious applause of the enormous mass of citizens was echoed by the town bells and the ships' sirens…

The human mass poured on to the streets, singing, and processions were formed, led by bands playing music.

The Fifth Season

Pinpricks of cold are back again, the incessant blasts of the bora.

Two geese in the mud, a hoe, a comet's tail, a chrysanthemum bloom.
That's what's in the frost this morning.
In a corner, standing behind the window panes, she runs her finger across that white iced landscape. Then she blows on her fingers to warm them, gazing silently at the garden.

The carpet of leaves, the dry branches.
The palm fans numb with cold.
A shovel stuck in the ground.
The fountain's jets of ice.

The cat rubs against her ankle, arches its back and its tail.
Elisa crouches and strokes it, seeking out the reflection of her face in those pupils.

Then she muses that everything's changed, ever since there's been that new empty space at home.
Ever since Christmas arrived. Ever since Greta, too, went away.

La Nazione
21 September 1920

The Address by Benito Mussolini

TRIESTE – Benito Mussolini addresses the Triestines… freely, openly, expressing his ideas without holding back any truth… "In the past fifty years Italy has achieved marvellous progress. First and foremost there is a point of fact, and that is the vitality of our breed, of our race… Besides the forty million Italians in Italy, there are ten million that have spilled over into every continent, across every ocean. And alongside this demographic development there's been commercial, industrial, agricultural and cultural development.

And don't talk to me of reaction, of reactionary political forms. Because if there is a country in the world where liberty is almost verging on license, that liberty which is the inalienable patrimony of every citizen, that country is none other than Italy…

If there is something that needs saying in Italy, that is that it's time to impose iron discipline on individuals and on multitudes…"

Fiume
November 1920

They walk fast, close together, under a sky so grey and opaque that it looks as if it's caked with slime.

Both of them wearing a dark cloak – the same tough woollen gabardine picked by mothers used to dealing hard-headedly both with daughters and with cloth – their sides touch as they chat.

Ever since Edith came back home – she ended up staying in Vienna a lot longer than expected – she and Greta have been seeing each other again, but their former closeness seems somehow to have dissolved, their adolescence now over, as if the two young women who met up again at summer's end were in part changed. Without acknowledging it even to themselves, they feel they are different people. Greta was not too surprised by the news that Edith has at last been engaged to her distant Viennese cousin. "I knew it," was her only comment. "… The person who talks the price down, ends up buying the goods."

And she thought the only person who couldn't see – who couldn't read her own self, who couldn't understand – was her friend.

On her return to Abbazia, Greta's found Edith to be more mature, strengthened by a newfound equilibrium, at times even predictable in the somewhat opaque meekness with which she seems to embrace a future into which she now sinks effortlessly, like currants in risen dough.

Greta, on the other hand, is more nervous and restless. So she is, at least, to Edith's eyes. At times difficult to make out, distant, her mind straying who knows where, yet at the same time immersed in the present – in Fiume's latest goings-on – with a dogged persistence which at times makes Edith recall the impetus with which Greta, as a child, would clamber up the branches of a tree.

There was a period when their closeness made even speech unnecessary: at times all that was needed was a glance, or a matey, understanding smile, and immediately they'd be sister spirits.

But something has changed between them in their crossing over into the world of adults, as if the hut at the bottom of the park could no longer hold them both: now each had a different gait, a different horizon. And different expectations, different goals. Today, however, they're walking close together, light-footed as before, electric: they're on their way to the station, where something awaits them that certainly doesn't happen every day.

The great lime-trees lining the avenue spread out their now denuded branches, but rounding a corner, the sea unfolds before them in the distance: and Greta even manages to catch the sound of the waves biting at the stanchions, a dense seething up against the pier. The dog suddenly appears, stiff-haired and wild-eyed, having perhaps just slipped out of a garden. They are paralyzed by surprise and, straight after, by fear.

The mastiff's sustained snarl displays the sharp whine of canines, a rasping, wide-jawed ferocity. Greta feels terror grip her, tingling spread from finger-tips along to her hands: she can't avert her gaze from the beast's maw as it slowly advances towards them.

Then a curt command calls it back: the dog runs towards its master, and both disappear into a garden.

Greta takes a moment or two to regain her composure, while she feels Edith relaxing her grip on her hand.

Then she walks on again with her friend, who in turn forces a smile. The station is close by: they're there. She feels as though there is in the air – glass-like – besides the smell of smoke, the dry, gripping chill that betokens the season's first frost.

As she goes up those few steps she senses a subtle disquiet, as if the encounter with that dog had turned into an omen of lurking danger.

★ ★ ★

The train draws slowly to a halt amid a prolonged hiss of air in the heart of the little station.

The Maestro is first to alight, holding his violin case in one hand, instinctively clasping it to his chest as if to guard it from knocks, and his light luggage in the other hand.

He is followed by his wife and children, then the long

line of musicians, each with his instrument which impresses the bystanders, and each glancing curiously around at people's faces and the unfamiliar place, which the newspapers have been full of for months. Then a roar of applause bursts out, as if the waiting crowd had only just fully realized that the scene is for real, that it's really him, that it's really his orchestra that's come with him and that by his very presence he backs Fiume's cause and its demands to be heard.

And suddenly a tenor voice rises strong above the noise of that ovation and starts to chant that name: *Toscanini Toscanini Toscanini.*

Instantly the name goes round, it grows into an excited tumult, swells and rises amid the buildings. The Maestro stands still, smiling, half abashed and half flattered.

Behind him, between two trailing crowds – like the somewhat frayed tails of a topcoat – the group accompanying him also comes to a halt, in a mass of bodies, instruments and hand luggage.

It's a sudden, unexpected gesture: out of its rigid case, Toscanini whips out his baton, a springy, ebony baton, to which is tied a blue ribbon that traces a note in the air.

Around him, every sound is stilled. And in that silence, hesitantly, looking at one another in astonishment and then twigging and gaining assurance, the musicians take their instruments out of their cases, which are left on the ground, at their feet: and in the space left free they form a broad semi-circle facing Toscanini.

Jammed against the wall, almost at the end, Tullio holds his breath. It seems to him that there's something sacred about that moment. Deep down, he hoped for it from the moment he got here. Not a concert for the few enclosed in the town theatre, which he knows will take place tomorrow evening, but a musical experience outside the conventions, on offer to everybody with no other ritual than that of bodily closeness and shared listening.

The opening notes trickle out muted, Tullio recognizing them as *Va' pensiero*: at first, still tremulous and subdued, then progressively more powerful and grieving with the force of the strings and the sottovoce of the woodwind. For an instant Tullio closes his eyes, leans against the wall.

Under closed eyelids, in darkness, he sees what he didn't realize he still had within him, still remembered.

A doll sticking out in the middle of nothingness in the wind that whines quietly.

A cloud of smoke rising – like a sudden blaze – and beginning to fill the gullies of a pock-marked landscape.

His father with the fishing-line over his shoulder above a field billowing with mist, where the mulberry bushes mark out the boundaries between the swathes of fog and the crooked edges of a watercourse.

The halo of the tips of the ears of wheat in fields of ripe grain.

A broad waste of stony rubble.

The line of Greta's torso.

Then he opens his eyes and spots her – she looks lost in thought, far away – as if an invisible compass had drawn a circle and set its centre right there, on Greta's slightly lowered face. Intently listening with the rest as she stands beneath that shelter.

Without moving, he goes on watching her. The line of her cheekbones and chin, her slender neck rising from the mantle that outlines her shoulders, her long brown hair curling slightly in the damp air. The hand she raises to her brow, her body backing a step from a man's sudden shove.

What is the desire for possession, the fear of losing the one you love, the tension that makes you feel you own a body you hardly know, the wounds it hides, its mysteries? He doesn't know, but he goes on looking at her. If he just waved his hand, if he tried somehow to attract Greta's attention which has strayed elsewhere, if she then noticed his gesture or at least guessed its intention, perhaps everything might – all of a sudden – derail on to a different track.

But Tullio keeps still. He doesn't move. He just lets the music take him over until it ends in silence.

And when the thunder of the applause begins to swamp everything around and people pour out, he realizes that now it's too late. He can no longer pick her out through the turmoil around him.

The right moment has passed, and apparently Greta has gone away.

La Nazione
13 November 1920

FIUME – Yesterday four new cases of bubonic plague were confirmed. Two of the cases involved military personnel, and two involved civilians.

The authorities are silent on the matter so as not to alarm the population.

Milan
November 1920

The small private room of the *Savini* restaurant has been fitted out for meetings which are not meant to attract attention, and its décor is discreet: soberly wall-papered, hung with valuable period prints, a blue and white vase with delicate grotesques in one corner, a Louis XVI sideboard along one wall beyond the walnut dining-table. On the sideboard, a crystal vase with a bunch of long-stemmed roses and a little brass handbell to be used as needed.

The restaurant – in the Galleria Vittorio Emanuele – is run by staff who are not only highly professional, but also utterly discreet.

The man isn't particularly tall, but his stout build, his gold-rimmed pince-nez, his perfectly groomed pepper-coloured beard and whiskers give him an air of distinction, as does also his beautifully tailored jacket and the heavy silver fob-watch that he extracts from his waistcoat pocket. Pippo

Naldi has an air of assurance and the briskly businesslike manner of one who is accustomed to handling the controls and the levers of power.

He is not solely a frequenter of the most exclusive bourse and business circles: his status as a wealthy financier has long enabled him to enter the holy of holies of Italian politics.

Sitting beside him – stiff and stern as a Templar in chainmail – elder statesman Giolitti's other envoy talks smoothly but precisely as one who is expert at weighing his words and bending them effortlessly to his meaning.

The third man sits opposite the other two.

His frame is massive, assertive. His jacket, made of heavy corduroy, looks tightly creased about the shoulders.

The strong features of his face seem to betray ancient attachments to a stock that loves to eat well, that appreciates fine wine: but even if that temptation to hedonism were his vocation, you can sense that it is held in check by a powerful inner tension, by a laborious discipline stubbornly maintained.

He's been eating sparingly and has hardly touched a drop. He's been listening a long time, and attentively.

The gravity of the moment seems to have clenched his jaws. His mouth now is a taut line.

His hand rests on the table on which is spread a snow-white Flemish linen cloth speckled with bread-crumbs: his fist aligned with the cutlery with the back of his hand touching the knife's blade as if to test it. His knuckles are the size of dried walnuts almost blanched by the tension. At length he spreads out his fingers over the table-napkin.

His palm cleaves to the linen cloth, and as he raises his head which has been bowed while he was listening, his gaze suddenly sharpens and reveals an underlying astuteness, cold and hard. Or perhaps merely alert, focused, as if intent on divining and gauging, on anticipating blows and niceties to be caught instantly.

He leaves room for the final words of a discourse now nearing its end which has suddenly opened up to him an unlooked-for scope for action, horizons quite unhoped-for.

Meanwhile, Naldi winds up: "… Enough of articles in your newspaper, then. Enough of appeals, subscriptions, propaganda. If you give us your word that from this moment on – from *now* – you will not back d'Annunzio in any way whatsoever and that you will leave him to his destiny… the destiny of a visionary… a destiny which in any case has already been marked out…"

This is followed by a little cough, a clearing of the throat.

"Then we can guarantee you that at the next elections your party…" only a slight pause "… will enjoy the fullest possible support from us."

His gaze has gone razor-sharp.

"Total and trustworthy support. Possibly a harbinger of great new developments. For yourself, for your political forces and… who knows… for the entire country."

Pippo Naldi slowly rises to his feet. The other two follow suit.

"Well, then, do you give us your word?"

The moment's pause is calculated, as if controlled by invisible strings.

The four-square jaws of the man who so far has sat and listened suddenly twitch.

Then his voice comes out firmly: "Agreed. I give you my word."

And, perhaps for the first time, the financier smiles, as does his ally.

The handshakes are firm and brisk. With repeated nods as he looks deep into his eyes, Naldi adds in a low voice, with satisfaction: "Don't worry, my dear sir. You won't regret it, you'll see."

The champagne cork pops and shoots against the wall. The champagne releases its fragrance in the long narrow flutes.

The timbre of the financier's voice is deep as he raises the goblet to his lips: "To the new era."

The man facing him smiles: "To the new era."

And this time Mussolini drinks.

La Nazione

17 November 1920

...The Treaty of Rapallo, shown here, concluded between the King of Italy and the Kingdom of Serbs, Croats and Slovenes, and signed at Rapallo on 12 November 1920, has been approved.

The King's Government is authorized to give full and complete effect to the Treaty...

With the Serbo-Croatian-Slovenian State, the Treaty of Rapallo sows the seed for further agreements intended to open up a fertile field of close cooperation between the two neighbouring peoples... for the general well-being and for peace in Europe.

Fiume, Government Palace
December 1920

S tanding at the window, d'Annunzio peers into the distance. The ships' impressive shapes are rimmed by the light of the setting sun as if by embroidery: two battleships, three tugs, eight destroyers. Overnight arrivals from Italy, they are now arrayed at the entrance to the harbour in decisive battle order.

The naval blockade is now complete. All contact with Fiume is totally interrupted from this moment.

So the government has made up its mind: it is ready to use force. Italians against Italians, as for hundreds and hundreds of years past.

The sea today is grey and turbulent, the sky a leaden pall.

D'Annunzio goes to his desk, sits down. He seems to hear his own words uttered a short while ago in his most recent address: he leaning forward from the palace balcony, the crowd packed in the square, thronging the stairways and the street that leads down to the pier. But he had felt a tightness in his chest, a weight that came close to overwhelming him. Even a feeling of nausea such as had never affected him before then.

Dumbfounded, the people listened.

I tell you that this balcony has now become hateful to me like the bars of a cage. I feel the urge to smash it and use its fragments for stoning.

True. He feels exhausted. A prisoner in his own palace. Caught among intriguing go-betweens, wheeler-dealers in fine suits, peremptory ultimatums from the government, furious, unremitting streams of ambassadors extraordinary, sometimes self-appointed, who represent no one but their own ambitions.

But that feeling of oppression is something else. Desertion by many of his comrades. Defections by his friends.

My heart aches, comrades, through having watched so many in whom I trusted fall away around me, through having suffered betrayal by so many before the cock crowed for the second time.

For an instant, he bows his head.

Admiral Millo has given way. He almost feels he understands him.

Really and truly, he did hold him in high esteem, that former Navy Minister – and governor of Dalmatia – who has always fought courageously: for his integrity, for his consistency. For the risks which, after all, he has taken, for the burdens, however unwieldy and unwelcome, that he has not hesitated to shoulder. But he knows that the King wrote to him in person, enjoining him to leave Fiume and to abandon its cause. A Prefect will now take his place.

D'Annunzio grasps his pen, then drops it again.

The treaty between Italy and Yugoslavia is now done and dusted. It was signed at Rapallo on 12 November, at dead of night. And it was fully implemented in all haste, without even awaiting approval by the Senate.

Italy did not gain Dalmatia, as had been agreed before the war. Some attempts at protest – he knows of one in Trieste and one in Venice – were nipped in the bud by dint of armoured vehicles and cavalry charges.

As for Fiume, it's been declared a small independent State, but he senses a different outcome.

He looks around the room. Once more he takes up the pen.

His thoughts swing like a pendulum, drift like a mine. He feels them fly and explode, resurface and then collapse once more amid doubts of every kind, and temptations: carve a way out. Fight on. Compromise. Never surrender. Rant to the crowd that has now dispersed: "I've been just a parenthesis. Now the sentence is up to you. You are this town, its history."

He picks up a sheet of paper from the desk, crumples it in the palm of his hand.

No, he can't make out Millo. It's treason. He can't make him out, he doesn't want to. He had undertaken a solemn bond with the Italians of Dalmatia. He had sworn loyalty. What's become of his promise?

A few hours back, as he watched the warships arrayed outside the harbour ready to attack, he had leaned over the balcony and had injected into his voice everything he was now feeling, from despair to fury, and from tension to rage, going by way of fear and stubbornness.

Millo has answered: "I obey." I answer: "I disobey." One man is lost.
One man stands fast.

Those had been his last words. The crowd had burst into a roar.

He had glanced at his hands and had seen them trembling.

15 December 1920

Disposition of naval forces.

Italian naval forces will have to provide support for the Army to take Fiume by assault.

    The following are my dispositions in this regard:

• The battleships Vittorio Arturo and Andrea Doria will leave the Pola anchorage and head for Fiume

• The light craft Fabrizi and Stocco will take up positions at the entrance to Fiume harbour

• The light craft Espero, Zefiro, La Farina and Bronzetti will position themselves parallel to the pier within one mile from it so as to be able to approach the Dante and the Mirabello which are moored there

• The Riboty and the Falco shall position themselves two miles off the pier

• The tugs Calipso, Titano and Marittimo will keep close to the Riboty at the mouth of the harbour.

Keep ready for action.

    Further orders will be issued very soon.

Signed
Admiral Caviglia

Fiume
December 1920

"Maybe I can still manage to get you out of here, Claire – to get you through the blockade. You've got to leave as soon as possible. You've got to get out of here immediately."

Paul's voice sounds tired to her ears, and seems to be coming from a long way off.

The bedsheets now emit a rustling sound that wafts a hint of perfume.

Silently, Claire muses about so much. That those six months have been lovely. That this town has bewitched her ever since the first day she set foot in it. That now all she feels like doing is smoke, curl up beneath the blankets, put off any decision as she sometimes used to do as a child, when everything seemed too big and the challenge made her weak at the knees and down her spine.

And she goes on musing about so much else as she

reaches out for him, to touch his body, his warmth.

She muses over the disjointed words – steeped in anguish, obsessive – which she's heard him utter in his agitated slumbers. She muses on how one can change one's mind while continuing to remain oneself and sensing that everything is getting uncertain, fluctuating like seaweed in the waves. No longer any true or false. Right or wrong. A world that escapes judgement: blurred, complex, crumbling. Just like the light in Fiume which had so struck her at first. The most liquid and bright she'd ever seen: maybe because it seems to hold the north's vivid chill but also the winds from the east and the languor of southern climes, their meek surrender to that sea.

No questions asked, no demands made. Promising nothing but the freedom to be together or to take leave light-heartedly, outside convention and hypocrisy, ownership or claims.

Honey licked off the fingers. Laughter in drinking Terrano, in between an article and a document, a proposal and a report. The figs they've devoured together, touching avidly: the thick drops from the fruit's flesh smearing the bedsheet, teeth suddenly clinking, tongues seeking each other.

His hand touching her, penetrating her hard or else with extreme tenderness, preparing her for love.

And love-making in bed or standing, in darkness or in the most pitiless light, guiding or letting oneself go.

She muses also that really she's betrayed everything that others expected of her: mockery, sarcasm, condemnation. Words that put a noose round that situation, that exploit, the entire Fiume business. While she has filled her articles with other things: doubt, suspicion, questioning. Complexities that cannot be caged in, flummoxing chiaroscuros. The rejection of black-and-white judgements.

But anyhow, that no longer matters, because her articles have never been published.

Claire reaches out to the bedside table, picks up the packet of cigarettes. The match's small flame lights up her profile for an instant. She inhales deeply, then passes the cigarette to Paul.

For a moment she listens to the rain beating at the window, steadily: it reminds her of other places, other moments. Of once familiar geographies. Land wrested from the marshes, the violet fields of lavender, the rosy salt-pans of a delta, the scent of eucalyptus and of gentians. Landscapes so remote that she wonders whether she'll ever be able to recognize them, whether she'll manage to feel they still belong to her. She lifts herself up on her side, looks at him. "D'you really think I could leave now that the fun's just about to start?"

Then she reads his glance, senses the hollowness of her words. She recognizes them as stupid and disloyal, incapable of real feigning. So she drops her vacuous tone and just smooths out a crease in the bedsheet.

She watches the cigarette smoke. The way it rises and disperses and makes the air quiver, and the emptiness, and the walls. The way it's now enveloping his profile.

Then she stubs out the cigarette butt and smiles. "I've got some bad news for you."

Paul waits without saying anything.

"I'm not leaving. I'm staying with you."

La Nazione
16 December 1920

At 6.15 this morning, eight vessels entered the harbour, several destroyers with two or three funnels and the Riboty… the names of the other ships could not be made out because of the fog.

Off Port'Albona a great ship can be seen approaching. It is thought to be the Andrea Doria, with the Pola commandant, Admiral Simonetti, on board… The landward blockade is now very tight: there is no way in or out of Fiume and its territory. The Regency has no means of communicating with the outside world except by means of its aircraft.

Captain Host-Venturi has been put in command of the city's defences and his first act has been to invite all foreigners to leave the State of Fiume within three days. He has further declared a curfew between 11pm and 5am and the severest penalties for officials or employees who abandon their posts or their tasks.

… One person who managed to get to Abbazia last night sends us this report: Fiume is perfectly calm. The citizenry are unanimous in wanting to follow d'Annunzio to the bitter end.

Fiume
24 December 1920, afternoon

Tullio walks up to a shop-window and looks at the covers of the books among the glassware knick-knacks.

In one corner, the little fir-tree, snowy with cotton-wool and adorned with red and gold globes and bright streamers, brings upon him a nostalgia that shades into something different, an incredulous, almost childlike, merriment.

He wonders whether to enter that shop or whether to go on looking around a bit longer in search of a more central store. Not that he expects any big finds. And Fiume has quite other urgent needs. But he does want to get a present for Greta, however modest and unpretentious. Just a bare festive gesture which he will place in her hands at the holidays' end, as soon as she goes back to school.

He's never enjoyed these rituals. But today he feels they have a new meaning, and he feels like joining in with everyone else in a Christmas Eve which people pretend is the same as so many previous ones. There's a smell of smoke in the air, and a vague promise of snow. The cold is now vivid and pungent. Off the sea, from time to time, a stiff wind blows. Objects have sharp clear profiles in that raw, flawless light.

The shops have little to offer, but have been dressed out in style, recalling the old days: garlands and decorated fir trees, white tallow candles in ancient polished candelabra, sprigs of holly and mistletoe held by gold ribbon, the red berries glowing like live coals amid the deep green of the foliage.

Tullio had felt uneasy as he roamed the streets this morning.

Upon waking, he had seen through the window the newly arrived warships of the Italian navy arrayed in the distance in attack formation at the entrance to the harbour. He had no trouble these days in recognizing the outlines of the torpedo boats and the great bulk of the battleships like gorged predators.

For days they had been lurking in the vicinity, but today they had struck him as being closer and locked in a more threatening and compact formation. He'd wondered whether this impression was an illusion induced by tiredness, the result of an almost wholly sleepless night: only towards morning had he managed to subside into brief and shallow slumber, when the winter dawn had already begun to outline furniture and objects: his desk, cluttered with papers, the gramophone shaped like a flower, the jumble of his jacket and clothes tossed on the chair at the foot of the bed.

On waking, he'd had some bitter coffee and had then hurried to the Palace to glean the latest news, counting on finding Paul there already.

The atmosphere in which he found himself on the staircases and in the corridors was the first thing that struck him: febrile yet calm at the same time, as if immersed in the expectation of something, with men scurrying this way and that with seeming urgency yet aimlessly.

The news his friend gave him was not at all reassuring.

From Rome, the Senate's ratification of the Treaty of Rapallo, notwithstanding abstention by the Socialists.

The ultimatum to d'Annunzio from General Caviglia, commanding the blockading forces, on behalf of the Italian government. D'Annunzio's brusque refusal to comply with that injunction, his intention to respond to an attack – were it actually to be made – meeting force with force. And his latest message to the legionaries, delivered in that hard, cutting tone which grew ever more tense and charged with anger and bitterness at the latest twist of events.

Anyone who doesn't wish to have his throat cut has until tomorrow evening to go through the barrier. Legionaries, every one of you is free to break your oath and obey the injunction. All he has to do is lay down his weapons, his gear… He will receive from the other side fatherly approval, an appropriate gratuity, and the promise of honourable inclusion in the association of amnestied deserters, which is one of the most flourishing and well remunerated within the Kingdom.

But not one of them had stirred. Not one had left.

"Will they attack?" Tullio, already at the door, had asked his friend.

"D'Annunzio doesn't think so. He doesn't think they will go that far."

Tullio had noted the bags under his eyes, the new set of his mouth, a fatigue similar to his own.

"And what do you think, Paul?"

Paul had looked at him silently, and the silence had dragged on awkwardly, hesitantly.

"I think... my God." He had broken off. "I think you're a nation that has given of its best – Michaelangelo, Leonardo, the Renaissance – at those moments when your history has sunk lowest through internal strife, wars. Through foreign oppression. And I wonder whether that means something."

Tullio had looked away. He had taken his time, then nodded. Then he had made a strange new gesture, which he certainly was not used to making between the two of them: without smiling, without replying, he had shaken him by the hand.

Yet now, amid the hustle and bustle of people in the street, Tullio feels calm.

Today they certainly won't attack. Not on a day like this. Not on Christmas Eve

Some people are carrying a wrapped present, others have a small fir-tree under their arm.

Children warmly clad in mufflers and gloves tug at their mothers outside the shop-windows.

A street-organ – he can't see where – has struck up *Stille Nacht*.

The air carries the scent of strong coffee and cinnamon, of roasted chestnuts and wine.

As he approaches a shop-window, Tullio rubs his hands together and blows a little warm cloud on his numbed palms, while he feels his feet freezing in his flimsy shoes.

A little lad with his beret rammed well down on his head goes past him, shelling hot chestnuts. A dog crosses the road and pisses at a corner. A young woman laughs heartily looking at the man walking beside her. A window is opened and closed again, letting out the sound of a child crying.

Tullio enters a little shop, which seems a reasonable compromise, given these lean times, wedged in between a multilingual bookshop and a pawnbroker's. In the shop-window he's spotted the book he was looking for: a copy of the odes of Catullus bound in red morocco, which felt delicate to the touch but which has already braved almost eighty years: it was printed in the mid eighteen-hundreds.

As he releases the handle of the door he's just closed behind him, he eyes his parcel with satisfaction: though it doesn't make a great show, being wrapped in brown paper without any hint of ribbon, he's sure it's the right gift.

It's just then that he hears the roar.

Far off, as from Fiume's outskirts, like the dull rumble of long-drawn-out thunder. Then comes the sound of bursts of gunfire, and individual shots.

Abbazia
24 December 1920, afternoon

G reta draws the string tight and ties the knot, then places the little packet beneath the decorated Christmas tree.

It's right that Elisa should get her present this year as well, she reflects as she sits on the carpet, while her gaze wanders across the room: the cherrywood table, the Thonet chairs all neatly lined up, the rosewood clock beside the etching on the wall and the great Biedermeier glass cabinet, perfectly dusted, with the Meissen porcelain ware that can be glimpsed through the cabinet's glass doors. And beyond that, the fireplace, the French window.

Everything as precise as embroidery, as her mother wished: preserving the past in apparently perfect geometry while really it has been blown apart.

What will Christmas mean without Arturo and without Papa?

But precisely because everything has been blown apart –

the very idea of Christmas – Greta has made every effort this year to give it a sense of continuity.

Elisa is still a child. She still has a right to feast-days and rituals. She has a right to build up memories that in some tomorrow can shield her from the senselessness of things, from the emptiness and the absences that lurk around us.

So, although these days her mother has hardly emerged from her room that's become her refuge, Greta has taken care that everything should be in its proper place, as in the past: the sprig of mistletoe at the entrance to augur an excellent new year, the candles in their candlesticks, the antique silverware polished mirror-bright, the Christmas-tree in its earthenware pot reaching the panes of the French window with its branches, mirroring in them the delicate beauty of its ornaments, the red thicket of the tiny candles, the metal tip set at the top of the tree like a fragile exclamation mark.

And if the feast won't be the same as ever – no dessert, no turkey, the bread somewhat darker – she has anyway laid out her savings on a present, though a small one, for Elisa: Perrault's fairy-tales and a new box of pastels.

And all at once she thinks of Tullio.

This is what's been happening to her lately: he slips into her thoughts and installs himself there, tenaciously, derailing everything else.

At first she was annoyed: angry with herself and with him, too, on account of feeling herself teetering all at once between familiar behaviours and certainties and visions too secret to be confessed.

She reaches out to the cat which has curled up beside her

and strokes its back, sensing its contented breathing, the warmth of its body, its purring.

And straight after – unreal, as if bellowed from the sea – a distant booming, from near Fiume.

Fiume
24 December 1920, evening

The shoving of people has thrust him out on to the street, as all of a sudden the shop's metal shutters come crashing down.

A woman runs into him, clutching a wailing infant and leading by the hand a little fair-haired girl wearing a skimpy coat who lets herself be dragged along in a daze. For an instant Tullio stops to observe the agitation, the feverish gestures, the fear: shops suddenly boarded up, people fleeing noisily, the streets emptying of people amid the tramp of running feet and female voices crying out, names yelled out repeatedly amid the spreading of the alarm that has turned the street into a crazed ants' nest.

Tullio starts walking along the walls. There's now only that one thought in his head.

Troops of armed legionaries rush through the city setting up strong-points which send him instantly hurtling back into the war which he thought was now long past. From behind barricades hurriedly thrown up with makeshift materials and hedgehogs he sees helmets protruding amid rifles and machine-guns. Gun-barrels peep out from some windows and elevated terraces and dormer windows.

So he starts running, too.

The huge thud takes him by surprise as he's racing up the stairs two at a time: he senses that it's just the first. The next two thuds reach him as he feverishly empties on to the floor a drawer of his desk in which he's rummaged in vain. Now all three bridges leading into the town have been blown up.

At last he finds what he's been looking for: the Zeiss was at the bottom of his back-pack, buried under his clothes on a chair. He snatches up the camera and rushes back to the stairs. The artillery fire seems to have got closer, heavier and more furious. The street is now deserted, glistening under a fine drizzle that seems to ooze out of things.

As he comes out, he cannons into Paul in the doorway. They stop and look at each other in silence, each with the same helpless expression. Then Paul grips his arm forcefully and says quietly: "Don't go. It's no use your going. You can tell the story without leaving here."

He hears what he says: he's already been through it. Roles have just been reversed. And the surrounding world: aims, conditions. Horizons of expectation, certainties. His hand upon Giulio's arm one afternoon in the war, his attempt to stop him doomed to come to nothing.

And as he relives that moment, he senses it to be so remote that he wonders whether it really occurred or whether he merely dreamt it, and all of a sudden he wonders whether there's an inscrutable design in what looks like sheer chance or whether chance is in fact destiny.

It is he now that frees his arm from that friendly grip, sensing that there's no alternative. Seizing his hand, he looks Paul in the eye: "We Italians are slaughtering each other as we did in the medieval times of the Communes. Who would ever have thought it? Not I."

They both give a start at a new shell-burst, looking round instinctively. The flash came from the harbour, which both of them know to be mined. Despite the slight haze which seems to have suddenly swathed the sea, they have no difficulty in making out the outline of the battleship which now looms not far off – unreal but ominous and threatening – with its array of torpedo boats and with its guns trained.

A dense pall of smoke rises above the Government Palace.

The side of a destroyer anchored in the heart of the harbour has been ripped open by an explosion that is still blazing. A drone of engines, as yet faint, draws their gaze upwards: Tullio recognizes the two biplanes. It's not hard for him to imagine. He follows their flight as they bank: they head for the vessel, descending over the torpedo boats.

The bursts of gunfire into the sky make the SVAs shudder.

"I guess we won't be capitulating in time for our Christmas feast," remarks Tullio bitterly. "But you can tell them to get the turkey cooked and keep the coffee hot."

Paul doesn't smile. He doesn't budge. The fine rain has soaked his hair, it streaks his face.

He's so still and tense that he seems rooted to the spot. Tullio adds quietly: "I must be off, Paul: it's my job.

Otherwise some day someone will swear that none of this ever happened."

Paul silently nods. The rain is getting heavier. It's slowly blurring the outline of things.

He watches Tullio striding away until he rounds a corner.

La Nazione

Saturday 25 December 1920

Has the action started?

FIUME – A report arrived yesterday evening that a military action had started between the legionaries and General Caviglia's forces, but the suspension of telephone and telegraph contact and the absence of other means of communication as well as the imposition of censorship have prevented us from ascertaining whether the report is true or false. We hope it is false and that Italy's history will be spared a fratricidal episode.

Fiume
26 December 1920

The burst of machine-gun fire reverberates violently in his ears: the pain twinges in his eardrums, the shock travels down his neck.

Then it's over, and everything swims back into focus.

The lime trees beyond the edge of the road, the pot-holes gouged out of the ground, the cartridge cases scattered at his feet, as he crouches looking down among boots and strides and rifle butts of the men squatting around him. In the distance, barely visible through the smoke that's already thinning and through the fine veil of mist, are the soldiers' grey helmets, an arm reaching up, a body lurching forwards and disappearing behind the silhouette of a tree-trunk only to reappear and then slip out of view.

The sky is clouded, lowering, livid and oppressive. The air is laden with moisture. The crackle of gunfire has sudden furious crescendos and brief uncertain silent breaks.

You can hear voices. Commands as sharp as sabre-strokes, the thud of a weight collapsing, feet scraping along the ground. Even a magpie's cry, the gurgling of water in a ditch. At times, from somewhere, a howl that sounds like surprise but may be pain.

Huddled behind sandbags and piled-up mattresses – makeshift barricades interspersed among the scrub and coils of barbed wire – Tullio briefly raises his head, lifts up his arm, snaps another photo.

He can feel the blood pounding in his temples, the tension in his neck.

Just like war, he's already remarked. Same as then.

At first he felt as if he was again going through the hailstorm of gunfire, the volleys of hand-grenades, the moving bodies, at times swallowed up in the smoke, like insects scrambling at the sudden collapse of their nest. But he's not up in the sky, amid towering ramparts of clouds: everything around him now is on the same level, vertical.

Then he concerned himself only with observing, synchronizing his hand movements, searching with his eyes among the sandbags, guessing the slackening in the gunfire and the brief gaps in the shelling. Then crawl, or stand, worming his way along a gap in the cover: and focus, snap. Quickly take out the plate. Slip in another frame.

At first he felt relieved at not wielding a weapon, that the clicks made by his finger are those of a camera shutter and not the lethal clicks of a trigger.

But his relief didn't last long, and suddenly felt like hypocrisy. Now he shares the same anguish, the same cold taste of tension, the same anxiety as the others, the fear. Squatting, balancing on his feet, he stops a moment to take a look. There's a young man on his right: pale-faced, gaunt-cheeked. There's a hint of a beard on his chin and a scar on his cheek. Tullio sees him raise an arm, flex his wrist and hand as he quickly tosses a grenade. He observes his profile creasing up, his gaze lingering and narrowing, then his body preparing to bend down again and squat low beside him.

Then there's the sudden shot.

Tullio hears it whistling sharply past. The lad slumps down at his feet almost without a sound: only his metal helmet clangs coldly as it violently strikes against a hard object. Tullio bends down over him, looks at his wide-staring eyes and the vein throbbing above his collar, the stain that is starting to soak his jacket around the shoulder. His face expresses surprise, and also terror. The young lad's torso and legs hang out in the open, over the edge of the ground cover.

He's got to move him. Take him away from there.

There's no time. He's got to do it on his own. He slides alongside the twitching body, grasps it around the hips, lifts it and begins to move back, while shots continue raining down.

The whistling this time is a whiplash. The pain is a sudden twinge. It goes through the temples and down the back of the neck, then bursts down his spinal column.

There's a flash of light amid the darkness and in it he seems to see a swarm of insects buzzing or stubble as hard as sharp stones in the fields where he used to run as a kid, with the crows gliding – black wings – and distant wisps of smoke. They outline Greta's body.

Shoulders, hips, breasts.

And that's it. Nothing else. They've gone too.

Abbazia
26 December 1920

She's tried in every possible way, sounded every note, but in vain.

At first advancing justifications which she'd rehearsed meticulously, then improvising desperately.

Imploring in the style of a convent girl, persisting with womanly dignity, and finally raising her voice to an unheard-of pitch, her expression switching from that of a suppliant to one of dogged determination.

But they wouldn't let her through the blockade checkpoint into Fiume. The officer who eventually stepped in – and who took down her particulars – even threatened to arrest her.

His tone was so cutting and hard that she felt almost stripped bare in that hapless humiliation which in the end forced her to cave in.

But it's not that that's making her head whirl. Not the

anxiety she's been in these last two days since hearing of the fighting in Fiume. It's a more overpowering and searing distress, one which remains shapeless and stops her from breathing.

Feeling helpless, she went back home. She forced herself to perform pointless tasks and practical, concrete duties.

In the end she dropped a plate, trod on the cat's paw, toppled the pile of firewood beside the hearth. And then sat beside Elisa, who had asked her to read her a fairy-tale.

Her eyes would now run words together, now skip a line or two, but somehow she did get to where it said the end.

"… the Marquis of Carabas, making deep bows, accepted the immense honour of the wedding.

Master Cat still wore his boots, but from then on was treated with respect and chased the castle mice only for fun, and not as a duty."

Now she feels the need to go out. To be on her own, in the open air, face to face with every one of her fears.

She is aware of Elisa looking at her as she opens the door on to the staircase and goes out without even saying goodbye.

She goes along the garden path, down towards the bay. In the distance, behind Abbazia, the clouds hang so low that they seem to have sprouted out of the earth like huge spongy fungi.

And all at once there floats into her consciousness – but coming from where? – a picture from her childhood.

A beach of golden sand, a man bending forward, intent on something.

She had approached in silence. Her mother was walking not far off, while Arturo was collecting sea-shells from among the seaweed along the foreshore. From behind the man's back, Greta peers at his hands, which move swiftly and deftly, bringing to life a lissome form, and all at once with a white quill – a long seagull feather – he's patiently sculpting the nipple of an already fully formed mermaid. The man bends down, blows away the sand scraped up by the feather's sharp stem, removes the excess matter from his idea of a breast, of symmetries: and in him there is a lover's passion and the power of a demiurge, a creator's freedom. But only now can she understand that, years after, as if only with time was she able to find the key to unlock the meaning of those actions, the desire expressed by those hands, the beauty of that figure. The need to sculpt in sand the details of one's aspirations.

Then she recalls that tall, foaming wave that had swallowed up the mermaid: her right flank, her face. Her long fish-tail. All that was left was a heap of sand with vague female features.

She wonders why this memory comes back to her now, so suddenly.

Who knows whether she will ever be able to decipher the laws which govern memory, she who is so often taken by surprise by overwhelming, unexpected memories.

She looks at the sea, the spray among the rocks, the great house at the top of the rise, the grey sky.

The air is chilly, but she breathes in deeply. She'd like to have snow around her, lots of snow.

La Nazione

31 December 1920

Hostilities suspended in Fiume.
Negotiations in progress.

During a meeting held in Abbazia, an agreement was signed which ends armed clashes in Fiume. Losses on the Fiume side amount to 22 legionaries and 5 civilians, including one woman. The regular army laments 25 deaths among military personnel and two civilians. The number of wounded is higher: 46 military and 15 civilians on the Fiume side; 139 military and 7 civilians among the regular forces.

The town suffered serious damage not only to the Government Palace, but also to a score of other buildings, including the gasworks and the railway depot.

The press has been told that Prime Minister Giolitti received a Parliamentary delegation drawn from different parties which requested information on the events in Fiume.

The Prime Minister in reply denied reports of d'Annunzio's death or injury and stated that the occupation of Fiume has only just been accomplished. He added that he had ordered that everything possible should be done to avoid bloodshed; he denied reports that private dwellings had been shelled. Some shots had been fired by the battleship Andrea Doria at the barracks and the

Government Palace and at the destroyer Espero…

The Hon. Mr Giolitti explained that it was necessary to expedite the action against Fiume so as to avoid external intervention by Yugoslavia. The *Corriere d'Italia* reports that after their conversation with Giolitti the parliamentarians declared their belief that the government's action had been fully justified.

Fiume
4 January 1921

Paul is squatting at the foot of the stretcher, his arms around his knees, his back leaning against the wall of the transport, which is already full.

He studies Tullio's ashen face, his shut eyes, his inert hands, the clotted blood at his shoulder which has now soaked through the bandages.

He thinks back to the parcel he's posted to Greta, hoping that the postal service will be back in operation within a few days: a book for her from Tullio – a Christmas present, he imagined – which it seemed right to him to send to her. He's attached to it a note in his own hand to bring her up to date about everything, and he's added his New York address underneath.

That's all he's been able to do for her.

For a moment, Paul shuts his eyes, breathes in the smells more deeply: the sweat of the men around him, the damp rising from the earth, the strong stench of disinfectant. And, further away, but still persistent with the *bora* blowing, hints of salt from the sea that cling to the lips and to the skin and seem to pervade one's clothing.

The men are squatting, sitting on the floor, or standing. Like the grass benumbed by the frost: each blade frozen at its own angle. Then the train moves off. He feels the first long heave, the gathering speed, the jolting that becomes more regular, smoke up his nose and in his throat.

Then, for the first time since he's boarded this train that will carry them away from Fiume, he gets up and looks out of a window. For a while, he doesn't focus on anything, immersed as he is in his thoughts.

Then things regain their shape and fit back into place out there: landscapes and distances reassemble in perspective. The clouds towering at the sky's edge, the flight of a bird over a cane thicket, children running after the train, hands waving goodbye.

Through that window, Paul has the impression of seeing a world which is both strange and familiar: little hamlets nestling in the shadow of their bell-tower, footpaths that score the hill-sides, narrow, winding terraced slopes of red earth, with vineyards clinging to the slopes and dry-stone boundary walls.

It's like retracing a pathway that can only be entered going the other way, and discovering new shapes and new connections among the usual elements of the landscape. Knowing that it isn't the world that's changed, but only one's way of looking at it. Realizing that it takes so little to transform a perspective.

He finds himself reflecting on so many things, as he gazes

at Tullio lying on his stretcher and goes back to sit beside him.

He reflects on the sixteen months he has spent in Fiume. On all the undoubted errors that were made, on the flights dashed, on the visionary dreams. On his office in Government Palace. On the shells that burst in that very spot on the second storey. On his unfinished reports, on the little that's been achieved, on so much more left undone.

He reflects on the systematic bombardment threatened by the army if they didn't agree to surrender, and on the adamant refusal to allow a truce for the evacuation of the elderly, women and children out of Fiume.

He reflects on d'Annunzio's final speech in dismissing the legionaries: the timbre of his voice, his silent pauses, his suddenly aged and ravaged face, the tremor in his hands.

And on Tullio, on his last words. On Giulio, killed as he had always lived, braving the most extreme challenges, unable to come to terms with life and its compromises: its balancing acts, what people call good sense, adapting to the times and to reality.

He reflects on those five days under fire. An awkward, inglorious episode, just one of those jolts of History which will soon be obliterated and which no one will remember.

He reflects upon a world which grinds everything down and digests every transgression, recording in its double-entry registers – its tidy book-keeping – every heresy and each new dream, every new enterprise or vision.

In one corner, a boy squatting on the floor pulls out his mouth-organ and begins to play quietly.

The empty sleeve of his left arm is pinned up to the shoulder, hiding only a stump.

Claire looks at Paul without speaking. Then she gets up and moves close to him.

Up to now she has respected his silence, his sense of defeat, his grief. His need to set himself apart, to keep himself to himself, and come to terms with his wounds.

As yet, she does not speak to him, she does not smile.

But perhaps she can hold his hand.

Epilogue

Jerusalem
September 1986

Keeping in step with her, the director of Yad Vashem walks by Greta's side.

He is accustomed to this gait, slow as that of the elderly who no longer know haste, and if they do know, aren't bothered.

And he finds that pace perfect for travelling through his entire museum: an institute that guards memories not in offices and corridors but in grottoes and green spaces, on the slopes of Har Hazikaran.

The Mount of Remembrance: a hill in Jerusalem.

And the memorial at the top of that hill is a garden. A garden, Greta suddenly reflects, that is gradually being transformed into an anarchic riot of trees and plants like the park where she grew up. In the beginning, the director explained, there were only carob trees, tough and tenacious as old dreams or calloused vices, their trunks wizened by cracks and their roots groping into emptiness. Then came olive trees: each one growing in its own way, with gnarled, anguished branches clutching space, air and light. Plants that can live on nothing, that barely know the seasons.

But beneath each tree is a stele. And on each stele is an inscription. A name, a surname, a nationality. Names of men and women who saved from extermination other men and other women guilty of being Jews.

She can still see the children's memorial, where she lingered in silence, next to the director. They exchanged no words in that dry, dark grotto.

The candle flames infinitely reflected in the mirrors were like swarms of fireflies against the rocky vault, like the summer fireflies in the Abbazia garden. But these fireflies won't find peace, thought Greta, in the long list of names rolled out by a voice: a voice not decked with sacred vestments, bare of any kind of liturgy. A recording voice, which, however, is naked.

Odette, aged eight…
Maria, four…
Eva, aged six…
Marta and Isaak, one…

Greta bowed her head. And then she could see them clearly, with her eyes closed. Some names wore long tresses, others had ears slightly sticking out and blue eyes, yet others had milky smiles and little windows between their teeth which whetted the sharp consonants and undid the aspirated syllables.

But how much does a name weigh, how tall is it? How does it sob, if it sobs, how does it laugh? How many times does it yawn, when it's really tired, how far can it run before it falls?

★ ★ ★

Lilia, aged ten…
Nora, five
Ester and Tobi… aged seven, three…

Almost one and a half million kids. She hadn't managed it with them: no one had managed it. No one had rescued them.

Says the Talmud: The righteous among the nations will share in the world to come.

These were the opening words of the letter which she had received from the Yad Vashem Institute.

Greta had read on in surprise, her hands shaking, her memories coming back to her in those distinct shapes that memories relived an infinity of times, never changing, in the depths of one's consciousness, take on: and it's like running over and over along a groove scored on a patch of ground, year in year out, keeping faith, like a grindstone rotating and carving a mark that records a wound.

Edith Levi had been the first.

They'd written to each other for years. Her letters – as well as Elisa's – had been for Greta the only remaining thread that connected her to her past, her link with Abbazia and Fiume.

It was an autumn day, she recalls. The autumn of '42. She had found her standing face to face outlined by the light in the doorway. Greta remembers, yes, it was blowing a *bora*. Shrill whistling wind, long sharp howls. From the joints in the woodwork of the windows came brief moans and sudden stabs of cold.

Edith was huddled in her overcoat, holding her daughter by the hand. She'd been widowed the previous year, and now had escaped from Abbazia.

The girl was fifteen, pale with fatigue and fear. Her great, intelligent and scared eyes roamed uneasily around the room as if seeking a resting-place between the books and the few objects among the books, between the curtains of the little verandah and the ever-open door to the breakfast room.

Greta had noticed her expression, she had recognized that bewilderment, sensed her heartache.

For a moment, just one moment, she had reflected that that could have been the glance of her own daughter – *her daughter* – if everything had gone differently.

Then she'd uprooted the thought like a weed, bending down to pick up the small suitcase at their feet. She had smiled at the girl, and asked her name.

Rebecca, she had answered quietly, looking at the bag in her hands: and she seemed to hang on that gesture, to gauge it with bated breath; she seemed to read in it the hope of a welcome into that house, of finding a refuge that she had lost.

Greta had stroked her face, but had felt it flinch in fear. Then she had remembered that that was the age in which no peace is to be had: not with the world, not with one's own body, not with anything within or without. And certainly not in war and not in flight, in a world which has just blown up around you.

She had insisted that they have the bed. She wanted them to sleep close together, to find at least in the close contact of their bodies the temporary security of natural warmth.

She herself, however, had not slept. Lying on the divan in her study, she had listened for hours to the wall clock ticking away and the last squalls of the *bora* and the muffled sounds from the street. And misgivings, suppositions, memories kept springing up full-bodied and overbearing, writhing like polecats, pressing forward fearsomely.

★ ★ ★

Bubbles bursting suddenly. Images rising from the depths, as if after being long compressed, and re-surfacing to recover their breath.

The low stone wall, the sunflower. The bodies of Edith and Arturo entwined along a branch as tightly as a vine tendril.

The light filtering through the fronds of the little hut of mysteries amid the gold of stripped corn cobs and the fruit swinging from the ceiling on the autumn Sukkot feast.

The crackling of dry leaves beneath the feet of two small girls who manage to exchange messages with their eyes and who still believe in the future.

Her hand on Tullio's chest and that heartbeat like a nestling in its nest.

The stroke of a paintbrush on the canvas, a letter from

Paris, a book flying out of the sky, a little tin soldier clutched like a trophy for bravery in a small boy's tiny hand.

And all at once in the darkness of that room, amid the jumble of blankets on the divan, and to the tune of the whistling *bora*, those misgivings had shrunk away like dabs of paint in the sunshine.

Next morning, she had reassured them. It would only be for a short while.

She'd hide them in the clinic, in her ward, in safety. They'd act invalid. Of course, it wouldn't be easy – she glanced at Rebecca as she said this, as if asking her pardon – but everything would be all right. No one would ever think of looking for them at the Trieste mental asylum. In other words, at the madhouse, as it was called by everyone in town.

Greta had reflected that, faced with madness and its mysteries, people had always attempted to stave off affliction, to protect themselves from the danger, to reject and shut away every kind of difference: in cages, pens, prisons. In ghettos and lazar-houses, in hospices and asylums.

But madness now lay elsewhere. Different from what it had always been, it was as if it had spilled over a dam and appeared to have inundated everywhere.

Perhaps the enclosure walls for the "mad" would keep madness out.

Just a few months, you'll see, just a few months. I'm sure everything will turn out right. I'm sure it won't be for long.

Edith and Rebecca looked at her, quietly wringing their hands: hungering for reassurance, straining to pick up the slightest hint of hope, anxious to believe her fully.

Instead, it had gone on for two and a half years: until the end of the war. Until the end of the occupation of the Adriatisches Küstenland, the far north-eastern littoral, stretching from Udine and Gorizia, taking in Trieste, as far as Fiume, Pula and Ljubljana, which was all under Nazi rule.

But Edith and Rebecca had somehow survived. And others after them, on the run.

That initial act of friendship – spontaneous, unplanned, improvised – had gradually evolved into a far-flung network, a last resort for the desperate: Greta's ward in Trieste had become one of the destinations to which the chief of police in Fiume directed Jews he was trying to save.

From Fiume, Split, Abbazia. From a territory soon destined to be part of the Reich and there to be meticulously cleansed so as to make it worthy of that future and racially pure.

★ ★ ★

Greta concentrates on his voice, forces herself to listen attentively, as the man standing before her keeps on speaking without pausing, amidst the knot of people around them.

… Since, from the autumn of 1942 until the end of the war, she exercised the noblest form of civil resistance by offering shelter and protection to dozens of Jews who were victims of Nazi-Fascism and rescuing them, at the risk of her own life, from certain deportation and death… we confer upon Dr Greta Vidal…

Greta keeps her gaze lowered.

One of the Righteous, one of the Righteous in the world. One of the Righteous among the Nations. That is how they've just defined her.

What it means, she doesn't know.

She's always told herself that any other person would have acted in the same way if they'd found themselves in her place.

It wasn't heroism, she knows that. It was like when as a child she used to stretch out her body and her arms and hands to reach a flower, a fruit, a nest, and could do nothing else but keep her balance and translate her daring into a forward spring and convert that spring into a leap so as not to succumb to the fear of heights and not to risk injury.

Or maybe she learnt it all when she was older, from him.

One can't choose what era to belong to, Greta…

She'd never forgotten Tullio's words, since that time: their strength, still intact and true, which was riveted to her conscience as if to some mysterious force of gravity.

…One can only choose how to belong to it.

That was her real credo. She still hung on to it.

Or maybe it was something else again that had led her to make that decision: nevertheless, the lives she tried to save would never have been enough. They would never make up for that one little life which she'd lost for ever by pushing it away from her.

So now she absents herself from everything: the ceremony, the people, the official tone of the speech, which moves her and embarrasses her at the same time, the stele which they are laying – her name and surname, her nationality – the smiles, the handshakes.

In the background, the desert. Overhead, the sky.

Splashes of yellow and green, streamers of light through the branches. A scrap of paper blown by the wind, the distant barking of a dog, a man's feet beside her, wearing a pair of light-coloured mocassins.

And all at once she finds herself thinking of what has been and what has not been, of what her life would be if everything had turned out differently.

No, Tullio: nothing glorious. Nothing glorious at all, in us. In what we would have become and in the future of our story. We gave up, as so many did, at the dawning of our age of so-called maturity. Accepting compromises and hypocrisies in a context of numb turbidity. And in that broth-like turbidity – nothing but little bubbles to give flavour which then goes rancid on the palate – life took other paths. I couldn't have known, at the outset, that the infection to your wound had isolated you for months on end in an obscure little hospital. Not hearing any news of you, I gave in to the idea that I'd been just a flutter for you, a thrill. When you sought me out, I had gone. To Padua, first, to study medicine. After that, to Trieste, to work. And in between, a short-lived marriage, a dreary meaningless experience as a short cut to normality. The persistence of your search – of which I knew nothing – got stranded only when you discovered I was married. So you didn't want to compromise what must have looked to you like serene equilibrium but was simply a capitulation. When I found this out and then sought you out myself, it was too late for us. Another life, different dimensions. Different latitudes, those of strangers. I remember you at the entrance to the school in that neat little town to which you had always belonged. Far enough from the borders not to feel the wounds. You were holding your children by the hand. The girl twittered away incessantly, the boy was laughing over something. Not

317

even your thunder-struck look – the long glance which locked us together – was able to unbalance things, to distract your children from you. How could I have the courage to present myself to you? Like two startled turtles, we shrank back into our shells. Maybe, if I'd asked it of you, you'd have dropped everything to get back with me. We were tied together not only by our memories, the steps we took together at crucial moments, regrets over what had been. And over what might still have been. We were tied together by dreams and emotions and desperate passion. Probably it could be called love. I have no other name for it. Yes, perhaps you'd have abandoned the certainties of your everyday life. But I never asked that of you. Nor did you ever suggest it.

It was late to tell you the whole story, it was late to tell you about her. It would have seemed to you like blackmail. I would only have hurt you.

It could have happened.
It had to happen…

The rest, in part, I heard later. Your joining the fascist party must at first have seemed to you to be a way of putting things in order. Of giving shape to a rebuilding with new horizons, new courage, faith. You, like so many, must have felt that that was what we needed. A sure guide, a strong man. The unquestioned authority of a Nation that at last really counted, that was able to make itself heard. I've often imagined your first doubts, your way of silencing them. Maybe leaving your job to apply your philosophy degree in school-teaching was part of a plan, Tullio. It was just your strategy. So as to survive. So as not to give up. So as to find yourself an untainted niche: your studies, your research, your students. So as not to make too many concessions to the cracks. But the cracks still kept widening. And undermining every hope, the certainties you had started with, the new world. Then that niche was no longer enough for you. Culture no longer protected you. You must have felt as if you were in Fiume, for those five seasons of ours. But what was under siege was your conscience. Or at least, I guess, what was left of it. I can still see, among so many others – but I don't remember in what newspaper – your signature below the manifesto launched by Benedetto Croce, our great philosopher. That manifesto was a cry of despair. It was a cry, more than a proclamation. It rang out like a defence of all freedom of expression. Like a last, forlorn barricade for those who still aspired to think. Then I remember your letter: out of the blue. The sudden emotion, my heart in my mouth, I had to sit down, breathless.

The foreign stamp. My astonishment at thinking of you being there. Just a few lines, letting me know you were alive. But they'd murdered a comrade of yours, who was living in exile in Paris like yourself. The killers – the long arm of the regime – had caught up with you. You were once again at a frontier, armed with nothing but your pen. A laconic note it was you sent me. You hadn't really changed. So at times you still thought of me, you were concerned about me. And it was from there, from Paris, that you again took to writing your thoughts intensely, to making your voice heard again. You came into your own again.

One can't choose which era to belong to, Greta...

You were right. One can't. Once again, it wasn't the right moment to tell you the whole story, to tell you about her. Then you left us all too soon. Long before verging on old age. The right moment, after a lifetime's waiting, ended up by never arriving.

It could have happened.
It had to happen.
It happened earlier. Later...

Then vertigo comes over her, as it has been doing for over fifty years, whenever, without warning or reason, the memory of her daughter takes hold of her.

She can still see her snuggled among the pillows, barely a few weeks old: catching the light on her little head, the barely visible down glows electrically in a funny little chick's halo.

Her fist is just showing through the folds of the bed-cover, like a tulip bulb: her tiny hand reaches out, extending wrinkled, groping fingers, feels for something soft and finds it rough, maybe searching for contact that isn't there.

Greta feels that same fear which had come over her then, at that moment. The fear of passing on to her the persistent fever that's been sapping her for weeks. The fear of feeding her on infected blood. The fear of being inept and at fault, of ending up by harming her. The fear of not being able to offer her a future. Of having to deny her that father of whom she had lost track now for months past.

And that's when it happens, for those eyes open wide suddenly, looking so large in that miniature face: their pupils are enormous, dilated, still lacking in shade and colour, and they now turn upon her a gaze that certainly cannot yet see her: that much she knows about newborn infants.

But precisely because she can't see, Greta feels that she can grasp realities that go beyond the appearance of things.

That is why she sees as an omen the sudden outburst of crying. A shrill, tense, desperate crying.

As if she were trying to convey to her her distress, and through that confirming a choice: perhaps it's really better for the two of them, what she's just decided.

So Greta turns to face the wall, while Claire picks up her daughter in her arms, rocks her gently and composedly, humming her a French lullaby: and her eyes shut again, her sobbing gradually subsides, and she finally finds peace in sleep.

All that remains is the sultry heat, and the fatigue, squashed down under the low ceiling of the little airless attic.

It could have happened.
It had to happen.
It happened earlier. Later.
Nearer. Farther off.

Just for a while. Only for a while. This was the reciprocal undertaking, the agreement made between them. Then I'd have her back. Paul and Claire had insisted. I sensed the sincerity of their support, their desire to be close to me. They reminded me of Tullio. They were pursuing their vocations, they lived a bit like visionaries. They didn't expect to be understood, they weren't anxious for acceptance. But they had always shown me an open heart, great and generous. I knew that my little daughter would end up in good hands. Just for a while. Only for a little while. Just long enough for me to recover from my fever and my exhaustion. And hopefully to find a job, a home for my little daughter and myself. A space bigger and more decent than that damp attic in an old district of Trieste, where I'd gone to live on my own since the previous winter. The need to study was my excuse, my enrolment at university. My mother had pretended to believe me, or had really believed me. I knew she had sunk back into her limbo, cut off from other people and even from herself. As for my father, he was now living in Salzburg, where he had set up a new business. He was living there with his latest mistress: twenty years younger and forty kilos lighter. Someone had let me know, with the usual solicitude which people always show you in such circumstances. Just for a while. Only for a little while. And once I was able to take care of her, I'd take the child back again to live with me. But almost five years went by before I was able to make the journey to New York, on my own. In the meantime, I had graduated.. And I had found myself a job. At last I was able to take her back – and to support her on my own – my own Laura, all ready to start school.

She was lovely, my daughter, then aged five. She had deep, dark eyes, long copper hair. She wrinkled her nose when she laughed or when she pouted. She only spoke English, of course. And a few words of French, which enabled us to communicate a little.

Say hello to aunty Greta, said Claire, leading her towards me.

I went down on my knees, presented my gift to her. I held back with all my strength from enfolding her in a hug. I'd have upset an equilibrium held up by magic. She quietly extracted from the box a doll dressed in white and pink. She gave me a nice, bright smile, and then ignored the doll and me as well. Instead, she went on playing with her dog. A spruce little Pekinese which kept brushing into people's faces in an impulse of universal love. And which would follow her meekly around wherever she moved. Then she started to play with her daddy. And Paul was an incomparable steed as he galloped around the house with Laura on his back. He'd pretend to shake her off his back and would then snatch her up again as she was sliding off his back and really risking a fall. That's when I understood, heart-wrenchingly. Laura was happy with them. Paul and Claire had no children. They never would have any. And as I gazed at the wrinkles on her nose – as she laughed and laughed, riding on Paul's back – I asked myself some fierce questions. Questions I'd never considered before. Was it right to take her away from mum and dad? Was it right for me to take back my daughter just because I'd brought her into the world, because I had my natural rights, because this made me happy? My return voyage home took forever, travelling back on the ship on my own. And a furious, brutal nausea raged in my gut. Yet I felt, I knew, it was right that way. And that was confirmed by that smile – the equilibrium it expressed, the serenity it radiated – in the photos that reached me punctually at every new stage of her life. Every birthday of her entire childhood. Her adolescence, without anything too dramatic. Her eighteenth birthday celebration. Her graduation from university with top grades, her wedding, the birth of her daughter. Then the accident occurred. In the evening, as she was returning home.

My daughter died in the crash. Twenty-six years and four months ago.

Just for an instant, I totter. Elisa, at my side, realizes. She grips my arm. She props me up.

> *It could have happened.*
> *It had to happen.*
> *It happened earlier. Later.*
> *Nearer. Farther off.*
> *It happened, but not to you...*

So runs a poem by Wisława Szymborska. Elisa showed it to me. That was when Elisa herself published her first verse collection. The one that most endeared her. The one for which she's so well known. As for myself, I no longer have the strength for lengthy reflections, for lengthy sentences. Silence is much better, sometimes.

Just names that were once lives, and candle flames around them.

Then the whole thing's over. She's almost feeling cold. Greta starts walking again.

She turns round just for a moment, casts one last glance over her shoulder.

She loves that tree, that spot, the shadows projected on to the pathway, the rustling of an eddy of wind gently going through the foliage and wandering off who knows where: and the olive tree that will bear her name and that has the gnarled and lop-sided trunk of trees that adapt to life, that are accustomed to its tribulations.

And she smiles. It's almost dark. There's a citrus fragrance in the air.

The languor is past.

It's time to get back.

Abbazia
May 2009

A seagull swoops low over the water, grabs his supper, flies off.

The bay is deserted at this time of day, but a little while ago a small girl slipped through a garden gate.

Now she's reading, sitting slightly further along. Leaning with her back against a rock, she slowly turns the pages of a book, immersed in a world all her own: I observe her concentrated expression, her pony-tail glinting against the sunlight, her crossed legs, bare and skinny, the hand she raises to her mouth so as to gnaw at a fingernail, then at another.

Beyond her can be glimpsed the footpath threading its way between the greenery of the coast, the white of the rocks and the blue of the sea.

Who knows where this photo was taken, which I'm still holding and which had lain hidden away inside a nondescript little chest whose corners are reinforced with metal and which locks with a key, just like any number such, mass-produced around the beginning of the last century. But confiscated a good long while ago.

It took ninety years before I was able to open it and discover what was inside.

I suddenly recall my grandfather, my hand clutching his, the timbre of his voice when he was telling me some story in a conspiratorial tone, as if he reserved for me and me alone all the sweetness remaining deep in his old soul which had outlived petty miseries, great setbacks and fragile triumphs.

I was only a little girl at the time of what seemed to me a fantastic adventure, my first away from home: I and he alone together as far as Washington to visit the capital.

I walk close to him, scared, in spaces that overawe me and turn words into whispers, along one of the many corridors of the National Gallery of Art.

At first, what strikes me is the silence. Then everything else, little by little. The light falling on sculptures and porcelain, a church-like sense of the sacred, the sudden sensation that my age is less than ever amid those halls, within those walls, beside those objects.

But perhaps the paintings hanging on the walls would remain just dead images – windows on to a buried world – if he did not not bring them so much to life with words of passion.

For *nonno* starts telling stories. He starts from a painting, and comes to a city. Or to a crib, or a battle: so bodies regain their volume and men, women and children come to life again and tell us their own stories, which are too big to fit inside the frames which hem them in hard on every side.

Van Gogh's *La Mousmé sitting*, Picasso's *Harlequin the*

musician, the three Magi coming from afar following the light of a star and captured, as they offer their gifts, by the paintbrush of Fra' Filippo Lippi. Or the *Madonna of the Pomegranate*, that little girl seated on an azure armchair, St George, his mantle flying in the wind, who fearlessly on horseback faces a dragon's gaping jaws.

And then the portraits. I'm won over by them.

What story does that gaze tell me, what enigma is hidden in the sadness of Giovanna Benci's gentle face, that expression of surrender and longing that Raphael one day captured, her eyes seemingly lost among the foliage that seems to radiate the bands of her chestnut curls into infinity, in a halo of shadows and lights?

"... and this boy, Alexandra, lived five hundred years ago. His name was Bindo Altoviti. See his clothes? Have a good look... They're made of damask, a precious fabric. Sometimes it was enriched with gold and silver thread, and the merchants' caravans from Syria carried it on adventurous journeys across the desert sands and along the Euphrates valley. But the boy didn't give it a thought. Or it didn't seem important to him. He was always dressed like a great lord. He had his own horse, a trained falcon to hunt with, a pair of black and white dogs which he fed with his own hand. He lived in Rome, in Italy. He was the son of a wealthy banker, and did not lack for comfort. He had money in plenty enough to be able to make loans to Popes and kings."

I go close up to the boy in the painting. I study his hand hanging idle, his gaze at once proud and sad, those locks of golden hair beneath the fabric of his black cap.

"What do you think he's thinking of, grandad? I don't think he's at all happy."

He keeps silent for a moment, as if rehearsing unspoken words, emotions.

"His family were from Florence. A beautiful city, Alexandra, with ancient palaces in white marble and hills with olive groves all around and an old bridge with arches across a river. But the boy's parents had been driven out because they had opposed the rulers of the city by force."

His eyes on the portrait. That gaze. My hand in his.

Now, I can feel it, he's far away. In a place I don't know. I dare not bring him back here, to where I am.

"Maybe he's just feeling homesick," his voice suddenly continues. "Maybe he finds exile humiliating, the sentence weighs on him. Maybe when he leaves home in the morning to join his father at work he thinks of his grandparents and his cousins far away in the courtyard of the house beside the river where his forebears once lived, he thinks of the face of a girl who had one day smiled at him as she looked down from a stone balcony. So he feels he's lost everything, and he feels profound homesickness."

I go on studying the boy's face, his full lips, his profile.

I don't find it hard to understand.

I, too, feel a great emptiness at times, and I experience sudden longings. Much too much for me.

Then the confiscation was over, and that chest came back home.

When it was handed over to me, I took it into my study and placed it on my desk. I stood there for a while eyeing it with unexpected uneasiness, wondering whether what I was about to do was right.

Then I reflected that my grandfather would be of the

same mind. I was his only grand-daughter, and we were very fond of one another. He told me of his past only in fragments, as if unsure whether to entrust it to my care or to spare me the irksome encumbrance of some inglorious heritage of his.

But his past is also a part of me. So I braved that lock, I gingerly raised that lid. Backing away, into the full light, I listened to the rain coming down.

Then I sat down, and I allowed myself to look.

A child's tissue is fragile: that's why everything that happens to us in our first years of life sinks deep roots within us.

It had been so long since I thought of my grandfather and of myself at that time: a child.

I can still see myself swept along by the tide of that enormous march of all those people filing through the streets of Washington in that August of 1963. We must really seem the most unlikely and mismatched couple since the time of Stan Laurel and Oliver Hardy, swallowed up amid everyone else by that procession: my grandfather wearing jacket and tie and with *The Times* sticking out of his pocket and I with my doll in my arms while I lick at my double lollipop. One can't live without lollipops or without newspapers. That's our view. I know very well why we're there. Grandad has told me everything.

So I walk beside him: I feel invincible, being with him. We both feel invincible, when we can stay together.

If granny were ever to see us now, she'd be sure to have a fit. But I'm smiling calmly: granny could never spot us amid that sea of people. So I peer at the bearded youths, at the girls with their long hair wearing flowery skirts and boots, at the slogans on boards and banners and on the back of T-shirts.

I've just learned to read. So I read, spelling the words out slowly. There are only two words written, so even I find them easy to understand. Simple words: *Work and freedom*.

The dust that's settled on my black shoes makes me want to bend down and trace with my finger a little sign, a letter, the A of my name.

Or maybe that isn't really true. Maybe I'm imagining it now as I relive the whole experience with my eyes closed, as I see that solemn little girl busily and steadily putting one foot in front of the other without a pause, taking care not to lose the rhythm, not to let grandad drag her along, not to show signs of weakness that would shame her: for instance saying that she's thirsty, that she's tired, that she'd like to go back home and drink lots and lots of lemonade. With oodles of sugar and lots of ice blocks to crunch quietly between her teeth, even though it hurts.

Having got as far as the Lincoln Memorial, her legs no longer hold her up.

But now all around a profound silence has descended, as if everyone was waiting.

I look up at my grandad's face: his eyes range slowly, in a calm, broad sweep, over the dense hugeness of the crowd which has now closed around us, and once again I sense that something – a memory, a call, who knows – for a few instants is transporting him far away, to a place I don't know, which clearly belongs to him alone.

Then suddenly the waiting is over. There's something *happening*, over there.

I realize it when I feel his hand squeezing mine harder

and I hear a man's voice over the loudspeakers announcing to all of us there *I have a dream*.

I thrust my hand into the little chest and began to pull everything out.

There were dozens of sealed envelopes, almost all of them with the same heading: *Bureau des Relations Extérieures. Fiume*. They had all the official air of embarrassing documents, of the sort which reasons of State prefer to keep under wraps or to censor. But one envelope carried another legend: *United States Embassy. Rome*.

I broke its wax seal and started to read those sheets, typed out ninety years ago. Nearly all the letters S had slipped on account of a faulty key, but the old black characters didn't seem at all faded.

The first amendment to our Constitution guarantees, besides freedom of religion, freedom of speech and freedom of the press... also the right to appeal to the government to right wrongs.

Only wrongs that affect us American citizens, or also those that affect other peoples, other injustices, other inequities?

Immersed in my reading, I no longer heard anything else around me.

... The great American dream is beautiful and terribly new...

Every people free, in the end, to dispose of itself and its future, following the end of a long war which has had devastating consequences.

I heard nothing else around, one sheet after another in the

silence, the paper rustling between my fingers.

... It's a dream that speaks of justice, of courage, and of truth.

Let's not allow it to go adrift.

Let's not allow it to be applied inequitably and, ultimately, hypocritically and arbitrarily.

Let's not let it be guaranteed only when it really coincides with the interests of the mighty, with the aims of the victors, of those who have the means to redraw the planet's geography...

Then I read the other letters, one by one, until the words on the page began to blur even through the lenses of my glasses.

One envelope was left at the bottom: the last one. I opened that, too. In it was a photograph.

I immediately recognized grandad Paul's face at the age of twenty, photographed in front of an aircraft with wings made of canvas and wood, perhaps a biplane from World War One, in which I knew he had fought.

The young man next to him was wearing an airman's jacket.

Between them was a girl: her expression was familiar. I moved further away: under the lamplight that adolescent but determined face was just like mine at eighteen. It was my face, but it wasn't me. Incredulously, I looked at my own smile.

Fiume, May 1920: these words were written on the back.

They were followed by the names.

Her name was Greta.

American bureaucracy is transparent and reliable.

Despite all the time that had gone by, it didn't prove too hard to reconstruct the whole story.

Paul and Claire behaved correctly: the birth certificate was never tampered with. The adoption was legal. Though I had the impression that that old letter of Greta's – so neat, and looking as if it had never been opened, preserved along with the family papers which I had decided to examine – addressed to my mother had for some reason never been delivered to her. Greta told her own story, spoke discreetly of Tullio, confided a couple of incidents.

The pages of the letter were tucked into an old book. I flipped through it. It was the poems of Catullus.

It had a dedication, and a date: *Christmas 1920.*

Little sails in the distance are racing over the water: a regatta. And it seems to be heading towards Fiume.

I didn't even know there was a city called Fiume until just a few days ago.

But there was a lot more that I didn't know. Paul's dreams, his past. The battles which he fought here, his defeats. Maybe also his delusions, his errors. All his controversial ideals, his passionate heterodoxy, the struggles against all sorts of prejudices, the goals he'd set himself for years, often risky and embarrassing and above all still unpopular, in a political career which never got him very far.

A Democrat only by choice. A Radical by vocation. An Idealist, even, by destiny, if there is such a thing in some sense and in some manner that drives us to flow in a current which is our own and in which we feel we must swim even without understanding why. Now I know that it is to him that I owe my own choices: everything I now am, for better or worse.

Like him, a Democrat by choice. A Radical, perhaps, by necessity.

From the volume of Catullus I pull out the little black and white photo. The girl is in the middle, shining, a single long tress of hair hanging down her shoulder, one lock hanging down over her forehead, she's lightly and brightly dressed. And she's looking up, past the camera. On either side of her, two young men. My maternal grandfathers, Tullio and Paul.

I study her. I ask myself so many questions. What music did she like? What books? What was her favourite dish? Did she suffer from any little phobia? Did she smoke or drink wine? What were her eyes looking at when that photo was taken, freezing for ever from that moment the expression of her fingers and her hands. I ask myself what her voice was like, what she dreamed of, what she was afraid of.

I find no answers. Not a single one. Yet our eyes meet, after almost a century's interval.

And then I understand the reason why I've come all this way, why I couldn't do without coming here.

Life is too complex to be left to the living.

I'd hesitated, I recall, before finding the words with which to ask him that question, and the courage to voice them. "Grandad, where do you go when from time to time you leave us… in thought… and you no longer seem to be on this earth, with us here?"

He did not strike me as being astonished. He had smiled for an instant. "It's hard to explain it to you, Alexandra. It's like when sometimes we try to recall a dream which we feel we've forgotten. It may be something that doesn't exist, but we have to make room for it inside ourselves, continue pondering it, search. It's like a new continent, like a fifth season."

He glanced outside, and I followed his gaze.

"Maybe somewhere there's another world, even if we haven't found it. Can you understand that?" he asked.

I shook my head. I didn't understand.

After all, I was only a child.

It's only now, forty years later, that I give that slight nod of understanding.

Now that I have indeed understood. Here, alone.

The tide of his fifth season – the long sea-swell of far-off dreams – has somehow reached me.

The little girl on the sea-shore has stuck her book into a backpack, has slipped on an outsize tee-shirt, has folded up her sunbathing mat. But before going on her way along the footpath she turned and looked at me, and smiled.

Or maybe I've just imagined it: that's how I want to remember her. However, in the dim light, I smile at her, I wave my hand at her.

And as I go on my way, I listen, in silence, to the world's voice returning.

Some notes on idealists, legionaries and clichés

Since collective History gate-crashes into this novel – bringing on stage certain figures that belong to the public life of those years – I deem it appropriate to mention some details that might interest the curious reader.

Perhaps what many in Italy know about the Fiume adventure comes from the few bare lines within which those events are compressed in the school-books, usually dismissing them as a nationalistic phenomenon which paved the way for Fascism.

In reality, as I foreshadowed in my Foreword, the complex character of the Fiume episode spills over simplistic theses and rigid interpretative grids, which tend to frame the Fiume enterprise within a "a mosaic that sets up the pattern of the irresistible rise of Fascism with an iron logic that encapsulates every incident within an obligatory plot" (Roberto Chiarini, 'L'impresa di Fiume nelle carte del maggiore Carlo Reina,' in

D'Annunzio politico, Atti del Convegno, Il Vittoriale, 9-10 ottobre 1985, in *Quaderni dannunziani*, 1-2, 1987, edited by Renzo De Felice and Pietro Gibellini).

The rich array of clues which can be drawn from this and other sources suggests that if the Fiume affair undoubtedly constituted a nationalistic experience and was in certain specific respects a fore-runner of Fascism, it also comprised a manifold cultural ferment, a profound urge for social renewal, economic transgressions, sexual freedoms, artistic expressions of alternative thinking and conflicting political aspirations, often teetering between conservatism and open insurrection, between nationalism and internationalism.

Fiume therefore embodied, between September 1919 and December 1920 an attempt – however contradictory and fanciful – to realize a sort of "experimental counter-culture." (This is mooted by Claudia Salaris, and the theme is canvassed by, among others, the American, Hakim Bey, in *T.A.Z. The Temporary Autonomous Zone, Ontological Anarchy, Poetic Terrorism*, Autonomedia, New York 1985.)

The city thus quickly became the favoured resort of a sort of political, cultural, artistic and intellectual "tourism" analogous to that centred on Paris in 1968.

Anyone interested in learning more is recommended to read, among other things, the detailed studies by Renzo De Felice, particularly *D'Annunzio politico 1918-1938*, Laterza, Roma-Bari 1978, but also the stimulating study by Claudia Salaris, *Alla festa della rivoluzione. Artisti e libertari con D'Annunzio a Fiume*, Il Mulino, Bologna 2002, as well as Mario Isnenghi's 'La nuova agorà. Fiume' (in *L'Italia in piazza. I luoghi della vita pubblica dal 1848 ai giorni nostri*, Mondadori, Milano 1994) and the studies by Michael Arthur Ledeen,

D'Annunzio a Fiume, Laterza, Roma-Bari 1975 and *D'Annunzio: the first Duce*, Transaction Publisher, 2000. For a better understanding of the atmosphere of the Fiume adventure it is also worth reading some of the novels written by contemporary participants. Essential among these are: *Il porto dell'amore*, Vianello, Treviso 1924, and *Le mie stagioni*, Longanesi, Milano 1963, by Giovanni Comisso, as well as *La quinta stagione o i centauri di Fiume*, Zanichelli, Bologna 1922, by Leone Kochnitzky. Also interesting in this regard are Filippo Tommaso Marinetti's *Taccuini 1915-1921*, edited by Alberto Bertoni, Il Mulino, Bologna 1987.

The historical framework

The micro-histories in this novel are the fruit of my imagination, but the historical setting is authentic: I've attempted a faithful reconstruction, though occasionally modifying the chronology of events to suit my narrative. I apologize to history fiends for taking these liberties.

The most apparently fictitious passages in my story did really happen: Guido Kepler's flight over Rome and Cesare Carminiani's over Paris, the visits to Fiume by Arturo Toscanini and Guglielmo Marconi, the departure of hundreds of poverty-stricken children from Fiume, during the prolonged blockade of the city, to be hosted in Milan, Florence and Bologna, and the threat by the legionaries to embark the little refugees on board a steamer to be escorted by a destroyer with orders to open fire on anyone attempting to prevent them from disembarking in Venice.

Also authentic are the destruction of the Udine district

of Sant'Osvaldo in August 1917 and the student demonstration at the Bologna railway station during the transit of the special train carrying Badoglio in September 1919 (though I have elaborated the incident).

Keller-Kepler's aerial duel probably did take place, and is recorded by some historians – see, for instance, Antonio Spinosa's book, *Il poeta armato*, Mondadori, Milano 1975 – and so did the incident involving Mussolini in Milan in the autumn of 1920.

"Isa" di Camerana is a historical figure, as is her role – incredible for those days – as leader of the *Disperata* legion. And naturally there is a historical basis for the use of the Orient Express as a clandestine courier to evade postal censorship, and for the roles of the reformist socialist Alceste De Ambris and of the American writer Henry Furst, on whom I partly based the character of Paul Forst, and also for the foundation of the Fiume League of Oppressed Peoples (an element of idealist endeavour which was decisive for my interest in the d'Annunzian adventure.)

Authentic also are the extracts from d'Annunzio's speeches and letters, the newspaper reports – sometimes minimally rephrased but always faithful as to content – and the texts of all the telegrams (from Nitti, Badoglio, Mussolini…) with the exception of the one supposed to have been dispatched to Badoglio by prime minister Nitti on 13 September 1919 and that dated 15 November 1919, whose words, however, faithfully record an actual event. The text of the second telegram read by Badoglio on board the train (13 September 1919) is made up of two different telegrams sent on 12 September 1919 by General Pittaluga and by General di Robilant to prime minister Nitti.

Finally, some points of historical fact regarding the final section of the novel: Italian naval ships were stationed outside Fiume harbour from 1st December 1920. Subsequently their positions were modified as described in the dispatch dated 15 December 1920, which is not an original text but my own narrative re-elaboration of what actually happened. The attack on the city was unleashed on 24 December – a date on which it is customary for newspapers not to be published – and lasted for five days. All the reports dealing with those hostilities – which have gone down in history as Bloody Christmas – are authentic, though some dates have been altered. For instance: the report dated 13 November in fact relates to 13 October and that dated 16 December is a combination of two different newspaper reports relating to December 2 and 24.

I must furthermore point out, so as to avoid any confusion, that the newspaper *La Nazione*, which is quoted several times in the novel, is not the current Florentine daily but a newspaper published in Trieste between 1918 and 1923 and founded by Silvio Enea Benco, subsequently editor of *Il Piccolo*, who had been copy editor of James Joyce's earliest article.

The Characters

Several characters in the novel are historical, or based on historical figures.

I need offer no information here about Badoglio, Mussolini or d'Annunzio, about whom a vast amount has been written.

It might, however, be of interest to give an account of some lesser known figures.

Giulio Kepler is loosely based on Guido Keller. A bizarre blend of swaggerer and bohemian, restless and unconventional, rebel and dreamer, sculptor and former airman in Francesco Baracca's squadron, Keller was born in Milan in 1892 of an old-established family of Swiss origin.

A vegetarian and a naturist, a friend of the writer Giovanni Comisso – who himself was a prominent actor in the Fiume affair – Keller founded the Fiume journal *Yoga* and its associated cultural and artistic movement. Transgressive and irreverent towards those in power, he organized several "piratical" exploits which kept the Fiume economy going during the prolonged trade embargo to which the town was subjected, with Red Cross supplies arriving only sporadically.

In Fiume he fathered a daughter out of wedlock, who seems to have subsequently been supported by Giovanni Comisso.

After the Fiume episode, Keller resumed his roving, restless life, pursuing visionary social utopias. He spent some time first in Turkey, then in Berlin – where he worked as a representative for the Italian embassy and mixed with the town's artistic *bohème* – and finally in Latin America. He visited Venezuela, Chile, Peru and Brazil, conceiving the dream of a union of the young South American republics free from outside interference and independent of the model of economic development exported by the United States.

He died as a result of an automobile accident near Rome in 1929.

A fuller picture of Keller is to be found in Sandro Pozzi's *Guido Keller nel pensiero nelle gesta*, Mediolanum, Milano 1933.

Though inspired, one might say, by deep personal admiration – and in that sense probably not a very lucid portrait – Pozzi's book contains some extremely interesting passages, such as Keller's autobiographical account of the flight over Rome.

The character of Paul Forst is based on Henry Furst, an American, born in New York in 1893, a polyglot and holder of three university degrees. Furst was, among other things, a writer, a literary critic, a teacher, a boxing manager. In Fiume he worked alongside Leon Kochnitzky, Ludovico Toepliz, Giovanni Comisso and others at the office for external affairs which was set up on 12 January 1920 with the task of dealing with the press and foreign propaganda.

An anti-Fascist at a time when few others were, during the 1930s he wrote numerous articles for the *New York Times Review of Books*, which was eventually banned by the regime in Italy, apparently on account of Furst's own pieces. Married to the writer Orsola Nemi, he divided his time between Rome and Camogli, near Genoa, and died at La Spezia in 1967. He maintained relations with Benedetto Croce, Eugenio Montale, Ernst Jünger, Mario Soldati and various other intellectuals.

The writer Kochnitzky wrote of him with regard to the Fiume period: "… he venerates no hierarchy, no principle of authority… Many execrate him because he's a foreigner… because he's intelligent and writes faultlessly in English, in French, in German and many other languages; because in conversation he comes out with Greek quotations… because he's unbearable, because he's highly entertaining. One fine day President Wilson's government itself could no longer bear this restless and troublesome citizen. The consular authorities were given orders to withdraw Henry Furst's passport and he was instructed to return immediately to the United States."

The rest of his story is the fruit of my imagination.

It seems certain, however, that Henry Furst cultivated the appalling vice of never lining up behind those currently in power. It's probably no coincidence that despite his lively participation in the cultural scene of the times and his copious literary output – he wrote several novels and worked enthusiastically as a critic and translator – he is almost totally forgotten today.

Leon Kochnitzky, born in Brussels in 1892 of a Russian father and a Polish mother, a poet and a musician, by contrast with the nationalist tendencies of the conservative wing of the Fiume expedition, was among those who endeavoured to give it a progressive, left-wing character, in the hope of turning Fiume into the outpost of an anti-imperialist league which would unite the poorer nations against the wealthy colonizing powers.

Ludovico Toeplitz de Grand Ry, born in Genoa in 1893, the polyglot son of the Polish Jewish banker Giuseppe Toeplitz, was appointed "ambassador" by the Fiume office for external affairs and founded the Anti-League of Nations, in open conflict with the logic and strategies emerging in Paris during the peace conference. Restless, a nomad and a visionary like the majority of his comrades, after the Fiume affair he worked in cinema, first in Rome and then in London.

After the promulgation of the race laws, he left Italy and

moved to Belgium. In 1950 he went to India where he settled for many years,

Alceste De Ambris, born in Licciana Nardi in the province of Massa Carrara in 1874, a revolutionary syndicalist and an organizer of agrarian strikes in the province of Parma at the beginning of the century, had been a political exile in Brazil. Joining the cause of Fiume, in January 1920 he took up the position of leader of the cabinet. He was the main author of Fiume's constitution, the Carnaro Charter. As regards foreign policy, while contacts were established with representatives of peoples and movements struggling for independence (Ireland, Egypt, Armenia...), De Ambris strove to link up the Fiume movement with the political forces of the Italian Left.

He subsequently joined the Arditi del Popolo people's brigade in the defence of Parma against the Fascists, fighting in the Filippo Corridoni proletarian legion. Assaulted by Fascists in Genoa in 1923, he removed to France. In Paris he organized labour cooperatives to support the numerous Italian political refugees. He died in Brive in 1934.

Incisa (Isa) di Camerana is also a historical figure. Along with some other young women (such as Alessandra Porro), she joined the Fiume enterprise, in which she was indeed assigned the role described in the novel. The Socialist leader Filippo Turati mentions her (actually in moralistic tones) in his letter of 20 March 1920, to his partner Anna Kuliscioff. Unfortunately I have been unable to discover more about this non-conformist young woman, whose role probably deserves exploring.

The *Questore* (police chief) of Fiume also appears as a background figure. I wish to record that he really lived.

His name is known to be Giovanni Palatucci. Posted to the Fiume *questura* to take charge of the foreigners department in 1937, beginning in March 1939, when he succeeded in saving eight hundred people from being handed over to the Gestapo, he strove to secure the escape of thousands of Jews.

While in Italy in 1943 the Nazi-Fascist "Social Republic" was proclaimed and the King and the Italian military high command fled to the South, and the anti-Fascist parties formed the Committees for National Liberation and organized armed resistance, Giovanni Palatucci continued to act as his conscience dictated.

Arrested on 13 September 1944 by SS Colonel Kappler, he was deported to the Dachau extermination camp, where he died a few days before the liberation.

He was 36 years of age. In 1990 the Yad Vashem declared him one of the Righteous among Nations.

Dates and places

I've taken some liberties with place, and, especially, with time.

For instance, I've located the historical Udine high school, the Liceo Classico Jacopo Stellini, in its present site, opposite the castle. In reality, the building, completed in 1915, was occupied by the Italian High Command during the early years of Italy's involvement in the Great War, and, after that, by the Austrians. At the time referred to in the novel, therefore, the school was located in the present Via del Ginnasio Vecchio.

As for the liberties I have taken with time for narrative purposes, I will mention only the most important:

• The killing of the legionary by the regular army took place in autumn, and the visit by the Duchess of Aosta on 4 November, the anniversary of the "victory" in the Great War.

• The Fiume delegation that arrives in Paris early in January 1920, on a diplomatic mission, is not admitted to the peace table, nor does it receive any acknowledgement of receipt of the letters to that effect sent to Clemenceau, President of the Peace Conference. Cesare Carminiani's flight over the French capital therefore takes place as a sign of protest directly after this event – in January – and not in May 1920, as I presented it in the novel.

• Guglielmo Marconi's visit to d'Annunzio and to the town, on board his yacht *Elettra* – whose radio transmitter broadcasts a speech by d'Annunzio – takes place not on 24 June but on 24 September, soon after the proclamation of *the Regency of the Carnaro*. The incident at the time caused a huge outcry. For a full account of the relations between d'Annunzio and Marconi, see Annamaria Andreoli's *Onde d'inchiostro. Marconi, D'Annunzio: storia di un'amicizia*, Abacus, 2004. The same author usefully explores d'Annunzio's multi-faceted – and often irritating – personality in *Il vivere inimitabile. Vita di Gabriele D'Annunzio*, Mondadori, Milan 2000.

• Arturo Toscanini visits Fiume on 20 November 1920 and gives his concert on the following evening in the town's Teatro Verdi. Relations between Toscanini and d'Annunzio – in terms of musical art, but also on the human level – are partially reconstructed in Carlo Santoli's *Gabriele D'Annunzio e Arturo Toscanini. Scritti*, Bulzoni, Roma 1999.

• The military actions ascribed to 24 December actually took place on two separate days: 24 and 26 December 1920.

Any reference to real persons – apart from those expressly mentioned in the notes – is to be put down to life's infinite possibilities and is to be considered pure coincidence.

Claudio Magris, whose words I have also quoted in my opening, points out that "the hopes of a generation in a particular historical season are part of that season's history and have thus also contributed to making us what we are, even if they have been unfulfilled or belied by the course of events... To feel and to put one's finger on what was deemed feasible or what was looked forward to in an actual situation – a different turn of events – helps us to understand more fully what actually happened, an understanding which is achievable only if we do not regard it as having been right from the start the only possible outcome."

We swim amid a swell that could bear us up or make us go under, rise or ebb in disillusionment, but in which nothing will ever be completely lost.

Acknowledgements

Once again, I wish to thank many people.

First and foremost, I thank my friends Mario Turello and Gianpietro Nimis, who were the first to read this novel: their comments have been invaluable. A special thank-you to Mario also for having got me a rare copy of Guglielmo Ferrero's book *Da Fiume a Roma* (Edizioni Athena, Milan, 1923), which I guard jealously.

My thanks to my friend Pierluigi Cappello, who was by my side at a key moment during the drafting of the novel: it is essentially to him that I owe the choice of the splendid poem by Wisława Szymborska.

My thanks to Franco Ferrarotti, for whose words about this story – when the story had just been completed – I am grateful and will never forget.

My thanks to Giovanna Pezzetta, for her "musical hint".

My thanks to Fulvio Salimbeni, lecturer in contemporary history at Udine University, who kindly subjected my Foreword to the novel to "historical validation".

My thanks to Luigi Bressan, who jovially checked my

transcription of the Venetian dialect spoken by a couple of my characters, saving me from mangling their speech.

My thanks to Marina Giovannelli, for the passion with which she continues to involve me in her inexhaustible reflections, written and unwritten.

My thanks to my friend Anna Marchese, who in the course of this past year has helped me to understand many things, giving me the courage which I should have given her.

My thanks to Marco Praloran, head of the Italian Department at the University of Lausanne, who believed in the rationale and the significance of my present research into *History, memory and Utopia*.

My thanks to the staff of Trieste's Biblioteca Civica Attilio Hortis, who so kindly allowed me to access texts and microfilms even at the height of renovation work and in the heat of August.

My thanks to my editor Ilde Buratti for her enthusiasm, her patience and her thoroughness.

My thanks to my agent Silvia Brunelli for having done all that she has done and for having done it so well.

To my daughter Silvia goes a special thank-you, on many grounds: not least the fact that the peace ensured by her compulsive reading often enabled me to devote myself to no less compulsive writing.

My husband Giuseppe has warned me off thanking him personally. He maintains that half his friends have made fun of him on account of the words I addressed to him at the opening of my previous novel and the other half on account of the words of thanks which I reserved for him at the end.

But I am a recidivist, and won't let go. I thank him again. And he knows why.